THE RUNAGATES CLUB

THE
RUNAGATES CLUB

JOHN BUCHAN

THOMAS NELSON AND SONS LTD
LONDON EDINBURGH PARIS MELBOURNE
TORONTO AND NEW YORK

THOMAS NELSON AND SONS LTD
Parkside Works Edinburgh 9
36 Park Street London W1
312 Flinders Street Melbourne C1
218 Grand Parade Centre   Cape Town

THOMAS NELSON AND SONS (CANADA) LTD
91–93 Wellington Street West   Toronto 1

THOMAS NELSON AND SONS
19 East 47th Street New York 17

SOCIÉTÉ FRANÇAISE D'EDITIONS NELSON
25 rue Henri Barbusse Paris V^e

———

First printed July 1928
First printed in this Edition September 1930
Reprinted 1933, 1938, 1950, 1952 , 1954

TO

LADY SALISBURY

♥

PREFACE

A LONDON dining-club is a curious organism, for it combines great tenacity of life with a chameleon-like tendency to change its colour. A club which begins as a haunt of roysterers may end as a blameless academic fraternity ; another, which at the start is a meeting-place of the intelligent, becomes in the progress of time a select coterie of sportsmen. So it has been with the institution of which I am the chronicler. It has changed its name and is now the Thursday Club, and the number of permissible members has been increased. Its dinners are admirable ; conversation at its board is dignified and a little serious ; it has enlarged its interests, and would not now refuse a Lord Chancellor or a Bishop.

But in its infancy it was different. Founded just after the close of the War by a few people who had been leading queer lives and wanted to keep together, it was a gathering of youngish men who met only for reminiscences and relaxation. It was officially limited to fifteen members—fifteen, because a dozen was dull, thirteen was unlucky, and fourteen had in those days an unpleasing flavour of President Wilson and his points. At first, until Burminster took it in hand, the food and wine were execrable ; hence the name of the Runagates Club, given it by Lamancha from the verse in the 68th Psalm : " He letteth the runagates continue in scarceness."

But all defects in the fare were atoned for by the talk, which, like that of Praed's Vicar,

> " slipped from politics to puns,
> And passed from Mahomet to Moses."

You could never tell what topic would engage the company, and no topic was left unadorned, for I do not suppose there has ever been a group with such varied experiences and attainments. Each man was in his own way an expert ; but, while knowledge might be specialized, the life of each had been preposterously varied. The War had flattened out grooves and set every man adventuring. So the lawyer and the financier were also soldiers ; the Greek scholar had captained a Bedawin tribe ; the traveller had dabbled in secret service ; the journalist had commanded a battalion ; the historian had been mate on a novel kind of tramp ; the ornithologist had watched more perilous things than birds ; the politician had handled a rougher humanity than an English electorate. Some of the members, like Lord Lamancha, Sir Edward Leithen, and Sir Arthur Warcliff, were familiar to the public ; others were known only to narrow circles ; but at the Runagates Club they were of one family and totem, like old schoolfellows.

Good talk is not for reproduction in cold print. But at those early dinners there were reminiscences which may well be rescued from oblivion, for all were story-tellers on occasion. Indeed, it became the fashion once a month for a member to entertain the company with a more or less complete narrative. From these I have made a selection which I now set forth.

CONTENTS

I. THE GREEN WILDEBEEST

SIR RICHARD HANNAY'S STORY

We carry with us the wonders we seek without us; there is all
Africa and her prodigies in us.

> SIR THOMAS BROWNE: *Religio Medici.*

THE RUNAGATES CLUB

I. THE GREEN WILDEBEEST

WE were talking about the persistence of race
qualities—how you might bury a strain for
generations under fresh graftings, but the aboriginal
sap would some day stir. The obvious instance
was the Jew, and Pugh had also something to say
about the surprises of a tincture of hill blood in
the Behari. Peckwether, the historian, was inclined to doubt. The old stock, he held, could
disappear absolutely as if by a chemical change,
and the end be as remote from the beginning as
—to use his phrase—a ripe Gorgonzola from a
bucket of new milk.

"I don't believe you're ever quite safe," said
Sandy Arbuthnot.

"You mean that an eminent banker may get up
one morning with a strong wish to cut himself
shaving in honour of Baal?"

"Maybe. But the tradition is more likely to be
negative. There are some things that for no particular reason he won't like, some things that
specially frighten him. Take my own case. I
haven't a scrap of real superstition in me, but I

hate crossing a river at night. I fancy a lot of my
blackguard ancestors got scuppered at moonlight
fords. I believe we're all stuffed full of atavistic
fears, and you can't tell how or when a man will
crack till you know his breeding."

"I think that's about the truth of it," said
Hannay, and after the discussion had rambled on
for a while he told us this tale.

Just after the Boer War (he said) I was on a
prospecting job in the north-eastern Transvaal.
I was a mining engineer, with copper as my
speciality, and I had always a notion that copper
might be found in big quantities in the Zoutpansberg foothills. There was of course Messina at
the west end, but my thoughts turned rather to
the north-east corner, where the berg breaks down
to the crook of the Limpopo. I was a young man
then, fresh from two years' campaigning with the
Imperial Light Horse, and I was thirsty for better
jobs than trying to drive elusive burghers up against
barbed wire and blockhouses. When I started
out with my mules from Pietersburg on the dusty
road to the hills, I think I felt happier than ever
before in my life.

I had only one white companion, a boy of
twenty-two called Andrew Du Preez. Andrew,
not Andries, for he was named after the Reverend
Andrew Murray, who had been a great Pope among
the devout Afrikanders. He came of a rich Free
State farming family, but his particular branch
had been settled for two generations in the Wak-

kerstroom region along the upper Pongola. The
father was a splendid old fellow with a head like
Moses, and he and all the uncles had been on commando, and most of them had had a spell in Ber-
muda or Ceylon. The boy was a bit of a freak
in that stock. He had been precociously intelligent, and had gone to a good school in the Cape
and afterwards to a technical college in Johannesburg. He was as modern a product as the others
were survivals, with none of the family religion
or family politics, very keen on science, determined
to push his way on the Rand—which was the Mecca
of all enterprising Afrikanders—and not very sorry
that the war should have found him in a place
from which it was manifestly impossible to join
the family banner. In October '99 he was on his
first job in a new mining area in Rhodesia, and as
he hadn't much health he was wise enough to stick
there till peace came.

I had known him before, and when I ran across
him on the Rand I asked him to come with me, and
he jumped at the offer. He had just returned from
the Wakkerstroom farm, to which the rest of his
clan had been repatriated, and didn't relish the
prospect of living in a tin-roofed shanty with a
father who read the Bible most of the day to find
out why exactly he had merited such misfortunes.
Andrew was a hard young sceptic, in whom the
family piety produced acute exasperation. . . . He
was a good-looking boy, always rather smartly
dressed, and at first sight you would have taken him
for a young American, because of his heavy hairless

chin, his dull complexion, and the way he peppered his ordinary speech with technical and business phrases. There was a touch of the Mongol in his face, which was broad, with high cheek bones, eyes slightly slanted, short thick nose, and rather full lips. I remembered that I had seen the same thing before in young Boers, and I thought I knew the reason. The Du Preez family had lived for generations close up to the Kaffir borders, and some-where had got a dash of the tar-brush.

We had a light wagon with a team of eight mules, and a Cape-cart drawn by four others; five boys went with us, two of them Shangaans, and three Basutos from Malietsie's location north of Pieters-burg. Our road was over the Wood Bush, and then north-east across the two Letabas to the Pufuri river. The countryside was amazingly empty. Beyer's commandos had skirmished among the hills, but the war had never reached the plains; at the same time it had put a stop to all hunting and prospecting, and had scattered most of the native tribes. The place had become in effect a sanctuary, and I saw more varieties of game than I had ever seen before south of the Zambesi, so that I wished I were on a hunting trip instead of on a business job. Lions were plentiful, and every night we had to build a *scherm* for our mules and light great fires, beside which we listened to their eerie serenades.

It was early December, and in the Wood Bush it was the weather of an English June. Even in the foothills, among the wormwood and wild

bananas, it was pleasant enough, but when we got
out into the plains it was as hot as Tophet. As far
as the eye could reach, the bushveld rolled its scrub
like the scrawled foliage a child draws on a slate,
with here and there a baobab swimming unsteadily
in the glare. For long stretches we were away from
water, and ceased to see big game—only Kaffir
queens and tick-birds, and now and then a wild
ostrich. Then on the sixth day out from Pieters-
burg we raised a blue line of mountains on the
north, which I knew to be the eastern extension
of the Zoutpansberg. I had never travelled this
country before, and had never met a man who had,
so we steered by compass, and by one of the old
bad maps of the Transvaal Government. That
night we crossed the Pufuri, and next day the landscape began to change. The ground rose, so that
we had a sight of the distant Lebombo hills to the
east, and mopani bushes began to appear—a sure
sign of a healthier country.

That afternoon we were only a mile or two from
the hills. They were the usual type of berg which
you find everywhere from Natal to the Zambesi—
cut sheer, with an overhang in many places, but
much broken up by kloofs and fissures. What
puzzled me was the absence of streams. The
ground was as baked as the plains, all covered with
aloe and cactus and thorn, with never a sign of
water. But for my purpose the place looked prom-
ising. There was that unpleasant metallic green
that you find in a copper country, so that everything seemed to have been steeped in a mineral

dye—even the brace of doves which I shot for luncheon.

We turned east along the foot of the cliffs, and presently saw a curious feature. A promontory ran out from the berg, connected by a narrow isthmus with the main *massif*. I suppose the superficial area of the top might have been a square mile or so ; the little peninsula was deeply cut into by ravines, and in the ravines tall timber was growing. Also we came to well-grassed slopes, dotted with mimosa and syringa bushes. This must mean water at last, for I had never found yellow-woods and stinkwoods growing far from a stream. Here was our outspan for the night, and when presently we rounded a corner and looked down into a green cup I thought I had rarely seen a more habitable place. The sight of fresh green herbage always intoxicated me, after the dust and heat and the ugly greys and umbers of the bushveld. There was a biggish kraal in the bottom, and a lot of goats and leggy Kaffir sheep on the slopes. Children were bringing in the cows for the milking, smoke was going up from the cooking fires, and there was a cheerful evening hum in the air. I expected a stream, but could see no sign of one : the cup seemed to be as dry as a hollow of the Sussex Downs. Also, though there were patches of mealies and Kaffir corn, I could see no irrigated land. But water must be there, and after we had fixed a spot for our outspan beside a clump of olive-woods, I took Andrew and one of our boys and strolled down to make inquiries.

I daresay many of the inhabitants of that kraal had never seen a white man before, for our arrival made a bit of a sensation. I noticed that there were very few young men about the place, but an inordinate number of old women. The first sight of us scattered them like plovers, and we had to wait for half an hour, smoking patiently in the evening sun, before we could get into talk with them. Once the ice was broken, however, things went well. They were a decent peaceable folk, very shy and scared and hesitating, but with no guile in them. Our presents of brass and copper wire and a few tins of preserved meat made a tremendous impression. We bought a sheep from them at a ridiculously small price, and they threw in a basket of green mealies. But when we raised the water question we struck a snag.

There was water, good water, they said, but it was not in any pan or stream. They got it morning and evening from up there—and they pointed to the fringe of a wood under the cliffs where I thought I saw the roof of a biggish *rondavel*. They got it from their Father ; they were Shangaans, and the word they used was not the ordinary word for chief, but the name for a great priest and medicine-man.

I wanted my dinner, so I forbore to inquire further. I produced some more Kaffir truck, and begged them to present it with my compliments to their Father, and to ask for water for two white strangers, five of their own race, and twelve mules. They seemed to welcome the proposition, and a string of them promptly set off uphill with their big calabashes. As we walked back I said something foolish to Andrew about having struck a Kaffir Moses who could draw water from the rock. The lad was in a bad temper. "We have struck an infernal rascal who has made a corner in the water supply and bleeds these poor devils. He's the kind of grafter I would like to interview with a sjambok."

In an hour we had all the water we wanted. It stood in a row of calabashes, and beside it the presents I had sent to the provider. The villagers had deposited it and then vanished, and our boys who had helped them to carry it were curiously quiet and solemnized. I was informed that the Father sent the water as a gift to the strangers without payment. I tried to cross-examine one of our Shangaans, but he would tell me nothing except that the water had come from a sacred place into which no man could penetrate. He also muttered something about a wildebeest which I couldn't understand. Now the Kaffir is the most superstitious of God's creatures. All the way from Pietersburg we had been troubled by the vivid imaginations of our outfit. They wouldn't sleep in one place because of a woman without a head who haunted it; they dared not go a yard along a particular road after dark because of a spook that travelled it in the shape of a rolling ball of fire. Usually their memories were as short as their fancies were quick, and five minutes after their protest they would be laughing like baboons. But that night they seemed to have been really impressed by something. They did not chatter or sing over their supper, but gossiped in undertones, and slept as near Andrew and myself as they dared.

Next morning the same array of gourds stood before our outspan, and there was enough water for me to have a tub in my collapsible bath. I don't think I ever felt anything colder.

I had decided to take a holiday and go shooting. Andrew would stay in camp and tinker up one of the wheels of the mule-wagon which had suffered from the bush roads. He announced his intention of taking a walk later and interviewing the water-merchant.

"For heaven's sake, be careful," I said. "Most likely he's a priest of sorts, and if you're not civil to him we'll have to quit this country. I make a point of respecting the gods of the heathen."

"All you English do," he replied tartly. "That's why you make such a damned mess of handling Kaffirs. . . . But this fellow is a business man with a pretty notion of cornering public utilities. I'm going to make his acquaintance."

I had a pleasant day in that hot scented wilderness. First I tried the low ground, but found nothing there but some old spoor of kudu, and a paauw which I shot. Then I tried the skirts of the berg to the east of the village, and found that the kloofs, which from below looked climbable, had all somewhere a confounded overhang which checked me. I saw no way of getting to the top of the plateau, so I spent the afternoon in exploring the tumbled glacis. There was no trace of copper here, for the rock was a reddish granite, but it was a jolly flowery place, with green dells among the crags, and an amazing variety of birds. But I was glad that I had brought a water-bottle, for I found no water ; it was there all right, but it was underground. I stalked a bushbuck ram and missed him, but I got one of the little buck like chamois which the Dutch call *klipspringer*. With it and the paauw strung round my neck I sauntered back leisurely to supper.

As soon as I came in sight of the village I saw that something had played the deuce with it. There was a great hubbub going on, and all the folk were collected at the end farthest away from our camp. The camp itself looked very silent. I could see the hobbled mules, but I could see nothing of any of our outfit. I thought it best in these circumstances to make an inconspicuous arrival, so I bore away to my left, crossed the hollow lower down where it was thick with scrub, and came in on the outspan from the south. It was very silent. The cooking fires had been allowed to go out, though the boys should have been getting ready the evening meal, and there seemed to be not a single black face on the premises. Very uneasy, I made for our sleeping tent, and found Andrew lying on his bed, smoking.

" What on earth has happened ? " I demanded. " Where are Coos and Klemboy and . . ."

" Quit," he said shortly. " They've all quit."

He looked sulky and tired and rather white in the face, and there seemed to be more the matter with him than ill temper. He would lay down his pipe, and press his hand on his forehead like a man with a bad headache. Also he never lifted his eyes to mine. I daresay I was a bit harsh, for I was hungry, and there were moments when I thought he was going to cry. However, at last I got a sort of story out of him.

He had finished his job on the wagon wheel in the morning, and after luncheon had gone for a walk to the wood above the village at the foot of the cliffs. He wanted to see where the water came from, and to have a word with the man who controlled it. Andrew, as I have told you, was a hard young realist, and, by way of reaction from his family, a determined foe of superstition, and he disliked the notion of this priest and his mumbo-jumbo. Well, it seemed that he reached the priest's headquarters—it was the big *rondavel* we had seen from below, and there was a kind of stockade stretching on both sides, very strongly fenced, so that the only entrance was through the *rondavel*. He had found the priest at home, and had, according to his account, spoken to him civilly and had tried to investigate the water problem. But the old man would have nothing to say to him, and peremptorily refused his request to be allowed to enter the enclosure. By-and-by Andrew lost his temper, and forced his way in. The priest resisted and there was a scuffle ; I daresay Andrew used his sjambok, for a backveld Dutchman can never keep his hands off a Kaffir.

I didn't like the story, but it was no use being angry with a lad who looked like a sick dog.

" What is inside ?   Did you find the water ? "
I asked.

" I hadn't time.   It's a thick wood and full of
beasts.   I tell you I was scared out of my senses
and had to run for my life."

" Leopards ? " I asked.   I had heard of native
chiefs keeping tame leopards.

" Leopards be damned.   I'd have faced leopards.
I saw a wildebeest as big as a house—an old brute,
grey in the nozzle and the rest of it green—green,
I tell you.   I took a pot shot at it and ran. . . .
When I came out the whole blasted kraal was
howling.   The old devil must have roused them.
I legged it for home. . . . No, they didn't follow,
but in half an hour all our outfit had cut their
stick . . . didn't wait to pick up their duds. . . .
Oh, hell, I can't talk.   Leave me alone."

I had laughed in spite of myself.   A wildebeest
is not ornamental at the best, but a green one must
be a good recipe for the horrors.   All the same I felt
very little like laughing.   Andrew had offended the
village and its priest, played havoc with the brittle
nerves of our own boys, and generally made the
place too hot to hold us.   He had struck some kind
of native magic, which had frightened him to the
bone for all his scepticism.   The best thing I could
do seemed to be to try and patch up a peace with
the water-merchant.   So I made a fire and put on
a kettle to boil, stayed my hunger with a handful
of biscuits, and started out for the *rondavel*.   But
first I saw that my revolver was loaded, for I
fancied that there might be trouble.   It was a

calm, bright evening, but up from the hollow where
the kraal lay there rose a buzz like angry wasps.

No one interfered with me ; indeed, I met no one
till I presented myself at the *rondavel* door. It was
a big empty place, joined to the stockades on both
sides, and opposite the door was another which
opened on to a dull green shade. I never saw a
scherm so stoutly built. There was a palisade of
tall pointed poles, and between them a thick wall
of wait-a-bit thorns interlaced with a scarlet-
flowered creeper. It would have taken a man with
an axe half a day to cut a road through. The only
feasible entrance was by the *rondavel*.

An old man was squatted on an earthen floor,
which had been so pounded and beaten that it
looked like dark polished stone. His age might
have been anything above seventy from the white-
ness of his beard, but there seemed a good deal of
bodily strength left in him, for the long arms which
rested on his knees were muscular. His face was
not the squat face of the ordinary Kaffir, but high-
boned and regular, like some types of well-bred
Zulu. Now that I think of it, there was probably
Arab blood in him. He lifted his head at the
sound of my steps, and by the way he looked at
me I knew that he was blind.

There he sat without a word, every line of his
body full of dejection and tragedy. I had suddenly
a horrible feeling of sacrilege. That that young
fool Andrew should have lifted his hand upon an
old man, and a blind man, and outraged some harmless *tabu* seemed to me an abominable thing. I

felt that some holiness had been violated, something ancient and innocent cruelly insulted. At that moment there was nothing in the world I wanted so much as to make restitution.

I spoke to him, using the Shangaan word which means both priest and king. I told him that I had been away hunting, and had returned to find that my companion had made bad mischief. I said that Andrew was very young, and that his error had been only the foolishness and hot-headedness of youth. I said—and my voice must have shown him that I meant it—that I was cut to the heart by what had happened, that I bowed my head in the dust in contrition, and that I asked nothing better than to be allowed to make atonement. . . . Of course I didn't offer money. I would as soon have thought of offering a tip to the Pope.

He never lifted his head, so I said it all over again, and the second time it was genuine pleading. I had never spoken like that to a Kaffir before, but I could not think of that old figure as a Kaffir, but as the keeper of some ancient mystery which a rude hand had outraged.

He spoke at last. "There can be no atonement," he said. "Wrong has been done, and on the wrong-doer must fall the penalty."

The words were wholly without menace ; rather he spoke as if he were an unwilling prophet of evil. He was there to declare the law, which he could not alter if he wanted.

I apologized, I protested, I pled, I fairly grovelled ;

I implored him to tell me if there was no way by
which the trouble could be mended ; but if I had
offered him a million pounds I don't believe that
that old fellow would have changed his tone. He
seemed to feel, and he made me feel it too, that a
crime had been committed against the law of
nature, and that it was nature, not man, that
would avenge it. He wasn't in the least un-
friendly ; indeed, I think he rather liked the serious
way I took the business and realized how sorry I
was ; his slow sentences came out without a trace
of bitterness. It was this that impressed me so
horribly—he was like an old stone oracle repeating
the commands of the God he served.

I could make nothing of him, though I kept at
it till the shadows had lengthened outside, and it
was almost dark within the *rondavel*. I wanted to
ask him at least to help me to get back my boys,
and to make our peace with the village, but I
simply could not get the words out. The atmosphere was too solemn to put a practical question
like that. . . .

I was turning to go away, when I looked at the
door on the far side. Owing to the curious forma-
tion of the cliffs the sinking sun had only now
caught the high tree-tops, and some ricochet of light
made the enclosure brighter than when I first
arrived. I felt suddenly an overwhelming desire
to go inside.

" Is it permitted, Father," I said, " to pass
through that door ? "

To my surprise he waved me on. " It is permitted," he said, "for you have a clean heart." Then he added a curious thing. "What was there is there no more. It has gone to the fulfilling of the law."

It was with a good deal of trepidation that I entered that uncanny *enceinte*. I remembered Andrew's terror, and I kept my hand on my revolver, for I had a notion that there might be some queer fauna inside. There was light in the upper air, but below it was a kind of olive-green dusk. I was afraid of snakes, also of tiger-cats, and there was Andrew's green wildebeest !

The place was only a couple of acres in extent, and though I walked very cautiously I soon had made the circuit of it. The *scherm* continued in a half-moon on each side till it met the sheer wall of the cliffs. The undergrowth was not very thick, and out of it grew tall straight trees, so that the wood seemed like some old pagan grove. When one looked up the mulberry sunset sky showed in patches between the feathery tops, but where I walked it was very dark.

There was not a sign of life in it, not a bird or beast, not the crack of a twig or a stir in the bushes ; all was as quiet and dead as a crypt. Having made the circuit I struck diagonally across, and presently came on what I had been looking for— a pool of water. The spring was nearly circular, with a diameter of perhaps six yards, and what amazed me was that it was surrounded by a parapet of hewn stone. In the centre of the grove there was a little more light, and I could see that

that stonework had never been made by Kaffir
hands.   Evening is the time when water comes to
its own ; it sleeps in the day, but it has its own
strange life in the darkness.   I dipped my hand in
it and it was as cold as ice.   There was no bubbling
in it, but there seemed to be a slow rhythmical
movement, as if fresh currents were always welling
out of the deeps and always returning.   I have
no doubt that it would have been crystal clear if
there had been any light, but, as I saw it, it was
a surface of darkest jade, opaque, impenetrable,
swaying to some magic impulse from the heart of
the earth.

It is difficult to explain just the effect it had on
me.   I had been solemnized before, but this grove
and fountain gave me the abject shapeless fear of
a child.   I felt that somehow I had strayed beyond
the reasonable world.   The place was clean against
nature.   It was early summer, so these dark aisles
should have been alive with moths and flying ants
and all the thousand noises of night.   Instead it
was utterly silent and lifeless, dead as a stone
except for the secret pulsing of the cold waters.

I had had quite enough.   It is an absurd thing
to confess, but I bolted—shuffled through the
undergrowth and back into the *rondavel*, where
the old man still sat like Buddha on the floor.

" You have seen ? " he asked.

" I have seen," I said—" but I do not know
what I have seen.   Father, be merciful to foolish
youth."

He repeated again the words that had chilled

me before. " What was there has gone to fulfil
the law."

I ran all the way back to our outspan, and took
some unholy tosses on the road, for I had got it
into my head that Andrew was in danger. I don't
think I ever believed in his green wildebeest, but
he had been positive that the place was full of
animals, and I knew for a fact that it was empty.
Had some fearsome brute been unloosed on the
world ?

I found Andrew in our tent, and the kettle I had
put on to boil empty, and the fire out. The boy
was sleeping heavily with a flushed face, and I saw
what had happened. He was practically a tee-
totaller, but he had chosen to swallow a good third
of one of our four bottles of whisky. The com-
pulsion must have been pretty strong which drove
him to drink.

After that our expedition went from bad to worse.
In the morning there was no water to be had, and
I didn't see myself shouldering a calabash and
going back to the grove. Also our boys did not
return, and not a soul in the kraal would come
near us. Indeed, all night they had kept up a
most distressing racket, wailing and beating little
drums. It was no use staying on, and, for myself,
I had a strong desire to get out of the neighbourhood. The experience of the night before had left
an after-taste of disquiet in my mind, and I wanted
to flee from I knew not what. Andrew was obviously a sick man. We did not carry clinical

thermometers in those days, but he certainly had
fever on him.

So we inspanned after breakfast, and a heavy job
trekking is when you have to do all the work
yourself. I drove the wagon and Andrew the
Cape-cart, and I wondered how long he would be
able to sit on his seat. My notion was that by
going east we might be able to hire fresh boys, and
start prospecting in the hill-country above the bend
of the Limpopo.

But the word had gone out against us. You
know the way in which Kaffirs send news for a
hundred miles as quick as the telegraph—by drum-
taps or telepathy—explain it any way you like.
Well, we struck a big kraal that afternoon, but not
a word would they say to us. Indeed, they were
actually threatening, and I had to show my revolver
and speak pretty stiffly before we got off. It was
the same next day, and I grew nervous about our
provisions, for we couldn't buy anything—not a
chicken or an egg or a mealie-cob. Andrew was a
jolly companion. He had relapsed into the primeval lout, and his manners were those of a cave-
man. If he had not been patently suffering, I
would have found it hard to keep my temper.

Altogether it was a bright look-out, and to crown
all, on the third morning Andrew went down like
a log with the worst bout of malaria I have ever
seen. That fairly put the lid on it. I thought it
was going to be black-water, and all my irritation
at the boy vanished in my anxiety. There was
nothing for it but to give up the expedition and

make the best speed possible to the coast. I made for Portuguese territory, and that evening got to the Limpopo. Happily we struck a more civil brand of native, who had not heard of our performances, and I was able to make a bargain with the headman of the village, who undertook to take charge of our outfit till it was sent for, and sold us a big native boat. I hired four lusty fellows as rowers, and next morning we started down the river.

We spent a giddy five days before I planted Andrew in hospital at Lourenço Marques. The sickness was not black-water, thank God, but it was a good deal more than ordinary malaria ; indeed, I think there was a touch of brain fever in it. Curiously enough I was rather relieved when it came. I had been scared by the boy's behaviour the first two days. I thought that the old priest had actually laid some curse on him ; I remembered how the glade and the well had solemnized even me, and I considered that Andrew, with a Kaffir strain somewhere in his ancestry, was probably susceptible to something which left me cold. I had knocked too much about Africa to be a dogmatic sceptic about the mysteries of the heathen. But this fever seemed to explain it. He had been sickening for it ; that was why he had behaved so badly to the old man, and had come back babbling about a green wildebeest. I knew that the beginnings of fever often make a man light-headed so that he loses all self-control and gets odd fancies. . . . All the same I didn't quite convince myself.

I couldn't get out of my head the picture of the
old man and his ominous words, or that empty
grove under the sunset.

I did my best for the boy, and before we reached
the coast the worst had passed. A bed was made
for him in the stern, and I had to watch him by
night and day to prevent him going overboard
among the crocodiles. He was apt to be violent,
for in this madness he thought he was being chased,
and sometimes I had all I could do to keep him in
the boat. He would scream like a thing demented,
and plead, and curse, and I noticed as a queer thing
that his ravings were never in Dutch but always in
Kaffir—mostly the Sesutu which he had learnt in
his childhood. I expected to hear him mention
the green wildebeest, but to my comfort he never
uttered the name. He gave no clue to what
frightened him, but it must have been a full-sized
terror, for every nerve in his body seemed to be
quivering, and I didn't care to look at his eyes.

The upshot was that I left him in bed in hospital,
as weak as a kitten, but with the fever gone and
restored to his right mind. He was again the good
fellow I had known, very apologetic and grateful.
So with an easy conscience I arranged for the re-
trieving of my outfit and returned to the Rand.

Well, for six months I lost sight of Andrew.
I had to go to Namaqualand, and then up to the
copper country of Barotseland, which wasn't as
easy a trek as it is to-day. I had one letter from
him, written from Johannesburg—not a very

satisfactory epistle, for I gathered that the boy
was very unsettled. He had quarrelled with his
family, and he didn't seem to be contented with
the job he had got in the goldfields. As I had
known him he had been a sort of school-book
industrious apprentice, determined to get on in the
world, and not in the least afraid of a dull job and
uncongenial company. But this letter was full of
small grouses. He wanted badly to have a talk
with me—thought of chucking his work and making
a trip north to see me ; and he ended with an under-
lined request that I should telegraph when I was
coming down-country. As it happened, I had no
chance just then of sending a telegram, and later
I forgot about it.

By-and-by I finished my tour and was at the
Falls, where I got a local Rhodesian paper. From
it I had news of Andrew with a vengeance. There
were columns about a murder in the bushveld—
two men had gone out to look for Kruger's treasure
and one had shot the other, and to my horror I
found that the one who was now lying in Pretoria
gaol under sentence of death was my unhappy
friend.

You remember the wild yarns after the Boer
War about a treasure of gold which Kruger in his
flight to the coast had buried somewhere in the
Selati country. That, of course, was all nonsense :
the wily ex-President had long before seen the main
funds safe in a European bank. But I daresay some
of the officials had got away with Treasury balances,
and there may have been bullion cached in the

bushveld. Anyhow, every scallywag south of the
Zambesi was agog about the business, and there
were no end of expeditions which never found a
single Transvaal sovereign. Well, it seemed that
two months before Andrew and a Dutchman called
Smit had started out to try their luck, and somewhere on the Olifants the two had gone out one
evening and only one had returned. Smit was
found by the native boys with a hole in his head,
and it was proved that the bullet came from
Andrew's rifle, which he had been carrying when
the two set out. After that the story became
obscure. Andrew had been very excited when
he returned and declared that he had " done it
at last," but when Smit's body was found he denied
that he had shot him. But it was clear that Smit
had been killed by Andrew's sporting ·303, and
the natives swore that the men had been constantly
quarrelling and that Andrew had always shown a
very odd temper. The Crown prosecutor argued
that the two believed they had found treasure,
and that Andrew had murdered Smit in cold blood
to prevent his sharing. The defence seemed to be
chiefly the impossibility of a guilty man behaving
as Andrew had behaved, and the likelihood of
his having fired at a beast in the dark and killed
his companion. It sounded to me very thin, and
the jury did not believe it, for their verdict was
wilful murder.

I knew that it was simply incredible that
Andrew could have committed the crime. Men
are queer cattle, and I wouldn't have put even

murder past certain fairly decent fellows I knew, but this boy was emphatically not one of them. Unless he had gone stark mad I was positive that he could never have taken human life. I knew him intimately, in the way you know a man you have lived alone with for months, and that was one of the things I could bank on. All the same it seemed clear that he had shot Smit. . . . I sent the longest telegram I ever sent in my life to a Scotch lawyer in Johannesburg called Dalgleish whom I believed in, telling him to move heaven and earth to get a reprieve. He was to see Andrew and wire me details about his state of mind. I thought then that temporary madness was probably our best line, and I believed myself that that was the explanation. I longed to take the train forthwith to Pretoria, but I was tied by the heels till the rest of my outfit came in. I was tortured by the thought that the hanging might have already taken place, for that wretched newspaper was a week old.

In two days I got Dalgleish's reply. He had seen the condemned man, and had told him that he came from me. He reported that Andrew was curiously peaceful and apathetic, and not very willing to talk about the business except to declare his innocence. Dalgleish thought him not quite right in his mind, but he had been already examined, and the court had rejected the plea of insanity. He sent his love to me and told me not to worry.

I stirred up Dalgleish again, and got a further reply. Andrew admitted that he had fired the rifle, but not at Smit. He had killed something, but what it was he would not say. He did not seem to be in the least keen to save his neck.

When I reached Bulawayo, on my way south, I had a brain-wave, but the thing seemed so preposterous that I could hardly take it seriously. Still I daren't neglect any chance, so I wired again to Dalgleish to try to have the execution postponed, until he got hold of the priest who lived in the berg above the Pufuri. I gave him full directions how to find him. I said that the old man had laid some curse on Andrew, and that that might explain his state of mind. After all, demoniacal possession must be equivalent in law to insanity. But by this time I had become rather hopeless. It seemed a futile thing to be wiring this rigmarole when every hour was bringing the gallows nearer.

I left the railroad at Mafeking, for I thought I could save the long circuit by De Aar by trekking across country. I would have done better to stick to the train, for everything went wrong with me. I had a breakdown at the drift of the Selons river and had to wait a day in Rustenburg, and I had trouble again at Commando Nek, so that it was the evening of the third day before I reached Pretoria. . . . As I feared, it was all over. They told me in the hotel that Andrew had been hanged that morning.

I went back to Johannesburg to see Dalgleish with a cold horror at my heart and complete mystification in my head. The Devil had taken an active hand in things and caused a hideous

miscarriage of justice.   If there had been anybody
I could blame I would have felt better, but the
fault seemed to lie only with the crookedness of
fate. . . . Dalgleish could tell me little.   Smit
had been the ordinary scallywag, not much of a
fellow and no great loss to the world ; the puzzle
was why Andrew wanted to go with him.   The boy
in his last days had been utterly apathetic—bore
no grudge against anybody—appeared at peace
with the world, but didn't seem to want to live.
The predikant who visited him daily could make
nothing of him.   He appeared to be sane enough,
but, beyond declaring his innocence, was not
inclined to talk, and gave no assistance to those
who were trying to get a reprieve . . . scarcely
took any interest in it. . . . He had asked repeatedly for me, and had occupied his last days in
writing me a long letter, which was to be delivered
unopened into my hand.   Dalgleish gave me the
thing, seven pages in Andrew's neat calligraphy,
and in the evening on his stoep I read it.

It was like a voice speaking to me out of the
grave, but it was not the voice I knew.   Gone was
the enlightened, commercially minded young man,
who had shed all superstition, and had a dapper
explanation for everything in heaven and earth.
It was a crude boy who had written those pages,
a boy in whose soul old Calvinistic terrors had been
awakened, and terrors older still out of primordial
African shadows.

He had committed a great sin—that was the
point he insisted upon, and by this sin he had set

free something awful to prey on the world. . . .
At first it seemed sheer raving mania to me, but as
I mused on it I remembered my own feelings in
that empty grove. I had been solemnized, and
this boy, with that in his blood which was not
in mine, had suffered a cataclysmic spiritual experience. He did not dwell on it, but his few
sentences were eloquent in their harsh intensity.
He had struggled, he had tried to make light of it,
to forget it, to despise it ; but it rode him like
a nightmare. He thought he was going mad. I
had been right about that touch of brain fever.

As far as I could make it out, he believed that
from that outraged sanctuary something real and
living had gone forth, something at any rate of
flesh and blood. But this idea may not have come
to him till later, when his mind had been for several
months in torture, and he had lost the power of
sleep. At first, I think, his trouble was only an
indefinite haunting, a sense of sin and impending
retribution. But in Johannesburg the *malaise* had
taken concrete form. He believed that through
his act something awful was at large, with infinite
power for evil—evil not only against the wrong-
doer himself but against the world. And he believed that it might still be stopped, that it was still
in the eastern bush. So crude a fancy showed how
his normal intelligence had gone to bits. He had
tumbled again into the backveld world of his childhood.

He decided to go and look for it. That was
where the tough white strain in him came out.

He might have a Kaffir's blind terrors, but he had
the frontier Boer's cast-iron courage. If you think
of it, it needed a pretty stout heart to set out to
find a thing the thought of which set every nerve
quivering. I confess I didn't like to contemplate
that lonely, white-faced, tormented boy. I think
he knew that tragedy must be the end of it, but
he had to face up to that and take the conse-
quences.

He heard of Smit's expedition, and took a half
share in it. Perhaps the fact that Smit had a
baddish reputation was part of the attraction. He
didn't want as companion a man with whom he had
anything in common, for he had to think his own
thoughts and follow his own course.

Well, you know the end of it. In his letter he
said nothing about the journey, except that he had
found what he sought. I can readily believe that
the two did not agree very well—the one hungry
for mythical treasure, the other with a problem
which all the gold in Africa could not solve. . . .
Somewhere, somehow, down in the Selati bushveld
his incubus took bodily form, and he met—or
thought he met—the thing which his impiety had
released. I suppose we must call it madness. He
shot his comrade, and thought he had killed an
animal. "If they had looked next morning they
would have found the spoor," he wrote. Smit's
death didn't seem to trouble him at all—I don't
think he quite realized it. The thing that mattered
for him was that he had put an end to a terror and
in some way made atonement. "Good-bye and

don't worry about me," were the last words, " I am quite content."

I sat a long time thinking, while the sun went down over the Magaliesberg. A gramophone was grinding away on an adjacent stoep, and the noise of the stamps on the Rand came like far-away drums. People at that time used to quote some Latin phrase about a new thing always coming out of Africa. I thought that it was not the new things in Africa that mattered, so much as the old things.

I proposed to revisit that berg above the Pufuri and have a word with the priest, but I did not get a chance till the following summer, when I trekked down the Limpopo from Main Drift. I didn't like the job, but I felt bound to have it out with that old man for Andrew's sake. You see, I wanted something more to convince the Wakkerstroom household that the boy had not been guilty, as his father thought, of the sin of Cain.

I came round the corner of the berg one January evening after a day of blistering heat, and looked down on the cup of green pasture. One glance showed me that there was not going to be any explanation with the priest. . . . A bit of the cliff had broken away, and the rock fall had simply blotted out the grove and the *rondavel*. A huge mass of débris sloped down from half-way up the hill, and buried under it were the tall trees through which I had peered up at the sky. Already it was feathered with thorn-bush and grasses. There were no patches of crops on the sides of the cup, and crumbling mud walls were all that remained of the kraal. The jungle had flowed over the village, and, when I entered it, great moon-flowers sprawled on the rubble, looking in the dusk like ghosts of a vanished race.

There was one new feature in the place. The landslip must have released the underground water, for a stream now flowed down the hollow. Beside it, in a meadow full of agapanthus and arum lilies, I found two Australian prospectors. One of them —he had been a Melbourne bank-clerk—had a poetic soul. "Nice little place," he said. "Not littered up with black fellows. If I were on a homesteading job, I reckon I'd squat here."

II. THE FRYING-PAN AND THE FIRE

THE DUKE OF BURMINSTER'S STORY

From the Bath, in its most exotic form, degenerate patrician youth passed to the coarse delights of the Circus, and thence to that parody of public duties which it was still the fashion of their class to patronize.

Von Letterbeck : *Imperial Rome.*

II. THE FRYING-PAN AND THE FIRE

PART I—THE FRYING-PAN

LAMANCHA had been staying for the week-end at some country house, and had returned full of wrath at the way he had been made to spend his evenings. "I thought I hated bridge," he said, "but I almost longed for it as a change from cracking my brain and my memory to find lines from poets I had forgotten to describe people I didn't know. I don't like games that make me feel a congenital idiot. But there was one that rather amused me. You invented a preposterous situation, and the point was to explain naturally how it came about. Drink, lunacy, and practical joking were barred as explanations. One problem given was the Bishop of London on a camel, with a string of sea-trout round his neck, playing on a penny whistle on the Hoe at Plymouth. There was a fellow there, a Chancery K.C., who provided a perfectly sensible explanation."

"I have heard of stranger things," said Sandy Arbuthnot, and he winked at Burminster, who flushed and looked uncomfortable. As the rest of our eyes took the same direction the flush deepened on that round, cheerful face.

"It's no good, Mike," said Arbuthnot. "We've been waiting months for that story of yours, and this is the place and the hour for it. We'll take no denial."

"Confound you, Sandy, I can't tell it. It's too dashed silly."

"Not a bit of it. It's full of profound philosophical lessons, and it's sheer romance, as somebody has defined the thing—strangeness flowering from the commonplace. So pull up your socks and get going."

"I don't know how to begin," said Burminster.

"Well, I'll start it for you. . . . The scene is the railway station of Langshiels on the Scottish Borders on a certain day last summer. On the platform are various gentlemen in their best clothes with rosettes in their buttonholes—all strictly sober, it being but the third hour of the afternoon. There are also the rudiments of a brass band. Clearly a distinguished visitor is expected. The train enters the station, and from a third-class carriage descends our only Mike with a muddy face and a scratched nose. He is habited in dirty white cord breeches, shocking old butcher boots, a purple knitted waistcoat, and what I believe is called a morning coat; over all this splendour a ticky ulster—clearly not his own since it does not meet—and on his head an unspeakable bowler hat. He is welcomed by the deputation and departs, attended by the band, to a political meeting in the Town Hall. But first—I quote from the local paper—'the Duke, who had arrived in sporting costume, proceeded to the Station Hotel, where he rapidly changed.' We want to know the reason of these cantrips."

Burminster took a long pull at his tankard, and looked round the company with more composure.

" It isn't much of a story, but it's true, and, like nearly every scrape I ever got into, Archie Roylance was at the bottom of it. It all started from a discussion I had with Archie. He was staying with me at Larristane, and we got talking about the old Border raiders and the way the face of the countryside had changed and that sort of thing. Archie said that, now the land was as bare as a marble-topped table and there was no cover on the hills to hide a tomtit, a man couldn't ride five miles anywhere between the Cheviots and the Clyde without being seen by a dozen people. I said that there was still plenty of cover if you knew how to use it—that you could hide yourself as well on bent and heather as in a thick wood if you studied the shadows and the lie of the land, same as an aeroplane can hide itself in an empty sky. Well, we argued and argued, and the upshot was that I backed myself to ride an agreed course, without Archie spotting me. There wasn't much money on it—only an even sovereign—but we both worked ourselves up into considerable keenness. That was where I fell down. I might have known that anything Archie was keen about would end in the soup.

" The course we fixed was about fifteen miles long, from Gledfoot bridge over the hills between Gled and Aller and the Blae Moor to the Mains of

4

Blae. That was close to Kirk Aller, and we agreed, if we didn't meet before, to forgather at the Cross Keys and have tea and motor home. Archie was to start from a point about four miles north-east of Gledfoot and cut in on my road at a tangent. I could shape any course I liked, but I couldn't win unless I got to the Mains of Blae before five o'clock without being spotted. The rule about that was that he must get within speaking distance of me— say three hundred yards—before he held me up. All the Larristane horses were at grass, so we couldn't look for pace. I chose an old hunter of mine that was very leery about bogs; Archie picked a young mare that I had hunted the season before and that he had wanted to buy from me. He said that by rights he ought to have the speedier steed, since, if he spotted me, he had more or less to ride me down.

"We thought it was only a pleasant summer day's diversion. I didn't want to give more than a day to it, for I had guests arriving that evening, and on the Wednesday—this was a Monday—I had to take the chair for Deloraine at a big Conservative meeting at Langshiels, and I meant to give a lot of time to preparing a speech. I ought to say that neither of us knew the bit of country beyond its general lines, and we were forbidden to carry maps. The horses were sent on, and at 9.30 a.m. I was at Gledfoot bridge ready to start. I was wearing khaki riding breeches, polo boots, an old shooting coat, and a pretty old felt hat. I mention my costume, for later it became important.

" I may as well finish with Archie, for he doesn't come any more into this tale. He hadn't been half an hour in the saddle when he wandered into a bog, and it took him till three in the afternoon to get his horse out. Consequently he chucked in his hand, and went back to Larristane. So all the time I was riding cunning and watching out of my right eye to see him on the skyline, he was sweating and blaspheming in a peat moss.

" I started from Gledfoot up the Rinks burn in very good spirits, for I had been studying the big Ordnance map and I believed I had a soft thing. Beyond the Rinks Hope I would cross the ridge to the top of the Skyre burn, which at its head is all split up into deep grassy gullies. I had guessed this from the map, and the people at Gledfoot had confirmed it. By one or other of these gullies I could ride in good cover till I reached a big wood of firs that stretched for a mile down the left bank of the burn. Archie, to cut in on me, had a pretty steep hill to cross, and I calculated that by the time he got on the skyline I would be in the shelter of one of the gullies or even behind the wood. Not seeing me on the upper Skyre, he would think that I had bustled a bit and would look for me lower down the glen. I would lie doggo and watch for him, and when I saw him properly started I meant to slip up a side burn and get into the parallel glen of the Hollin. Once there I would ride like blazes, and either get to the Blae Moor before him—in which case I would simply canter at ease up to the Mains of Blae—or, if I saw him ahead of me, fetch a circuit among the plantings and come in on the farm from the other side. That was the general lay out, but I had other dodges in hand in case Archie tried to be clever.

"So I tittuped along the hill turf beside the Rinks burn, feeling happy and pretty certain I would win. My horse, considering he was fresh from the grass, behaved very well, and we travelled in good style. My head was full of what I was going to say at Langshiels, and I thought of some rather fine things —'Our opponents would wreck the old world in order to build a new, but you cannot found any system on chaos, not even Communism'—I rather fancied that. Well, to make a long story short, I got to the Rinks Hope in thirty minutes, and there I found the herd gathering his black-faced lambs.

"Curiously enough I knew the man—Prentice they called him—for he had been one of the young shepherds at Larristane. So I stopped to have a word with him, and watched him at work. He was short-handed for the job, and he had a young collie only half-trained, so I offered to give him a hand and show my form as a mounted stockman. The top of that glen was splendid going, and I volunteered to round up the west hirsel. I considered that I had plenty of time and could spare ten minutes to help a pal.

"It was a dashed difficult job, and it took me a good half-hour, and it was a mercy my horse didn't get an over-reach among the mossy well-heads. However, I did it, and when I started off again both I and my beast were in a lather of sweat. That

must have confused me, and the way I had been
making circles round the sheep, for I struck the
wrong feeder, and instead of following the one that
led to the top of the Skyre burn I kept too much to
my left. When I got to the watershed I looked
down on a country utterly different from what I
had expected. There was no delta of deep gullies,
but a broad green cup seamed with stone walls,
and below it a short glen which presently ran out
into the broader vale of the Aller.

" The visibility was none too good, so I could not
make out the further prospect. I ought to have
realized that this was not the Skyre burn. But
I only concluded that I had misread the map, and
besides, there was a big wood lower down which
I thought was the one I had remarked. There was
no sign of Archie as yet on the high hills to my right,
so I decided I had better get off the skyline and
make my best speed across that bare green cup.

" It took me a long time, for I had a lot of trouble
with the stone dykes. The few gates were all
fastened up with wire, and I couldn't manage to
undo them. So I had to scramble over the first
dyke, and half pull down the next, and what with
one thing and another I wasted a shocking amount
of time. When I got to the bottom, I found that
the burn was the merest trickle, not the strong
stream of the Skyre, which is a famous water for
trout. But there, just ahead of me, was the big
wood, so I decided I must be right after all.

" I had kept my eye lifting to the ridge on the
right, and suddenly I saw Archie. I know now

that it wasn't he, but it was a man on a horse and it looked his living image. He was well down the hillside and he was moving fast. He didn't appear to have seen me, but I realized that he would in a minute, unless I found cover.

" I jogged my beast with the spur, and in three seconds was under cover of the fir-wood. But here I found a track, and it struck me that it was this track which Archie was following, and that he would soon be up with me. The only thing to do seemed to be to get inside the wood. But this was easier said than done, for a great wall with broken bottles on the top ran round that blessed place. I had to do something pretty quick, for I could hear the sound of hoofs behind me, and on the left there was nothing but the benty side of a hill.

" Just then I saw a gate, a massive thing of close-set oak splints, and for a mercy it was open. I pushed through it and slammed it behind me. It shut with a sharp click as if it was a patent self-locking arrangement. A second later I heard the noise of a horse outside and hands trying the gate. Plainly they couldn't open it. The man I thought was Archie said ' Damn ' and moved away.

" I had found sanctuary, but the question now was how to get out of it. I dismounted and wrestled with the gate, but it was as firm as a rock. About this time I began to realize that something was wrong, for I couldn't think why Archie should have wanted to get through the gate if he hadn't seen me, and, if he had seen me, why he hadn't shouted, according to our rules. Besides, this wasn't a wood, it was the grounds of some house, and the map had shown no house in the Skyre glen. . . . The only thing to do was to find somebody to let me out. I didn't like the notion of riding about in a stranger's policies, so I knotted my bridle and let my beast graze, while I proceeded on foot to prospect.

" The ground shelved steeply, and almost at once my feet went from under me and I slithered down a bank of raw earth. You see there was no grip in the smooth soles of my polo boots. The next I knew I had banged hard into the back of a little wooden shelter which stood on a sunny mantelpiece of turf above the stream. I picked myself up and limped round the erection, rubbing the dirt from my eyes, and came face to face with a group of people.

" They were all women, except one man, who was reading aloud to them, and they were all lying in long chairs. Pretty girls they seemed to be from the glimpse I had of them, but rather pale, and they all wore bright-coloured cloaks.

" I daresay I looked a bit of a ruffian, for I was very warm and had got dirty in slithering down, and had a rent in my breeches. At the sight of me the women gave one collective bleat like a snipe, and gathered up their skirts and ran. I could see their cloaks glimmering as they dodged like woodcock among the rhododendrons.

" The man dropped his book and got up and faced me. He was a young fellow with a cadaverous face and side-whiskers, and he seemed to be in

a funk of something, for his lips twitched and his
hands shook as if he had fever. I could see that
he was struggling to keep calm.

" ' So you've come back, Mr. Brumby,' he said.
' I hope you had a g-good time ? '

" For a moment I had a horrid suspicion that he
knew me, for they used to call me ' Brummy ' at
school. A second look convinced me that we had
never met, and I realized that the word he had used
was Brumby. I hadn't a notion what he meant,
but the only thing seemed to be to brazen it out.
That was where I played the fool. I ought to have
explained my mistake there and then, but I still
had the notion that Archie was hanging about, and
I wanted to dodge him. I dropped into a long
chair, and said that I had come back and that it was
a pleasant day. Then I got out my pipe.

" ' Here, you mustn't do that,' he said. ' It
isn't allowed.'

" I put the pipe away, and wondered what lunatic
asylum I had wandered into. I wasn't permitted
to wonder long, for up the path from the rhododendrons came two people in a mighty hurry. One
was an anxious-faced oldish man dressed like a
valet, and the other a middle-aged woman in nurse's
uniform. Both seemed to be excited, and both to
be trying to preserve an air of coolness.

" ' Ah, Schwester,' said the fellow with the
whiskers. ' Here is Mr. Brumby back again and
none the worse.'

" The woman, who had kind eyes and a nice
gurgling voice, looked at me reproachfully.

" ' I hope you haven't taken any harm, sir,' she said. ' We had better go back to the house, and Mr. Grimpus will give you a nice bath and a change, and you'll lie down a bit before luncheon. You must be very tired, sir. You'd better take Mr. Grimpus's arm.'

" My head seemed to be spinning, but I thought it best to lie low and do what I was told till I got some light. Silly ass that I was, I was still on the tack of dodging Archie. I could easily have floored Grimpus, and the man with the whiskers wouldn't have troubled me much, but there was still the glass-topped wall to get over, and there might be heftier people about—grooms and gardeners and the like. Above all, I didn't want to make any more scenes, for I had already scared a lot of sick ladies into the rhododendrons.

" So I went off quite peaceably with Grimpus and the sister, and presently we came to a house like a small hydropathic, hideously ugly but beautifully placed, with a view south to the Aller valley. There were more nurses in the hall, and a porter with a jaw like a prize-fighter. Well, I went up in a lift to the second floor, and there was a bed-room with a balcony, and several trunks, and brushes on the dressing-table lettered H. B. They made me strip and get into a dressing-gown, and then a doctor arrived, a grim fellow with gold spectacles and a soft, bedside manner. He spoke to me soothingly about the beauty of the weather and how the heather would soon be in bloom on the hill ; he also felt my pulse and took my blood pressure, and talked for a long time in a corner with the sister. If he said there was anything wrong with me he lied, for I had never felt fitter in my life except for the bewilderment of my brain.

"Then I was taken down in a lift to the basement, and Grimpus started out to give me a bath. My hat! that was a bath! I lay in six inches of scalding water, while a boiling cataract beat on my stomach; then it changed to hot hail and then to gouts that hit like a pickaxe; and then it all turned to ice. But it made me feel uncommonly frisky. After that they took me back to my bedroom and I had a gruelling massage, and what I believe they call violet rays. By this time I was fairly bursting with vim, but I thought it best to be quite passive, and when they told me I must try to sleep before luncheon, I only grinned and put my head on the pillow like a child. When they left me I badly wanted to smoke, but my pipe had gone with my clothes, and I found laid out for me a complete suit of the man Brumby's flannels.

"As I lay and reflected I began to get my bearings. I knew where I was. It was a place called Craigiedean, about six miles from Kirk Aller, which had been used as a shell-shock hospital during the War and had been kept on as a home for nervous cases. It wasn't a private asylum, as I had thought at first; it called itself a Kurhaus, and was supposed to be the last thing in science outside Germany. Now and then, however, it got some baddish cases, people who were almost off their rocker, and I fancied that Brumby was one. He was apparently my double, but I didn't believe in exact doubles, so I guessed that he had just arrived, and hadn't given the staff time to know him well before he went off on the bend. The horseman whom I had taken for Archie must have been out scouring the hills for him.

" Well, I had dished Archie all right, but I had also dished myself. At any moment the real Brumby might wander back, and then there would be a nice show up. The one thing that terrified me was that my identity should be discovered, for this was more or less my own countryside, and I should look a proper ass if it got about that I had been breaking into a nerve-cure place, frightening women, and getting myself treated like a gentle loony. Then I remembered that my horse was in the wood and might be trusted to keep on grazing along the inside of the wall where nobody went. My best plan seemed to be to wait my chance, slip out of the house, recover my beast, and find some way out of the infernal park. The wall couldn't be everywhere, for, after all, the place wasn't an asylum.

" A gong sounded for luncheon, so I nipped up, and got into Brumby's flannels. They were all right for length, but a bit roomy. My money and the odds and ends from my own pockets were laid out on the dressing-table, but not my pipe and pouch, which I judged had been confiscated.

" I wandered downstairs to a big dining-room, full of little tables, with the most melancholy outfit seated at them that you ever saw in all your days.

The usual thing was to have a table to oneself, but sometimes two people shared one—husband and wife, no doubt, or mother and daughter. There were eight males including me, and the rest were females of every age from flappers to grandmothers. Some looked pretty sick, some quite blooming, but all had a watchful air, as if they were holding themselves in and pursuing some strict régime. There was no conversation, and everybody had brought a book or a magazine which they diligently studied. In the centre of each table, beside the salt and pepper, stood a little fleet of medicine bottles. The sister who led me to my place planted down two beside me.

" I soon saw the reason of the literary absorption. The food was simply bestial. I was hungry and thirsty enough to have eaten two beefsteaks and drunk a quart of beer, and all I got was three rusks, a plate of thin soup, a purée of vegetables, and a milk pudding in a teacup. I envied the real Brumby, who at that moment, if he had any sense, was doing himself well in a public-house. I didn't dare to ask for more in case of inviting awkward questions, so I had plenty of leisure to observe the company. Nobody looked at anybody else, for it seemed to be the fashion to pretend you were alone in a wilderness, and even the couples did not talk to each other. I made a cautious preliminary survey to see if there was any one I knew, but they were all strangers. After a time I felt so lonely that I wanted to howl.

" At last the company began to get up and

straggle out. The sister whom I had seen first—
the others called her Schwester and she seemed to
be rather a boss—appeared with a bright smile
and gave me my medicine. I had to take two pills
and some horrid drops out of a brown bottle. I
pretended to be very docile, and I thought that I'd
take the chance to pave the way to getting to my
horse. So I said that I felt completely rested, and
would like a walk that afternoon. She shook her
head.

" ' No, Mr. Brumby. Dr. Miggle's orders are
positive that you rest to-day.'

" ' But I'm feeling really very fit,' I protested.
' I'm the kind of man who needs a lot of exercise.'

" ' Not yet,' she said with a patient smile. ' At
present your energy is morbid. It comes from an
irregular nervous complex, and we must first cure
that before you can lead a normal life. Soon you'll
be having nice long walks. You promised your
wife, you know, to do everything that you were
told, and it was very wrong of you to slip out last
night and make us all so anxious. Dr. Miggle says
that must *never* happen again.' And she wagged
a reproving finger.

" So I had a wife to add to my troubles. I began
now to be really worried, for not only might
Brumby turn up any moment, but his precious
spouse, and I didn't see how I was to explain to
her what I was doing in her husband's trousers.
Also the last sentence disquieted me. Dr. Miggle
was determined that I should not bolt again, and
he looked a resolute lad. That meant that I

would be always under observation, and that at night my bedroom door would be locked.

"I made an errand to go up to my room, while Grimpus waited for me in the hall, and had a look at the window. There was a fine thick Virginia creeper which would make it easy to get to the floor beneath, but it was perfectly impossible to reach the ground, for below was a great chasm of a basement. There was nothing doing that way, unless I went through the room beneath, and that meant another outrage and probably an appalling row.

"I felt very dispirited as I descended the stairs, till I saw a woman coming out of that identical room. . . . Blessed if it wasn't my Aunt Letitia!

"I needn't have been surprised, for she gave herself out as a martyr to nerves, and was always racing about the world looking for a cure. She saw me, took me for Brumby, and hurried away. Evidently Brumby's doings had got about, and there were suspicions of his sanity. The moment was not propitious for following her, since Grimpus was looking at me.

"I was escorted to the terrace by Grimpus, tucked up in a long chair, and told to stay there and bask in the sun. I must not read, but I could sleep if I liked. I never felt less like slumber, for I was getting to be a very good imitation of a mental case. I must get hold of Aunt Letitia. I could see her in her chair at the other end of the terrace, but if I got up and went to her she would take me for that loony Brumby and have a fit.

"I lay cogitating and baking in the sun for about

two hours. Then I observed that sisters were bringing out tea or medicines to some of the patients, and I thought I saw a chance of a move. I called one of them to me, and in a nice invalidish voice complained that the sun was too hot for me and that I wanted to be moved to the other end where there was more shade. The sister went off to find Grimpus, and presently that sportsman appeared.

" ' I've had enough of this sun-bath,' I told him, ' and I feel a headache coming. I want you to shift me to the shade of the beeches over there.'

" ' Very good, sir,' he said, and helped me to rise, while he picked up chair and rugs. I tottered delicately after him, and indicated a vacant space next to Aunt Letitia. She was dozing, and mercifully did not see me. The chair on my other side was occupied by an old gentleman who was sound asleep.

" I waited for a few minutes and began to wriggle my chair a bit nearer. Then I made a pellet of earth from a crack in the paving stones and jerked it neatly on to her face.

" ' Hist ! ' I whispered. ' Wake up, Aunt Letty.'

" She opened one indignant eye, and turned it on me, and I thought she was going to swoon.

" ' Aunt Letty,' I said in an agonized voice. ' For heaven's sake don't shout. I'm not Brumby. I'm your nephew Michael.'

" Her nerves were better than I thought, for she managed to take a pull on herself and listen to me while I muttered my tale. I could see that she hated the whole affair, and had some kind of grievance against me for outraging the sanctity of her pet cure. However, after a bit of parleying, she behaved like a brick.

" ' You are the head of our family, Michael,' she said, ' and I am bound to help you out of the position in which your own rashness has placed you. I agree with you that it is essential to have no disclosure of identity. It is the custom here for patients to retire to their rooms at eight-thirty. At nine o'clock I shall have my window open, and if you enter by it you can leave by the door. That is the most I can do for you. Now please be silent, for I am ordered to be very still for an hour before tea.'

" You can imagine that after that the time went slowly. Grimpus brought me a cup of tea and a rusk, and I fell asleep and only woke when he came at half-past six to escort me indoors. I would have given pounds for a pipe. Dinner was at seven, and I said that I would not trouble to change, though Brumby's dress-clothes were laid out on the bed. I had the needle badly, for I had a horrid fear that Brumby might turn up before I got away.

" Presently the doctor arrived, and after cooing over me a bit and feeling my pulse, he started out to cross-examine me about my past life. I suppose that was to find out the subconscious complexes which were upsetting my wits. I decided to go jolly carefully, for I suspected that he had either given Brumby the once-over or had got some sort of report about his case. I was right, for the first

thing he asked me was about striking my sister
at the age of five. Well, I haven't got a sister,
but I had to admit to beating Brumby's, and I
said the horrible affair still came between me and
my sleep. That seemed to puzzle him, for apparently I oughtn't to have been thinking about it ;
it should have been buried deep in my unconscious
self, and worrying me like a thorn in your finger
which you can't find. He asked me a lot about my
nurse, and I said that she had a brother who went
to gaol for sheep-stealing. He liked that, and said
it was a fruitful line of inquiry. Also he wanted to
know about my dreams, and said I should write
them down. I said I had dreamed that a mare
called Nursemaid won the Oaks, but found there
was no such animal running. That cheered him up
a bit, and he said that he thought my nurse might
be the clue. At that I very nearly gave the show
away by laughing, for my nurse was old Alison
Hyslop, who is now the housekeeper at Larristane,
and if anybody called her a clue she'd have their
blood.

"Dinner was no better than luncheon—the same
soup and rusks and vegetables, with a bit of ill-
nourished chicken added. This time I had to
take three kinds of medicine instead of two. I told
the sister that I was very tired, and Grimpus took
me upstairs at eight o'clock. He said that Dr.
Miggle proposed to give me another go of violet
rays, but I protested so strongly that I was too
sleepy for his ministrations that Grimpus, after
going off to consult him, announced that for that

evening the rays would be omitted. You see I was afraid that they would put me to bed and remove my clothes, and I didn't see myself trapesing about the country in Brumby's pyjamas.

"As Grimpus left me I heard the key turn in the lock. It was as well that I had made a plan with Aunt Letitia.

"At nine o'clock I got out of my window. It was a fine night, with the sun just setting and a young moon. The Virginia creeper was sound, and in less than a minute I was outside Aunt Letitia's window. She was waiting in a dressing-gown to let me in, and I believe the old soul really enjoyed the escapade. She wanted to give me money for my travels, but I told her that I had plenty. I poked my nose out, saw that the staircase and hall were empty, and quietly closed the door behind me.

"The big hall door was shut, and I could hear the prize-fighting porter moving in his adjacent cubby hole. There was no road that way, so I turned to the drawing-room, which opened on the terrace. But that was all in darkness, and I guessed that the windows were shuttered. There was nothing for it but to try downstairs. I judged that the servants would be at supper, so I went through a green-baize swing-door and down a long flight of stone steps.

"Suddenly I blundered into a brightly lit kitchen. There was no one in it, and beyond was a door which looked as if it might lead to the open air. It actually led to a scullery, where a maid was busy at a tap. She was singing to herself a song called 'When the kye come hame,' so I knew she belonged to the countryside. So did I, and I resolved to play the bold game.

" ' Hey, lassie,' I said. ' Whaur's the road out o' this hoose ? I maun be back in Kirk Aller afore ten.'

" The girl stopped her singing and stared at me. Then in response to my grin she laughed.

" ' Are ye frae Kirk Aller ? ' she asked.

" ' I've gotten a job there,' I said. ' I'm in the Cally station, and I cam' up about a parcel for ane o' the leddies here. But I come frae farther up the water, Larristane way.'

" ' D'ye say sae ? I'm frae Gledside mysel'. What gars ye be in sic a hurry ? It's a fine nicht and there's a mune.'

" She was a flirtatious damsel, but I had no time for dalliance.

" ' There's a lassie in Kirk Aller will take the heid off me if I keep her waitin'.'

" She tossed her head and laughed. ' Haste ye then, my mannie. Is it Shanks' powny ? '

" ' Na, na, I've a bicycle ootbye.'

" ' Well, through the wash-hoose and up the steps and roond by the roddydendrums and ye're in the yaird. Guid-nicht to you.'

" I went up the steps like a lamplighter and dived into the rhododendrons, coming out on the main avenue. It ran long and straight to the lodge gates, and I didn't like the look of it. My first business was to find my horse, and I had thought out more or less the direction. The house stood on the right bank of the burn, and if I kept to my left I would cross the said burn lower down and could then walk up the other side. I did this without trouble. I forded the burn in the meadow, and was soon climbing the pine-wood which clothed the gorge. In less than twenty minutes I had reached the gate in the wall by which I had entered.

" There was no sign of my horse anywhere. I followed the wall on my left till it curved round and crossed the burn, but the beast was not there, and it was too dark to look for hoof marks. I tried to my right and got back to the level of the park, but had no better luck. If I had had any sense I would have given up the quest, and trusted to getting as far as Gledfoot on my own feet. The horse might be trusted to turn up in his own time. Instead I went blundering on in the half-light of the park, and presently I blundered into trouble.

" Grimpus must have paid another visit to my room, found me gone, seen the open window, and started a hue-and-cry. They would not suspect my Aunt Letitia, and must have thought that I had dropped like a cat into the basement. The pursuit was coming down the avenue, thinking I had made for the lodge gates, and as ill-luck would have it, I had selected that moment to cross the drive, and they spotted me. I remember that out of a corner of one eye I saw the lights of a fly coming up the drive, and I wondered if Brumby had selected this inauspicious moment to return.

" I fled into the park with three fellows after me. Providence never meant me for a long-distance

runner, and besides, I was feeling weak from lack
of nourishment. But I was so scared of what
would happen if I was caught that I legged it
like a miler, and the blighters certainly didn't
gain on me.

"But what I came to was the same weary old
wall with the bottle glass on the top of it. I was
pretty desperate, and I thought I saw a way. A
young horse-chestnut tree grew near the wall and
one bough overhung it. I made a jump at the
first branch, caught it, and with a bit of trouble
swung myself up into the crutch. This took time,
and one of the fellows came up and made a grab
at my leg, but I let him have Brumby's rubber-
soled heel in the jaw.

"I caught the bigger branch and wriggled along
it till I was above and beyond the wall. Then the
dashed thing broke with my twelve stone, and I
descended heavily on what looked like a highroad.

"There was no time to spare, though I was a
bit shaken, for the pursuit would not take long to
follow me. I started off down that road looking
for shelter, and I found it almost at once. There
was a big covered horse-van moving ahead of me,
with a light showing from the interior. I sprinted
after it, mounted the step, and stuck my head
inside.

"'Can I come in?' I panted. 'Hide me for
ten minutes and I'll explain.'

"I saw an old, spectacled, whiskered face. It
was portentously solemn, but I thought I saw a
twinkle in the eye.

" ' Ay,' said a toothless mouth, ' ye can come in.'
A hand grabbed my collar, and I was hauled inside.
That must have been just when the first of my pur-
suers dropped over the wall."

PART II—THE FIRE

" I had got into a caravan which was a sort of
bedroom, and behind the driver's seat was a double
curtain.   There I made myself inconspicuous while
the old man parleyed with the pursuit.

" ' Hae ye seen a gentleman ? ' I could hear a
panting voice.   ' Him that drappit ower the wa' ?
He was rinnin' hard.'

" ' What kind of a gentleman ? '

" ' He had on grey claithes—aboot the same
height as mysel'.'   The speaker was not Grimpus.

" ' Naebody passed me,' was the strictly truthful
answer.   ' Ye'd better seek the ither side o' the
road among the bracken.   There's plenty hidy-
holes there.   Wha's the man ? '

" ' Ane o' the doctor's folk.'   I knew, though I
could not see, that the man had tapped his forehead
significantly.   ' Aweel, I'll try back.   Guid-nicht
to ye.'

" I crept out of my refuge and found the old man
regarding me solemnly under the swinging lamp.

" ' I'm one of the auld-fashioned Radicals,' he
announced, ' and I'm for the liberty o' the indi-
vidual.   I dinna hold wi' lockin' folks up because a
pernicketty doctor says they're no wise.   But I'd

be glad to be assured, sir, that ye're no a dangerous lunattic. If ye are, Miggle has nae business to be workin' wi' lunattics. His hoose is no an asylum.'

" ' I'm as sane as you are,' I said, and as shortly as I could I told him my story. I said I was a laird on Gledwater-side—which was true, and that my name was Brown—which wasn't. I told him about my bet with Archie, and my ride and its disastrous ending. His face never moved a muscle ; probably he didn't believe me, but because of his political principles he wasn't going to give me away.

" ' Ye can bide the night with me,' he said. ' The morn we'll be busy and ye can gang wherever ye like. It's a free country in spite o' our God-forsaken Government.'

" I blessed him, and asked to whom I was indebted for this hospitality.

" ' I'm the Great McGowan,' he said. ' The feck o' the pawraphernalia is on ahead. We open the morn in Kirk Aller.'

" He had spoken his name as if it were Mussolini or Dempsey, one which all the world should know. I knew it too, for it had been familiar to me from childhood. You could have seen it any time in the last twenty years flaming upon hoardings up and down the Lowlands—The Great McGowan's Marvellous Multitudinous Menagerie—McGowan's Colossal Circassian Circus—The Only Original McGowan.

" We rumbled on for another half-mile, and then turned from the road into a field. As we bumped over the grass I looked out of the door and saw

about twenty big caravans and wagons at anchor
There was a strong smell of horses and of cooking
food, and above it I seemed to detect the odour of
unclean beasts. We took up our station apart
from the rest, and after the proprietor had satisfied
himself by a brief inspection that the whole outfit
was there, he announced that it was time to retire
Mr. McGowan had apparently dined, and he did
not offer me food, which I would have welcomed,
but he mixed me a rummer of hot toddy. I
wondered if it would disagree with the various
medicines I had been compelled to take, and make
me very sick in the night. Then he pointed out
my bunk, undressed himself as far as his shirt,
pulled a nightcap over his venerable head, and in
five minutes was asleep. I had had a wearing day,
and in spite of the stuffiness of the place it wasn't
long before I dropped off also.

"I awoke next morning to find myself alone in
the caravan. I opened the window and saw that
a fine old racket was going on. The show had
started to move, and as the caravans bumped over
the turf various specimens inside were beginning
to give tongue. It was going to be a gorgeous day
and very hot. I was a little bit anxious about my
next move, for Kirk Aller was unpleasantly near
Craigiedean and Dr. Miggle. In the end I decided
that my best plan would be to take the train to
Langshiels and there hire a car to Larristane,
after sending a telegram to say I was all right, in
case my riderless steed should turn up before me.
I hadn't any headgear, but I thought I could buy

something in Kirk Aller, and trust to luck that nobody from the Kurhaus spotted me in the street. I wanted a bath and a shave and breakfast, but I concluded I had better postpone them till I reached the hotel at Langshiels.

"Presently Mr. McGowan appeared, and I could see by his face that something had upset him. He was wearing an old check dressing-gown, and he had been padding about in his bare feet on the dewy grass.

"'Ye telled me a story last night, Mr. Brown,' he began solemnly, 'which I didna altogether believe. I apologize for being a doubting Thomas. I believe every word o't, for I've just had confirmation.'

"I mumbled something about being obliged to him, and he went on.

"'Ay, for the pollis were here this morning— seeking you. Yon man at Craigiedean is terrible ill-set against ye, Mr. Brown. The pollisman— his name's Tam Doig, I ken him fine—says they're looking for a man that personated an inmate, and went off wi' some o' the inmate's belongings. I'm quotin' Tam Doig. I gave Tam an evasive answer, and he's off on his bicycle the other road, but—I ask ye as a freend, Mr. Brown—what are precisely the facts o' the case?'

"'Good God!' I said. 'It's perfectly true. These clothes I'm wearing belong to the man Brumby, though they've got my own duds in exchange. He must have come back after I left. What an absolutely infernal mess! I suppose they could have me up for theft.'

" ' Mair like obtaining goods on false pretences, though I think ye have a sound answer. But that's no the point, Mr. Brown. The doctor is set on payin' off scores. Ye've entered his sawnatorium and gone through a' the cantrips he provides, and ye've made a gowk o' him. He wants to make an example o' *you*. Tam Doig was sayin' that he's been bleezin' half the night on the telephone, an' he'll no rest till ye're grippit. Now ye tell me that ye're a laird and a man o' some poseetion, and I believe ye. It wad be an ill job for you and your freends if ye was to appear before the Shirra.'

" I did some rapid thinking. So far I was safe, for there was nothing about the clothes I had left behind to identify me. I was pretty certain that my horse had long ago made a bee-line for the Larristane stables. If I could only get home without being detected, I might regard the episode as closed.

" ' Supposing I slip off now,' I said. ' I have a general notion of the land, and I might get over the hills without anybody seeing me.'

" He shook his head. ' Ye wouldn't travel a mile. Your description has been circulated and a' body's lookin' for ye—a man in a grey flannel suit and soft shoes wi' a red face and nae hat. Guid kens what the doctor has said about ye, but the countryside is on the look-out for a dangerous, and maybe lunattic, criminal. There's a reward offered of nae less than twenty pound.'

" ' Can you not take me with you to Kirk Aller ? ' I asked despairingly.

" ' Ay, ye can stop wi' me. But what better wad ye be in Kirk Aller ? That's where the Procurator Fiscal bides.'

" Then he put on his spectacles and looked at me solemnly.

" ' I've taken a fancy to ye, Mr. Brown, and ye can tell the world that. I ask you, are ye acquaint wi' horses ? '

" I answered that I had lived among them all my life, and had been in the cavalry before I went into the Air Force.

" ' I guessed it by your face. Horses have a queer trick o' leavin' their mark on a body. Now, because I like ye, I'll make a proposeetion to ye that I would make to no other man. . . . I'm without a ring-master. Joseph Japp, who for ten years has had the job with me, is lyin' wi' the influenzy at Berwick. I could make shift with Dublin Davie, but Davie has no more presence than a messan dog, and forbye Joseph's clothes wouldna fit him. When I cast my eyes on ye this mornin' after hearin' Tam Doig's news, I says to mysel', " Thou art the man." '

" Of course I jumped at the offer. I was as safe in Kirk Aller, as Joseph Japp's under-study, as I was in my own house. Besides, I liked the notion ; it would be a good story to tell Archie. But I said it could only be for one night, and that I must leave to-morrow, and he agreed. ' I want to make a good show for a start in Kirk Aller—forbye, Joseph will be ready to join me at Langshiels.'

" I borrowed the old boy's razor and had a shave

and a wash, while he was cooking breakfast. After we had fed he fetched my predecessor's kit. It fitted me well enough, but Lord ! I looked a proper blackguard. The cord breeches had been recently cleaned, but the boots were like a pair of dilapidated buckets, and the coat would have made my tailor weep. Mr. McGowan himself put on a frock-coat and a high collar, and spruced himself up till he looked exactly like one of those high-up Irish dealers you see at the Horse Show—a cross between a Cabinet Minister and a Methodist parson. He said the ring-master should ride beside the chief exhibit, so we bustled out and I climbed up in front of a wagon which bore a cage containing two very low-spirited lions. I was given a long whip, and told to make myself conspicuous.

" I didn't know Kirk Aller well, so I had no fear of being recognized either as myself or as the pseudo-Brumby. The last time I had been there was when I had motored over from Larristane to dine with the Aller Shooting Club. My present entry was of a more sensational kind. I decided to enjoy myself and to attract all the notice I could, and I certainly succeeded. Indeed, you might say I received an ovation. As it happened it was a public holiday, and the streets were pretty full. We rumbled up the cobbled Westgate, and down the long High Street, with the pavements on both sides lined with people, and an attendant mob of several hundred children. The driver was a wizened little fellow in a jockey cap, but I was the principal figure on the box. I gave a fine exhibition with my whip, and when we slowed down I picked out conspicuous figures in the crowd and chaffed them. I thought I had better use Cockney patter, as being more in keeping with my job, and I made a happy blend of the table-talk of my stud-groom and my old batman in the regiment. It was rather a high-class performance and you'd be surprised how it went down. There was one young chap with a tremendous head of hair that I invited to join his friends in the cage, and just then one of the dejected lions let out a growl, and I said that Mamma was calling to her little Percy. And there was an old herd from the hills, who had been looking upon the wine-cup, and who, in a voice like a fog-horn, wanted to know what we fed the beasts on. Him I could not refrain from answering in his own tongue. 'Braxy, my man,' I cried, 'the yowes ye lost when we were fou last Boswell's Fair.' I must have got home somehow, for the crowd roared, and his friends thumped the old chap on the back and shouted: 'That's a guid ane! He had you there, Tam.'

"My triumphant procession came to an end on the Aller Green, where the show was to be held. A canvas palisade had been set up round a big stretch of ground, and the mob of children tailed off at the gate. Inside most of our truck had already arrived. The stadium for the circus had been marked off, and tiers of wooden seats were being hammered together. A big tent had been set up, which was to house the menagerie, and several smaller tents were in process of erection.

I noticed that the members of the troupe looked
at me curiously till Mr. McGowan arrived and
introduced me. 'This is Mr. Brown, a friend of
mine,' he said, 'who will take on Joe Japp's job
for the night.' And, aside to me, 'Man, I heard
ye comin' down the High Street. Ye did fine.
Ye've a great natural talent for the profession.'
After that we were all very friendly, and the whole
company had a snack together in one of the tents
—bread and cheese and bottled beer.

"The first thing I did was to make a bundle of
Brumby's clothes, which Mr. McGowan promised
to send back to Craigiedean when the coast was
clear. Then I bribed a small boy to take a telegram to the post office—to Archie at Larristane,
saying I had been detained and hoped to return
next day. After that I took off my coat and
worked like a beaver. It was nearly six o'clock
before we had everything straight, and the show
opened at seven, so we were all a bit the worse
for wear when we sat down to high tea. It's a
hard job an artiste's, as old McGowan observed.

"I never met a queerer, friendlier, more innocent
company, for the proprietor seemed to have set out
to collect originals, and most of them had been with
him for years. The boss of the menagerie was an
ex-sailor, who had a remarkable way with beasts ;
he rarely spoke a word, but just grinned and
whistled through broken teeth. The clown, who
said his name was Sammle Dreep, came from
Paisley, and was fat enough not to need the con-
ventional bolster. Dublin Davie, my second in

command, was a small Irishman who had been an ostler, and limped owing to having been with the Dublin Fusiliers at Gallipoli. The clown had a wife who ran the commissariat, when she wasn't appearing in the ring as Zenobia, the Pride of the Sahara. Then there were the Sisters Wido—a young married couple with two children; and the wife of a man who played the clarionet figured in the bill as Elise the Equestrienne. I had a look at the horses, which were the ordinary skinny, broad-backed, circus ponies. I found out later that they were so well trained that I daresay they could have done their turns in the dark.

"At a quarter to seven we lit the naphtha flares and our orchestra started in. McGowan told me to get inside Japp's dress clothes, and rather unwillingly I obeyed him, for I had got rather to fancy my morning's kit. I found there was only a coat and waistcoat, for I was allowed to retain the top-boots and cords. Happily the shirt was clean, but I had a solitaire with a sham diamond as big as a shilling, and the cut of the coat would have been considered out-of-date by a self-respecting waiter in Soho. I had also a scarlet silk handkerchief to stuff in my bosom, a pair of dirty white kid gloves, and an immense coach whip.

"The menagerie was open, but that night the chief attraction was the circus, and I don't mind saying that about the best bit of the circus was myself. In one of the intervals McGowan insisted on shaking hands and telling me that I was wasted in any other profession than a showman's. The fact is I was rather above myself, and entered into what you might call the spirit of the thing. We had the usual Dick Turpin's ride to York, and an escape of Dakota Dan (one of the Sisters Wido) from Red Indians (the other Wido, Zenobia, and Elise, with about a ton of feathers on their heads). The Equestrienne equestered, and the Widos hopped through hoops, and all the while I kept up my patter and spouted all the rot I could remember.

"The clown was magnificent. He had a Paisley accent you could have cut with a knife, but he prided himself on talking aristocratic English. He had a lot of badinage with Zenobia about her life in the desert. One bit I remember. She kept on referring to bulbuls, and asked him if he had ever seen a bull-bull. He said he had, for he supposed it was a male coo-coo. But he was happiest at my expense. I never heard a chap with such a flow of back-chat. A funny thing—but when he wasn't calling me 'Little Pansy-face,' he addressed me as 'Your Grace' and 'Me Lord Dook,' and hoped that the audience would forgive my négligé attire, seeing my coronet hadn't come back from the wash.

"Altogether the thing went with a snap from beginning to end, and when old McGowan, all dressed up with a white waistcoat, made a speech at the end and explained about the next performances, he got a perfect hurricane of applause. After that we had to tidy up. There was the usual trouble with several procrastinating drunks, who wanted to make a night of it. One of them got into the ring and tried to have a row with me. He was a big loutish fellow with small eyes and red hair, and had the look of a betting tout. He stuck his face close to mine and bellowed at me:

" ' I ken ye fine, ye —— ! I seen ye at Lanerick last back-end. . . . Ye ca'd yoursel' Gentleman Geordie, and ye went off wi' my siller. By God, I'll get it out o' ye, ye —— welsher.'

" I told him that he was barking up the wrong tree, and that I was not a bookie and had never been near Lanerick; but he refused to be convinced. The upshot was that Davie and I had to chuck him out, blaspheming like a navvy and swearing that he was coming back with his pals to do me in.

" We were a very contented lot of mountebanks at supper that night. The takings were good and the menagerie also had been popular, and we all felt that we had been rather above our form. McGowan, for whom I was acquiring a profound affection, beamed on us, and produced a couple of bottles of blackstrap to drink the health of the Colossal Circassian Circus. That old fellow was a nonesuch. He kept me up late—for I stopped with him in his caravan—expounding his philosophy of life. It seemed he had been intended for the kirk, but had had too much *joie de vivre* for the pulpit. He was a born tramp, and liked waking up most days in a new place, and he loved his queer outfit and saw the comedy of it. ' For three-and-thirty years I've travelled the country,' he said, ' and I've been a public benefactor, Mr. Brown. I've put colour into many a dowie life, and I've been a godsend to the bairns. There's no vulgarity in my performances—they're a' as halesome as spring water.' He quoted Burns a bit, and then he got on to politics, for he was a great Radical, and maintained that Scotland was about the only true democracy, because a man was valued precisely for what he was and no more. ' Ye're a laird, Mr. Brown, but ye're a guid fellow, and this night ye've shown yourself to be a man and a brither. What do you and me care for mawg-nates ? We take no stock in your Andra Carnegies and your Dukes o' Burminster.' And as I dropped off to sleep he was obliging with a verse of ' A man's a man for a' that.'

" I woke in excellent spirits, thinking what a good story I should have to tell when I returned to Larristane. My plan was to get off as soon as possible, take the train to Langshiels, and then hire. I could see that McGowan was sorry to part with me, but he agreed that it was too unhealthy a countryside for me to dally in. There was to be an afternoon performance, so everybody had to hustle, and there was no reason for me to linger. After breakfast I borrowed an old ulster from him, for I had to cover up my finery, and a still older brown bowler to replace the topper I had worn on the preceding day.

" Suddenly we heard a fracas, and the drunk appeared who had worried me the night before He had forced his way in and was pushing on

through an expostulating crowd. When he saw
me he made for me with a trail of blasphemy. He
was perfectly sober now and looked very ugly.

" ' Gie me back my siller,' he roared. ' Gie me
back the five-pund note I won at Lanerick when I
backed Kettle o' Fish.' If I hadn't warded him off
he would have taken me by the throat.

" I protested again that he was mistaken, but
I might as well have appealed to a post. He swore
with every variety of oath that I was Gentleman
Geordie, and that I had levanted with his winnings.
As he raved I began to see a possible explanation
of his madness. Some bookmaker, sporting my
sort of kit, had swindled him. I had ridden several
times in steeplechases, and he had seen me and got
my face in his head, and mixed me up with the
fraudulent bookie.

" It was a confounded nuisance, and but for the
principle of the thing I would have been inclined
to pay up. As it was we had to fling him out, and
he went unwillingly, doing all the damage he could.
His parting words were that he and his pals weren't
done with me, and that though he had to wait fifty
years he would wring my neck.

" After that I thought I had better waste no
time, so I said good-bye to McGowan and left the
show-ground by the back entrance close to the
Aller. I had a general notion of the place, and
knew that if I kept down the river I could turn
up a lane called the Water Wynd, and get to the
station without traversing any of the main streets.
I had ascertained that there was a train at 10.30

which would get me to Langshiels at 11.15, so that I could be at Larristane for luncheon.

" I had underrated the persistence of my enemy. He and his pals had picketed all the approaches to the show, and when I turned into the Water Wynd I found a fellow there, who at the sight of me blew a whistle. In a second or two he was joined by three others, among them my persecutor.

" ' We've gotten ye noo,' he shouted, and made to collar me.

" ' If you touch me,' I said, ' it's assault, and a case for the police.'

" ' That's your game, is it ? ' he cried. ' Na, na, we'll no trouble the pollis. They tell me the Law winna help me to recover a bet, so I'll just trust to my nieves. Will ye pay up, ye ——, or take the bloodiest bashin' ye ever seen ? '

" I was in an uncommon nasty predicament. There was nobody in the Wynd but some children playing, and the odds were four to one. If I fought I'd get licked. The obvious course of safety was to run up the Wynd towards the High Street, where I might find help. But that would mean a street row and the intervention of the police, a case in court, and the disclosure of who I was. If I broke through and ran back to McGowan I would be no further forward. What was perfectly clear was that I couldn't make the railway station without landing myself in the worst kind of mess.

" There wasn't much time to think, for the four men were upon me. I hit out at the nearest, saw him go down, and then doubled up the Wynd and into a side alley on the right.

" By the mercy of Providence this wasn't a cul-de-sac, but twisted below the old walls of the burgh, and then became a lane between gardens. The pursuit was fairly hot, and my accursed boots kept slipping on the cobbles and cramped my form. They were almost upon me before I reached the lane, but then I put on a spurt, and was twenty yards ahead when it ended in a wall with a gate. The gate was locked, but the wall was low, and I scrambled over it, and dropped into the rubbish heap of a garden.

" There was no going back, so I barged through some gooseberry bushes, skirted a lawn, squattered over a big square of gravel, and charged through the entrance gates of a suburban villa. My enemies plainly knew a better road, for when I passed the entrance they were only a dozen yards off on my left. That compelled me to turn to the right, the direction away from Kirk Aller. I was now on a highway where I could stretch myself, and it was not long before I shook off the pursuit. They were whiskyfied ruffians and not much good in a hunt. It was a warm morning, but I did not slacken till I had put a good quarter of a mile between us. I saw them come round a turn, lumbering along, cooked to the world, so I judged that I could slow down to an easy trot.

" I was cut off from my lines of communication, and the only thing to do was to rejoin them by a detour. The Aller valley, which the railway to

Langshiels followed, gave me a general direction. I remembered that about six miles off there was a station called Rubersdean, and that there was an afternoon train which got to Langshiels about three o'clock. I preferred to pick it up there, for I didn't mean to risk showing my face inside Kirk Aller again.

"By this time I had got heartily sick of my adventures. Being chased like a fox is amusing enough for an hour or two, but it soon palls. I was becoming a regular outlaw—wanted by the police for breaking into a nursing home and stealing a suit, and very much wanted by various private gentlemen on the charge of bilking. Everybody's hand seemed to be against me, except old McGowan's, and I had had quite enough of it. I wanted nothing so much as to be back at Larristane, and I didn't believe I would tell Archie the story, for I was fed up with the whole business.

"I didn't dare go near a public-house, and the best I could do for luncheon was a bottle of ginger-beer and some biscuits which I bought at a sweetie-shop. To make a long story short, I reached Rubersdean in time, and as there were several people on the platform I waited till the train arrived before showing myself. I got into a third-class carriage at the very end of it.

"The only occupants were a woman and a child, and my appearance must have been pretty bad, for the woman looked as if she wanted to get out when she saw me. But I said it was a fine day and 'guid for the crops,' and I suppose she was reassured by my Scotch tongue, for she quieted down. The child was very inquisitive, and they discussed me in whispers. 'What's that man, Mamaw?' it asked. 'Never mind, Jimmie.' 'But I want to ken, Mamaw.' 'Wheesht, dearie. He's a crool man. He kills the wee mawpies.' At that the child set up a howl, but I felt rather flattered, for a rabbit-trapper was a respectable profession compared to those with which I had recently been credited.

"At the station before Langshiels they collect the tickets. I had none, so when the man came round I could only offer a Bank of England five-pound note. He looked at it very suspiciously, asked me rudely if I had nothing smaller, consulted the station-master, and finally with a very ill grace got me change out of the latter's office. This hung up the train for a good five minutes, and you could see by their looks that they thought I was a thief. The thing had got so badly on my nerves that I could have wept. I counted the minutes till we reached Langshiels, and I was not cheered by the behaviour of my travelling companion. She was clearly convinced of the worst, and when we came out of a tunnel she was jammed into the farthest corner, clutching her child and her bag, and looking as if she had escaped from death. I can tell you it was a thankful man that shot out on to the platform at Langshiels. . . .

"I found myself looking into the absolutely bewildered eyes of Tommy Deloraine. . . . I saw a lot of fellows behind him with rosettes and scared faces, and I saw what looked like a band. . . .

"It took me about a hundredth part of a second to realize that I had dropped out of the frying-pan into the fire. You will scarcely believe it, but since I had rehearsed my speech going up the Rinks burn, the political meeting at Langshiels had gone clean out of my head. I suppose I had tumbled into such an utterly new world that no link remained with the old one. And as my foul luck would have it, I had hit on the very train by which I had told Deloraine I would travel.

"'For heaven's sake, Tommy, tell me where I can change.' I hissed. 'Lend me some clothes or I'll murder you.'

.   .   .   .   .   .

"Well, that was the end of it. I got into a suit of Tommy's at the Station Hotel—luckily he was about my size—and we proceeded with the brass band and the rosetted committee to the Town Hall. I made a dashed good speech, though I say it who shouldn't, simply because I was past caring what I did. Life had been rather too much for me the last two days."

Burminster finished his tankard, and a light of reminiscence came into his eye.

"Last week," he said, "I was passing Buckingham Palace. One of the mallards from St. James's Park had laid away, and had hatched out a brood somewhere up Constitution Hill. The time had come when she wanted to get the ducklings back to the water. There was a big crowd, and through the midst of it marched two bobbies with the mother-duck between them, while the young ones waddled behind. I caught the look in her eye, and, if you believe me, it was the comicalest mixture of relief and embarrassment, shyness, self-consciousness, and desperation.

"I would like to have shaken hands with that bird. I knew exactly how she felt."

III. DR. LARTIUS

JOHN PALLISER-YEATES'S STORY

The idols have spoken vanity, and the diviners have seen a lie, and
have told false dreams ; they comfort in vain ; therefore they went
their way as a flock.

Zechariah **x. 2.**

III. DR. LARTIUS

IN the early spring Palliser-Yeates had 'flu, and had it so badly that he was sent to recruit for a fortnight on the Riviera. There, being profoundly bored, he wrote out and sent to us this story. He would not give the name of the chief figure, because he said he was still a serving soldier, and his usefulness, he hoped, was not exhausted. The manuscript arrived opportunely, for some of us had just been trying, without success, to extract from Sandy Arbuthnot the truth of certain of his doings about which rumour had been busy.

I

In the second week of January 1917, a modest brass plate appeared on a certain door in Regent Street, among modistes and hat-makers and vendors of cosmetics. It bore the name of Dr. S. Lartius. On the third floor were the rooms to which the plate was the signpost, a pleasant set, newly decorated with powder-blue wallpapers, curtains of orange velveteen, and sham marqueterie. The milliners' girls who frequented that staircase might have

observed, about eleven in the morning, the figure
of Dr. Lartius arriving. They did not see him
leave, for they had flown to their suburban homes
long before the key turned of an evening in the
doctor's door.

He was a slim young man of the middle height,
who held himself straighter than the usual run of
sedentary folk. His face was very pale, and his
mop of hair and fluffy beard were black as jet. He
wore large tortoise-shell spectacles, and, when he
removed them, revealed slightly protuberant and
very bright hazel eyes, which contrasted oddly with
his pallor. Had such a figure appeared on the
stage, the gallery experts, familiar with stage
villains, would have unhesitatingly set him down
as the anarchist from Moscow about to assassinate
the oppressive nobleman and thereby give the hero
his chance. But his clothes were far too good for
that part. He wore a shiny top-hat and an expen-
sive fur coat, and his neat morning coat, fine linen,
unobtrusive black tie, and pearl pin suggested the
high finance rather than the backstairs of revo-
lution.

It appeared that Dr. Lartius did a flourishing
business. Suddenly London had begun to talk
about him. First there were the people that
matter, the people who are ever on the hunt for a
new sensation and must always be in the first flight
of any fad. Lady A. told the Duchess of B.
about a wonderful new man who really had Power
—no ordinary vulgar spiritualist, but a true Seeker
and Thinker. Mr. D., that elderly gossip, carried

the story through many circles, and it grew with the telling. The curious began to cultivate Dr. Lartius, and soon the fame of him came to the ears of those who were not curious, only anxious or broken-hearted ; and because the last were a great multitude, and were ready to give their all for consolation, there was a busy coming and going on Dr. Lartius's staircase.

His way with his clients was interesting. He had no single method of treatment, and varied his manner according to the motives of the inquirer. The merely inquisitive he entertained with toys. " I am no professor of an art," he told them laughingly. " I am a student, groping on the skirts of great mysteries." And to the more intelligent he would propound an illustration. " Take the mathematics of the Fourth Dimension," he would say. " I can show you a few simple mechanical puzzles, which cannot be explained except by the aid of abstruse mathematics, and not always then. But these puzzles tell you nothing about the Fourth Dimension, except that there is a world about us inexplicable on the rule of three dimensions. It is the same with my toys—my crystal ball, my pool of ink, my star-maps, even those superinduced moods of abstraction in which we seem to hear the noise of wings and strange voices. They only tell me that there is more in earth and heaven than is dreamed of in man's philosophy."

But his toys were wonderful. The idle ladies who went there for a thrill were not disappointed. In the dusky room, among the strange rosy lights, their hearts seemed to be always fluttering on the brink of a revelation, and they came away excited and comforted, for Dr. Lartius was an adept at delicate flattery. Fortune-telling in the ordinary sense there was none, but this young man seemed to have an uncanny knowledge of private affairs, which he used so discreetly that even those who had most reason to desire secrecy were never disquieted. For such entertainments he charged fees—high fees, as the fur coat and the pearl pin required "You wish to be amused," he would say, "and it is right that you should pay me for it."

Even among the idle clients there was a sprinkling of the earnest. With these he had the air of a master towards initiates ; they were fellow-pilgrims with him on the Great Road. He would talk to them by the hour, very beautifully, in a soft musical voice. He would warn them against charlatans, those who sought to prostitute a solemn ritual to purposes of vulgar gain. He would unroll for them the history of the great mystics and tell of that secret science known to the old adepts, which had been lost for ages, and was now being recovered piecemeal. These were the most thrilling hours of all, and the fame of Dr. Lartius grew great in the drawing-rooms of the Elect. "And he's such a gentleman, my dear—so well-bred and sympathetic and unworldly and absolutely honest ! "

But from others he took no fees. The sad-faced women, mostly in black, who sat in his great velvet chair and asked broken questions, found a very different Dr. Lartius. He was no longer fluent and silver-tongued ; sometimes he seemed almost embarrassed. He would repeat most earnestly that he was only a disciple, a seeker, not a master of hidden things. On such occasions the toys were absent, and if some distracted mother sought knowledge that way she was refused. He rarely had anything definite to impart. When Lady H.'s only son was about to exchange from the cavalry to the Foot Guards and his mother wanted to know how the step would affect his chances of survival, she got nothing beyond the obvious remark that this was an infantry war and he would have a better prospect of seeing fighting. Very rarely, he spoke out. Once to Mrs. K., whose boy was a prisoner, he gave a full account of life in a German prison-camp, so that, in the absence of letters, her imagination had henceforth something to bite on. Usually his visitors were too embarrassed to be observant, but one or two noted that he was uncommonly well informed about the British Army. He never made a mistake about units, and seemed to know a man's battalion before he was told it. And when mothers poured out details to him— for from the talk of soldiers on leave and epistolary indiscretions a good deal of information circulated about London—he now and then took notes.

Yet, though they got little from him that was explicit, these visitors, as a rule, went away comforted. Perhaps it was his gentle soothing manner. Perhaps, as poor Lady M. said, it was that he seemed so assured of the spiritual life that they felt that

their anxieties were only tiny eddies on the edg
of a great sea of peace. At any rate, it was th
afflicted even more than the idly curious who spok
well of Dr. Lartius.

Sometimes he had masculine clients—fathers o
fighting sons, who said they came on their wives
behalf, elderly retired Generals who preferre
spiritualism to golf, boys whose nerves were i
tatters and wanted the solace which in other age
and lands would have been found in the confes
sional. With these last Dr. Lartius became a new
man. He would take off his spectacles and lool
them in the face with his prominent lustrous eyes
and talk to them with a ring in his pleasant voice
It was not what he said so much, perhaps, as hi
manner of saying it, but he seemed to have a singu
lar power over boys just a little bit loose from thei
moorings. " Queer thing," said one of these
" but one would almost think you had been a
soldier yourself." Dr. Lartius had smiled an
resumed his spectacles. " I am a soldier, but in a
different war. I fight with the sword of the spiri
against the hidden things of darkness."

Towards the end of March the brass plat
suddenly disappeared. There was a great flutter
ing in the dovecotes of the Elect when the new
went round that there had been trouble with th
police. It had been over the toys, of course, an
the taking of fees. The matter never came int
court, but Dr. Lartius had been warned to clea
out, and he obeyed. Many ladies wrote indignan
letters to the Home Secretary about persecution

letters which cited ominous precedents from the
early history of the Christian Church.

But in April came consolation. The rumour
spread that the Seekers were not to lose their guide.
Mr. Greatheart would still be available for the comforting of pilgrims. A plate with the name of
Dr. S. Lartius reappeared in a quiet street in
Mayfair. But for the future there would be no
question of fees. It was generally assumed that
a few devout women had provided a fund for the
sustenance of the prophet.

In May his fame was greater than ever. One
evening Lady Samplar, the most ardent of his
devotees, spoke of him to a certain General who
was a power in the land. The General was popular
among the women of her set, but a notorious
scoffer. Perhaps this was the secret of his popularity, for each hoped to convert him.

" I want you to see him yourself," she said.
" Only once. I believe in him so firmly that I am
willing to stake everything on one interview.
Promise me you will let me take you. I only want
you to see him and talk to him for ten minutes.
I want you to realize his unique personality, for
if you once *feel* him you will scoff no more."

The General laughed, shrugged his shoulders, but
allowed himself to be persuaded. So it came about
that one afternoon in early June he accompanied
Lady Samplar to the flat in Mayfair. " You must
go in alone," she told him in the ante-room. " I
have spoken about you to him, and he is expecting
you. I will wait for you here."

For half an hour the General was closeted with
Dr. Lartius. When he returned to the lady his face
was red and wrathful.

"That's the most dangerous fellow in London,"
he declared. "Look here, Mollie, you and your
friends have been playing the fool about that man.
He's a German spy, if there ever was one.
caught him out, for I trapped him into speaking German. You say he's a Swiss, but I swear no
Swiss ever spoke German just as he speaks it.
The man's a Bavarian. I'll take my oath he is!"

It was a very depressed and rather frightened lady
who gave him tea a little later in her drawing-room.

"That kind of sweep is far too clever for you
innocents," she was told. "There he has been
for months pumping you all without your guessing
it. You say he's a great comfort to the mourners.
I daresay he is, but the poor devils tell him everything that's in their heads. That man has a unique
chance of knowing the inside of the British Army.
And how has he used his knowledge ? That's what
I want to know."

"What are you going to do about it ? " she
quavered.

"I'm going to have him laid by the heels," he
said grimly, as he took his departure. "Interned
—or put up against a wall, if we can get the evidence. I tell you he's a Boche pure and simple
—not that there's much purity and simplicity
about him."

The General was as good as his word, but in one
matter he was wrong. The credentials of the

prophet's Swiss nationality were good enough. There was nothing for it but to deport him as an undesirable, so one fine morning Dr. S. Lartius got his marching orders. He made no complaint, and took a dignified farewell of his friends. But the Faithful were not silent, and the friendship between Lady Samplar and the General died a violent death. The thing got into the papers. Dr. Lartius figured in many unrecognizable portraits in the press, and a bishop preached a sermon in a City church about the worship of false gods.

II

As Dr. Lartius, closely supervised by the French police, pursued his slow and comfortless journey to the Swiss frontier, he was cheered by several proofs that his fame had gone abroad and that he was not forgotten. At Paris there were flowers in his dingy hotel bedroom, the gift of an unknown admirer, and a little note of encouragement in odd French. At Dijon he received from a strange lady another note telling him that his friends were awaiting him in Berne. When he crossed the border at Pontarlier there were more flowers and letters. The young man paid little attention to such tributes. He spent the journey in quiet reading and meditation, and when he reached Berne did not seem to expect any one to greet him, but collected his luggage and drove off unobtrusively to an hotel.

He had not been there an hour when a card was
brought to him bearing the name of Ernst Ulrici,
Doctor of Philosophy in the University of Bonn.

"Dr. Lartius," said the visitor, a middle-aged
man with a peaked grey beard and hair cut *en
brosse*. "It is an honour to make your acquaintance. We have heard of your fine work and your
world-moulding discoveries."

The young man bowed gravely. "I am only a
seeker," he said. "I make no claim to be a master
—yet. I am only a little way on the road to en-
lightenment."

"We have also heard," said the other, "of how
shamelessly the British Government has persecuted
learning in your person."

The reply was a smile and a shrug. "I make no
complaint. It is natural that my studies should
seem foolishness to the children of this world."

Dr. Ulrici pressed him further on the matter of
Britain, but could wake no bitterness.

"There is war to-day," he said at last. "You
are of German race. Your sympathies are with
us ?"

"I have no nationality," was the answer. "All
men are my brothers. But I would fain see this
bloodshed at an end."

"How will it end ?" came the question.

"I am no prophet," said Dr. Lartius. "Yet I
can tell that Germany will win, but how I can tell
I cannot tell."

The conversation lasted long and explored many
subjects. The German led it cunningly to small

matters, and showed a wide acquaintance with the
young man's science. He learned that much of his
work had been done with soldiers and soldiers' kin,
and that in the process of it he had heard many
things not published in the newspapers. But
when he hinted, ever so delicately, that he would be
glad to buy the knowledge, a flush passed over the
other's pale face and his voice sharpened.

"I am no spy," he said. "I do not prostitute
my art for hire. It matters nothing to me which
side wins, but it matters much that I keep my soul
clean."

So Dr. Ulrici tried another tack. He spoke of
the mysteries of the craft, and lured the young man
into the confession of hopes and ideals. There
could be no communion with the dead, he was told,
until communion had first been perfected with the
spirits of the living. "Let the time come," said
Dr. Lartius, "when an unbroken fellowship can
be created between souls separated by great tracts
of space, and the key has been found. Death is an
irrelevant accident. The spirit is untouched by it.
Find the *trait d'union* between spirits still in their
fleshly envelope, and it can be continued when that
envelope is shed."

"And you have progressed in this affair?" asked
Ulrici, with scepticism in his tone.

"A few stages," said the other, and in the ardour
of exposition he gave proofs. He had clients, he
said, with whom he had established the mystic
catena. He could read their thoughts even now,
though they were far away, share in their mental

changes, absorb the knowledge which they acquired.

"Soldiers ? " asked the German.

"Some are soldiers. All are the kin of soldiers."

But Ulrici was still cold. "That is a great marvel," he said, "and not easy to believe."

Dr. Lartius was fired "I will give you proofs," he said, with unwonted passion in his voice. "You can test them at your leisure. I know things which have not yet come to pass, though no man has spoken to me of them. How do I know them ? Because they have come within the cognizance of minds attuned to my own."

For a moment he seemed to hesitate. Then he spoke of certain matters—a little change in the method of artillery barrages, a readjustment in the organization of the British Air Force, an alteration in certain British commands.

"These may be trivial things," he said. "I do not know. I have no technical skill. But they are still in the future. I offer them to you as proofs of my knowledge."

"So ? " said the other. "They are indeed small things, but they will do for a test. . . ."

Then he spoke kindly, considerately, of Dr. Lartius's future.

"I think I will go to Munich," said the young man. "Once I studied at the University there, and I love the bright city. They are a sympathetic people and respect knowledge."

Dr. Ulrici rose to take his leave. "It may be I am able to further your plans, my friend," he said.

Late that night in a big sitting-room in another hotel, furnished somewhat in the style of an official bureau, Ulrici talked earnestly with another man, a heavy, bearded man, who wore the air of a prosperous bagman, but who was addressed with every token of respect.

" This Lartius fellow puzzles me. He is a transparent fanatic, with some odd power in him that sets him above others of his kidney. I fear he will not be as useful to us as we had hoped. If only we had known of him sooner and could have kept him in England."

" He can't go back, I suppose ? "

" Impossible, sir. But there is still a chance. He has some wild theory that he has established a link with various people, and so acquires automatically whatever new knowledge they gain. Some of these people are soldiers. He has told me things—little things—that I may test this power of his. I am no believer in the spiritualist mumbo-jumbo, but I have lived long enough not to reject a thing because it is new and strange. About that we shall see. If there is anything in it there will be much. Meantime I keep closely in touch with him."

" What is he going to do ? "

" He wants to go to Munich. I am in favour of permitting it, sir. Our good Bavarians are somewhat light in the head, and are always seeking a new thing. They want a little ghostly consolation at present, and this man will give it them. He believes most firmly in our German victory."

The other yawned and flung away the end of his
cigar. "The mountebank seems to have some
glimmerings of sense," he said.

III

So it came about that in August of the year 1917
Dr. Lartius was settled in comfortable rooms off the
Garmischstrasse in the Bavarian capital, and a new
plate of gun-metal and oxidized silver, lettered in
the best style of *art nouveau*, advertised his name
to the citizens of Munich.

Fortune still attended the young man, for, as in
London, he seemed to spring at once into fame.
Within a week of his arrival people were talking
about him, and in a month his chambers were
crowded. Perhaps his friend Ulrici had spoken
a word in the right place. It was the great season
before Caporetto, and Dr. Lartius spoke hearten-
ing things to his clients. Victory was near and
the days of glory; but when asked about the
date of peace he was coy. Peace would come, but
not yet; for the world there was another winter
of war.

His methods were the same as those which had
captured Lady Samplar and her friends. To the
idly curious he showed toys; to the emotional he
spoke nobly of the life of the spirit and the locked
doors of hidden knowledge which were now almost
ajar. Rich ladies, bored with the dullness of the
opera season and the scarcity of men, found in him

a new interest in life. To the sorrowful he gave
the comfort which he had given to his London
circle—no more. His personality seemed to exhale
hope and sympathy, and mourners, remembering
his pleasant voice and compelling eyes, departed
with a consolation which they could not define.

That was for the ordinary run of clients; but
there were others—fellow-students they professed
themselves—to whom he gave stronger meat. He
preached his doctrine of the mystic community of
thought and knowledge between souls far apart,
and now and then he gave proofs such as he had
given to Ulrici. It would appear that these proofs
stood the test, for his reputation grew prodigiously.
He told them little things about forthcoming
changes in the Allied armies, and the event always
proved him right. They were not things that
mattered greatly; but if he could disclose triviali-
ties, some day his method might enable him to
reveal a mighty secret. So more than one *General-
stabschef* came to sit with him in his twilit room.

About once a month he used to go back to Berne,
and was invariably met at the station by Ulrici.
He had been given a very special passport, which
took him easily and expeditiously over the frontier,
and he had no trouble with station commandants.
In these visits he would be closeted with Ulrici
for hours. Occasionally he would slip out of his
hotel at night for a little, and when Ulrici heard
of it he shrugged his shoulders and laughed. "He
is young," he would say with a leer. "Even a
prophet must have his amusements." But he

was wrong, for Dr. Lartius had not the foibles he suspected.

The winter passed slowly, and the faces in the Munich streets grew daily more pinched and wan, clothing more shabby, and boots more down at heel. But there was always comfort for seekers in the room in the Garmischstrasse. Whoever lost faith, it was not Dr. Lartius. Peace was coming, and his hearers judged that he had forgotten his scientific detachment from all patriotisms and was becoming a good German.

Then in February of the New Year came the rumour of the great advance preparing in the West. The High Command had promised speedy and final victory in return for a little more endurance. Dr. Lartius seemed to have the first news of it. " It is Peace," he said, " Peace before winter ; " and his phrase was repeated everywhere and became a popular watchword. So, when the news came at the end of March of the retreat of the French and English to the gates of Amiens, the hungry people smiled to each other and said, " He is right, as always. It is Peace." Few now cared much about victory, except the high officers and the very rich, but on Peace all were determined.

April passed into May, and ere the month was out came glorious tidings. Ludendorff had reached the Marne, and was within range of Paris. About this time his closest disciples marked a change in Dr. Lartius. He seemed to retire into himself, and to be struggling with some vast revelation. His language was less intelligible, but far more impressive. Ulrici came up from Berne to see him, for he had stopped for some months his visits to Switzerland. There were those who said his health was breaking, others that he was now, in very truth, looking inside the veil. This latter was the general view, and the fame of the young man became a superstition.

"You tell us little now about our enemies," Ulrici complained.

"*Mystica catena rupta est*," Dr. Lartius quoted sadly. "My friends are your enemies, and they are suffering. Their hearts and nerves are breaking. Therefore the link is thin and I cannot feel their thoughts. That is why I am so sad, for against my will the sorrow of my friends clouds me."

Ulrici laughed in his gross way. "Then the best omen for us is that you fall into melancholia ? When you cut your throat we shall know that we have won."

Yet Ulrici was not quite happy. The young prophet was in danger of becoming a Frankenstein's monster, which he could not control. For his popular fame was now a thing to marvel at. It had gone abroad through Germany, and to all the fighting fronts, and the phrase linked to it was that of "Peace before winter." Peace had become a conviction, an obsession. Ulrici and his friends would have preferred the word to be "Victory."

In the early days of July a distinguished visitor came from Berlin to the Garmischstrasse. He was an *Erster Generalstabsoffizier*, high in the confidence

of the Supreme Command. He sat in the shaded
room and asked an urgent question.

"I am not a Delphian oracle," said Dr. Lartius,
"and I do not prophesy. But this much I can tell
you. The hearts of your enemies have become like
water, and they have few reserves left. I am not
a soldier, so you can judge better than I. You say
you are ready to strike with a crushing force. If
you leave your enemies leisure they will increase
and their hearts may recover."

"That is my view," said the soldier. "You have
done much for the German people in the past, sir.
Have you no word now to encourage them?"

"There will be peace before winter. This much
I can tell, but how I know I cannot tell."

"But on what terms?"

"That depends upon your armies," was the
oracular reply.

The staff officer had been gazing intently at the
speaker. Now he rose and switched on the electric
light.

"Will you oblige me by taking off your glasses,
sir?" he asked, and there was the sharpness of
command in his voice.

Dr. Lartius removed his spectacles, and for some
seconds the two men looked at each other.

"I thank you," said the soldier at last. "For a
moment I thought we had met before. You reminded me of a man I knew long ago. I was
mistaken."

After that it was noted by all that the melancholy
of Dr. Lartius increased. His voice was saddened,

and dejection wrapped him like a cloud. Those of
the inner circle affected to see in this a good omen.
" He is *en rapport* with his English friends," they
said. " He cannot help himself, and their despair
is revealed in him. The poor Lartius! He is
suffering for the sins of our enemies." But the
great public saw only the depression, and as August
matured, and bad news filtered through the land,
it gave their spirits an extra push downhill.

In those weeks only one word came from the
Garmischstrasse. It was " Peace—peace before
winter." The phrase became the universal formula
whispered wherever people spoke their minds. It
ran like lightning through the camps and along the
fronts, and in every workshop and tavern. It
became a passion, a battle-cry. The Wise Doctor of
Munich had said it. Peace before winter—Peace
at all costs—only Peace.

In September Ulrici was in communication with
a certain bureau in Berlin. " The man is honest
enough, but he is mad. He has served his purpose.
It is time to suppress him." Berlin agreed, and
one morning Ulrici departed from Berne.

But when he reached the Garmischstrasse he
found the flamboyant plate unscrewed from the
door and the pleasant rooms deserted.

For a day or two before Dr. Lartius had been
behaving oddly. He gave out that he was ill, and
could not receive ; but he was very busy indoors
with his papers. Then late one evening, after a
conversation on the telephone with the railway
people, he left his rooms, with no luggage but a

small dressing-case, and took the night train for Innsbruck. His admirable passport franked him anywhere. From Innsbruck he travelled to the Swiss frontier, and when he crossed it, in the darkness of the September evening and in an empty carriage, he made a toilet which included the shaving of his silky black beard. He was whistling softly and seemed to have recovered his spirits. At Berne he did not seek his usual hotel, but went to an unfrequented place in a back street, where, apparently, he was well known. There he met during the course of the day various people, and their conversation was not in the German tongue.

That night he again took train, but it was westward to Lausanne and the French border.

IV

In the early days of November, when the Allies were approaching Maubeuge and Sedan, and the German plenipotentiaries were trying to dodge the barrage and get speech with Foch, two British officers were sitting in a little room at Versailles. One was the General we have already met, the quondam friend of Lady Samplar. The other was a slim young man who wore the badges of a lieutenant-colonel and the gorget patches of the staff. He had a pale face shaven clean, black hair cut very short, and curious, bright, protuberant hazel eyes. He must have seen some service, for he had two rows of medal ribbons on his breast.

" Unarm, Eros," quoted the General, looking at the last slip on a pile of telegrams. " 'The long day's task is done.' It has been a grim business, and, Tommy, my lad, I think you had the most difficult patch of the lot to hoe. . . . It was largely due to you that the Boche made his blunder on 15th July, and stretched his neck far enough to let Foch hit him."

The young man grinned. " I wouldn't like to go through it again, sir. But it didn't seem so bad when I was at it, though it is horrible to look back on. The worst part was the loneliness."

" You must have often had bad moments."

" Not so many. I only remember two as particularly gruesome. One was when I heard you slanging me to Lady Samplar, and I suddenly felt hopelessly cut off from my kind. . . . The other was in July, when von Mudra came down from Berlin to see me. He dashed nearly spotted me, for he was at the Embassy when I was in Constantinople."

The General lifted a flamboyant plate whereon the name of Dr. S. Lartius was inscribed in letters of oxidized silver. " You've brought away your souvenir all right. I suppose you'll have it framed as a trophy for your ancestral hall. By the way, what did the letter S stand for ? "

" When I was asked," said the young man, " I said ' Sigismund.' But I really meant it for ' Spurius '—the chap, you remember, who held the bridge with Horatius."

IV. THE WIND IN THE PORTICO

HENRY NIGHTINGALE'S STORY

A dry wind of the high places . . . not to fan nor to cleanse, even a full wind from those places shall come unto me.

Jeremiah iv. 11, 12.

IV. THE WIND IN THE PORTICO

NIGHTINGALE was a hard man to draw. His doings with the Bedawin had become a legend, but he would as soon have talked about them as claimed to have won the War. He was a slim dark fellow about thirty-five years of age, very short-sighted, and wearing such high-powered double glasses that it was impossible to tell the colour of his eyes. This weakness made him stoop a little and peer, so that he was the strangest figure to picture in a burnous leading an army of desert tribesmen. I fancy his power came partly from his oddness, for his followers thought that the hand of Allah had been laid on him, and partly from his quick imagination and his flawless courage. After the War he had gone back to his Cambridge fellowship, declaring that, thank God, that chapter in his life was over.

As I say, he never mentioned the deeds which had made him famous. He knew his own business, and probably realized that to keep his mental balance he had to drop the curtain on what must have been the most nerve-racking four years ever spent by man. We respected his decision and kept off Arabia. It was a remark of Hannay's that drew from him the following story. Hannay

was talking about his Cotswold house, which was
on the Fosse Way, and saying that it always
puzzled him how so elaborate a civilization as
Roman Britain could have been destroyed utterly
and left no mark on the national history beyond
a few roads and ruins and place-names. Peckwether, the historian, demurred, and had a good
deal to say about how much the Roman tradition
was woven into the Saxon culture. "Rome only
sleeps," he said ; "she never dies."

Nightingale nodded. "Sometimes she dreams
in her sleep and talks. Once she scared me out
of my senses."

After a good deal of pressing he produced this
story. He was not much of a talker, so he wrote
it out and read it to us.

There is a place in Shropshire which I do not
propose to visit again. It lies between Ludlow
and the hills, in a shallow valley full of woods. Its
name is St. Sant, a village with a big house and
park adjoining, on a stream called the Vaun, about
five miles from the little town of Faxeter. They
have queer names in those parts, and other things
queerer than the names.

I was motoring from Wales to Cambridge at the
close of the long vacation. All this happened before
the War, when I had just got my fellowship and
was settling down to academic work. It was a fine
night in early October, with a full moon, and I
intended to push on to Ludlow for supper and
bed. The time was about half-past eight, the road

was empty and good going, and I was trundling
pleasantly along when something went wrong
with my headlights. It was a small thing, and I
stopped to remedy it beyond a village and just
at the lodge-gates of a house.

On the opposite side of the road a carrier's cart
had drawn up, and two men, who looked like indoor
servants, were lifting some packages from it on to
a big barrow. The moon was up, so I didn't need
the feeble light of the carrier's lamp to see what they
were doing. I suppose I wanted to stretch my
legs for a moment, for when I had finished my job
I strolled over to them. They did not hear me
coming, and the carrier on his perch seemed to be
asleep.

The packages were the ordinary consignments
from some big shop in town. But I noticed that
the two men handled them very gingerly, and that,
as each was laid in the barrow, they clipped off the
shop label and affixed one of their own. The new
labels were odd things, large and square, with some
address written on them in very black capital
letters. There was nothing in that, but the men's
faces puzzled me. For they seemed to do their
job in a fever, longing to get it over, and yet in a
sweat lest they should make some mistake. Their
commonplace task seemed to be for them a matter
of tremendous importance. I moved so as to get
a view of their faces, and I saw that they were white
and strained. The two were of the butler or valet
class, both elderly, and I could have sworn that
they were labouring under something like fear.

I shuffled my feet to let them know of my presence, and remarked that it was a fine night.   They
started as if they had been robbing a corpse.   One
of them mumbled something in reply, but the other
caught a package which was slipping, and in a
tone of violent alarm growled to his mate to be
careful.   I had a notion that they were handling
explosives.

I had no time to waste, so I pushed on.   That
night, in my room at Ludlow, I had the curiosity
to look up my map and identify the place where I
had seen the men.   The village was St. Sant, and it
appeared that the gate I had stopped at belonged to
a considerable demesne called Vauncastle.   That
was my first visit.

At that time I was busy on a critical edition of
Theocritus, for which I was making a new collation
of the manuscripts.   There was a variant of the
Medicean Codex in England, which nobody had
seen since Gaisford, and after a good deal of trouble
I found that it was in the library of a man called
Dubellay.   I wrote to him at his London club, and
got a reply, to my surprise, from Vauncastle Hall,
Faxeter.   It was an odd letter, for you could see
that he longed to tell me to go to the devil, but
couldn't quite reconcile it with his conscience.
We exchanged several letters, and the upshot was
that he gave me permission to examine his manuscript.   He did not ask me to stay, but mentioned
that there was a comfortable little inn in St. Sant.

My second visit began on the 27th of December,
after I had been home for Christmas.   We had had

a week of severe frost, and then it had thawed
a little ; but it remained bitterly cold, with leaden
skies that threatened snow. I drove from Faxeter,
and as we ascended the valley I remember thinking
that it was a curiously sad country. The hills were
too low to be impressive, and their outlines were
mostly blurred with woods ; but the tops showed
clear, funny little knolls of grey bent that suggested
a volcanic origin. It might have been one of those
backgrounds you find in Italian primitives, with
all the light and colour left out. When I got a
glimpse of the Vaun in the bleached meadows it
looked like the " wan water " of the Border ballads.
The woods, too, had not the friendly bareness of
English copses in winter time. They remained
dark and cloudy, as if they were hiding secrets.
Before I reached St. Sant, I decided that the landscape was not only sad, but ominous.

I was fortunate in my inn. In the single street
of one-storied cottages it rose like a lighthouse,
with a cheery glow from behind the red curtains
of the bar parlour. The inside proved as good as the
outside. I found a bedroom with a bright fire,
and I dined in a wainscoted room full of preposterous old pictures of lanky hounds and hollow-
backed horses. I had been rather depressed on my
journey, but my spirits were raised by this comfort, and when the house produced a most respectable bottle of port I had the landlord in to drink
a glass. He was an ancient man who had been a
gamekeeper, with a much younger wife, who was
responsible for the management. I was curious to

hear something about the owner of my manuscript, but I got little from the landlord. He had been with the old squire, and had never served the present one. I heard of Dubellays in plenty—the land-lord's master, who had hunted his own hounds for forty years ; the Major, his brother, who had fallen at Abu Klea ; Parson Jack, who had had the living till he died ; and of all kinds of collaterals. The "Deblays" had been a high-spirited, open-handed stock, and much liked in the place. But of the present master of the Hall he could or would tell me nothing. The Squire was a "great scholard," but I gathered that he followed no sport and was not a convivial soul like his predecessors. He had spent a mint of money on the house, but not many people went there. He, the landlord, had never been inside the grounds in the new master's time, though in the old days there had been hunt break-fasts on the lawn for the whole countryside, and mighty tenantry dinners. I went to bed with a clear picture in my mind of the man I was to inter-view on the morrow. A scholarly and autocratic recluse, who collected treasures and beautified his dwelling and probably lived in his library. I rather looked forward to meeting him, for the bonhomous sporting squire was not much in my line.

After breakfast next morning I made my way to the Hall. It was the same leaden weather, and when I entered the gates the air seemed to grow bitterer and the skies darker. The place was muffled in great trees which even in their winter bareness made a pall about it. There was a long avenue of ancient sycamores, through which one caught only rare glimpses of the frozen park. I took my bearings, and realized that I was walking nearly due south, and was gradually descending. The house must be in a hollow. Presently the trees thinned, I passed through an iron gate, came out on a big untended lawn, untidily studded with laurels and rhododendrons, and there before me was the house front.

I had expected something beautiful—an old Tudor or Queen Anne façade or a dignified Georgian portico. I was disappointed, for the front was simply mean. It was low and irregular, more like the back parts of a house, and I guessed that at some time or another the building had been turned round, and the old kitchen door made the chief entrance. I was confirmed in my conclusion by observing that the roofs rose in tiers, like one of those recessed New York sky-scrapers, so that the present back parts of the building were of an impressive height.

The oddity of the place interested me, and still more its dilapidation. What on earth could the owner have spent his money on ? Everything— lawn, flower-beds, paths—was neglected. There was a new stone doorway, but the walls badly needed pointing, the window woodwork had not been painted for ages, and there were several broken panes. The bell did not ring, so I was reduced to hammering on the knocker, and it must have been ten minutes before the door opened. A pale butler, one of the men I had seen at the carrier's cart the October before, stood blinking in the entrance.

He led me in without question, when I gave my name, so I was evidently expected. The hall was my second surprise. What had become of my picture of the collector ? The place was small and poky, and furnished as barely as the lobby of a farmhouse. The only thing I approved was its warmth. Unlike most English country houses, there seemed to be excellent heating arrangements.

I was taken into a little dark room with one window that looked out on a shrubbery, while the man went to fetch his master. My chief feeling was of gratitude that I had not been asked to stay, for the inn was paradise compared with this sepulchre. I was examining the prints on the wall, when I heard my name spoken and turned round to greet Mr. Dubellay.

He was my third surprise. I had made a portrait in my mind of a fastidious old scholar, with eye-glasses on a black cord, and a finical *weltkind*-ish manner. Instead I found a man still in early middle age, a heavy fellow dressed in the roughest country tweeds. He was as untidy as his demesne, for he had not shaved that morning, his flannel collar was badly frayed, and his finger-nails would have been the better for a scrubbing brush. His face was hard to describe. It was high-coloured, but the colour was not healthy ; it was friendly, but it was also wary ; above all, it was *unquiet*. He gave me the impression of a man whose nerves were all wrong, and who was perpetually on his guard.

He said a few civil words, and thrust a badly tied brown paper parcel at me.

"That's your manuscript," he said jauntily.

I was staggered. I had expected to be permitted to collate the codex in his library, and in the last few minutes had realized that the prospect was distasteful. But here was this casual owner offering me the priceless thing to take away.

I stammered my thanks, and added that it was very good of him to trust a stranger with such a treasure.

"Only as far as the inn," he said. "I wouldn't like to send it by post. But there's no harm in your working at it at the inn. There should be confidence among scholars." And he gave an odd cackle of a laugh.

"I greatly prefer your plan." I said "But I thought you would insist on my working at it here."

"No, indeed," he said earnestly. "I shouldn't think of such a thing. . . . Wouldn't do at all. . . . An insult to our freemasonry. . . . That's how I should regard it."

We had a few minutes' further talk. I learned that he had inherited under the entail from a cousin, and had been just over ten years at Vaun-castle. Before that he had been a London solicitor. He asked me a question or two about Cambridge—wished he had been at the University—much hampered in his work by a defective education. I was a Greek scholar?—Latin, too, he presumed.

Wonderful people the Romans. . . . He spoke quite freely, but all the time his queer restless eyes were darting about, and I had a strong impression that he would have liked to say something to me very different from these commonplaces—that he was longing to broach some subject but was held back by shyness or fear. He had such an odd appraising way of looking at me.

I left without having been asked to a meal, for which I was not sorry, for I did not like the atmosphere of the place. I took a short cut over the ragged lawn, and turned at the top of the slope to look back. The house was in reality a huge pile, and I saw that I had been right and that the main building was all at the back. Was it, I wondered, like the Alhambra, which behind a front like a factory concealed a treasure-house ? I saw, too, that the woodland hollow was more spacious than I had fancied. The house, as at present arranged, faced due north, and behind the south front was an open space in which I guessed that a lake might lie. Far beyond I could see in the December dimness the lift of high dark hills.

That evening the snow came in earnest, and fell continuously for the better part of two days. I banked up the fire in my bedroom and spent a happy time with the codex. I had brought only my working books with me and the inn boasted no library, so when I wanted to relax I went down to the tap-room, or gossiped with the landlady in the bar parlour. The yokels who congregated in the former were pleasant fellows, but, like all the folk

on the Marches, they did not talk readily to a
stranger, and I heard little from them of the Hall.
The old squire had reared every year three thousand
pheasants, but the present squire would not allow
a gun to be fired on his land, and there were only
a few wild birds left. For the same reason the
woods were thick with vermin. This they told me
when I professed an interest in shooting. But of
Mr. Dubellay they would not speak, declaring that
they never saw him. I daresay they gossiped wildly
about him, and their public reticence struck me as
having in it a touch of fear.

The landlady, who came from a different part
of the shire, was more communicative. She had
not known the former Dubellays and so had no
standard of comparison, but she was inclined to
regard the present squire as not quite right in the
head. "They do say," she would begin ; but she,
too, suffered from some inhibition, and what promised to be sensational would tail off into the
commonplace. One thing apparently puzzled the
neighbourhood above others, and that was his
rearrangement of the house. "They do say," she
said in an awed voice, "that he have built a great
church." She had never visited it—no one in the
parish had, for Squire Dubellay did not allow
intruders—but from Lyne Hill you could see it
through a gap in the woods. "He's no good
Christian," she told me, "and him and Vicar has
quarrelled this many a day. But they do say as
he worships summat there." I learned that there
were no women servants in the house, only the

men he had brought from London. "Poor be-
nighted souls, they must live in a sad hobble," and
the buxom lady shrugged her shoulders and giggled.

On the last day of December I decided that I
needed exercise and must go for a long stride.
The snow had ceased that morning, and the dull
skies had changed to a clear blue. It was still very
cold, but the sun was shining, the snow was firm
and crisp under foot, and I proposed to survey the
country. So after luncheon I put on thick boots
and gaiters, and made for Lyne Hill. This meant
a considerable circuit, for the place lay south of
the Vauncastle park. From it I hoped to get a
view of the other side of the house.

I was not disappointed. There was a rift in the
thick woodlands, and below me, two miles off, I
suddenly saw a strange building, like a classical
temple. Only the entablature and the tops of the
pillars showed above the trees, but they stood out
vivid and dark against the background of snow.
The spectacle in that lonely place was so startling
that for a little I could only stare. I remember
that I glanced behind me to the snowy line of
the Welsh mountains, and felt that I might have
been looking at a winter view of the Apennines two
thousand years ago.

My curiosity was now alert, and I determined to
get a nearer view of this marvel. I left the track
and ploughed through the snowy fields down to
the skirts of the woods. After that my troubles
began. I found myself in a very good imitation
of a primeval forest, where the undergrowth had

een unchecked and the rides uncut for years.
sank into deep pits, I was savagely torn by briars
nd brambles, but I struggled on, keeping a line as
est I could. At last the trees stopped. Before
ne was a flat expanse which I knew must be a lake,
nd beyond rose the temple.

It ran the whole length of the house, and from
where I stood it was hard to believe that there were
buildings at its back where men dwelt. It was a
ine piece of work—the first glance told me that
—admirably proportioned, classical, yet not following exactly any of the classical models. One could
imagine a great echoing interior, dim with the smoke
of sacrifice, and it was only by reflecting that I
realized that the peristyle could not be continued
down the two sides, that there was no interior, and
hat what I was looking at was only a portico.

The thing was at once impressive and preposterous. What madness had been in Dubellay when
he embellished his house with such a grandiose
garden front ? The sun was setting and the
shadow of the wooded hills darkened the interior,
so I could not even make out the back wall of the
portico. I wanted a nearer view, so I embarked
on the frozen lake.

Then I had an odd experience. I was not tired,
the snow lay level and firm, but I was conscious
of extreme weariness. The biting air had become
warm and oppressive. I had to drag boots that
seemed to weigh tons across that lake. The place
was utterly silent in the stricture of the frost, and
from the pile in front no sign of life came.

I reached the other side at last and found myself
in a frozen shallow of bulrushes and skeleton
willow-herbs. They were taller than my head,
and to see the house I had to look upward through
their snowy traceries. It was perhaps eighty feet
above me and a hundred yards distant, and, since
I was below it, the delicate pillars seemed to spring
to a great height. But it was still dusky, and the
only detail I could see was on the ceiling, which
seemed either to be carved or painted with deeply
shaded monochrome figures.

Suddenly the dying sun came slanting through
the gap in the hills, and for an instant the whole
portico to its farthest recesses was washed in clear
gold and scarlet. That was wonderful enough, but
there was something more. The air was utterly
still, with not the faintest breath of wind—so still
that, when I had lit a cigarette half an hour before,
the flame of the match had burned steadily upward
like a candle in a room. As I stood among the
sedges not a single frost crystal stirred. . . . But
there was a wind blowing in the portico.

I could see it lifting feathers of snow from the
base of the pillars and fluffing the cornices. The
floor had already been swept clean, but tiny flakes
drifted on to it from the exposed edges. The
interior was filled with a furious movement, though
a yard from it was frozen peace. I felt nothing
of the action of the wind, but I knew that it was
hot, hot as the breath of a furnace.

I had only one thought, dread of being overtaken
by night near that place. I turned and ran. Ran

with labouring steps across the lake, panting and
stifling with a deadly hot oppression, ran blindly
by a sort of instinct in the direction of the village.
I did not stop till I had wrestled through the big
wood, and come out on some rough pasture above
the highway. Then I dropped on the ground,
and felt again the comforting chill of the December air.

The adventure left me in an uncomfortable
mood. I was ashamed of myself for playing the
fool, and at the same time hopelessly puzzled, for
the oftener I went over in my mind the incidents
of that afternoon the more I was at a loss for an
explanation. One feeling was uppermost, that I
did not like this place and wanted to be out of it.
I had already broken the back of my task, and by
shutting myself up for two days I completed it ;
that is to say, I made my collation as far as I had
advanced myself in my commentary on the text.
I did not want to go back to the Hall, so I wrote
a civil note to Dubellay, expressing my gratitude
and saying that I was sending up the manuscript
by the landlord's son, as I scrupled to trouble him
with another visit.

I got a reply at once, saying that Mr. Dubellay
would like to give himself the pleasure of dining
with me at the inn before I went, and would receive the manuscript in person.

It was the last night of my stay in St. Sant, so
I ordered the best dinner the place could provide,
and a magnum of claret, of which I discovered a
bin in the cellar. Dubellay appeared promptly

at eight o'clock, arriving, to my surprise, in a car.
He had tidied himself up and put on a dinner
jacket, and he looked exactly like the city solicitors
you see dining in the Junior Carlton.

He was in excellent spirits, and his eyes had lost
their air of being on guard. He seemed to have
reached some conclusion about me, or decided
that I was harmless. More, he seemed to be
burning to talk to me. After my adventure I was
prepared to find fear in him, the fear I had seen
in the faces of the men-servants. But there was
none ; instead, there was excitement, overpower-
ing excitement.

He neglected the courses in his verbosity.
His coming to dinner had considerably startled
the inn, and instead of a maid the landlady herself waited on us. She seemed to want to get the
meal over, and hustled the biscuits and the port
on to the table as soon as she decently could.
Then Dubellay became confidential.

He was an enthusiast, it appeared, an enthusiast with a single hobby. All his life he had
pottered among antiquities, and when he succeeded to Vauncastle he had the leisure and
money to indulge himself. The place, it seemed,
had been famous in Roman Britain—Vauni
Castra—and Faxeter was a corruption of the
same. " Who was Vaunus ? " I asked. He
grinned, and told me to wait.

There had been an old temple up in the high
woods. There had always been a local legend
about it, and the place was supposed to be

haunted. Well, he had had the site excavated
and he had found—— Here he became the
cautious solicitor, and explained to me the law of
treasure trove. As long as the objects found
were not intrinsically valuable, not gold or jewels,
the finder was entitled to keep them. He had
done so—had not published the results of his
excavations in the proceedings of any learned
society—did not want to be bothered by tourists.
I was different, for I was a scholar.

What had he found ? It was really rather hard
to follow his babbling talk, but I gathered that he
had found certain carvings and sacrificial imple-
ments. And—he sunk his voice—most important
of all, an altar, an altar of Vaunus, the tutelary
deity of the vale.

When he mentioned this word his face took on a
new look—not of fear but of secrecy, a kind of
secret excitement. I have seen the same look on
the face of a street-preaching Salvationist.

Vaunus had been a British god of the hills,
whom the Romans in their liberal way appear to
have identified with Apollo. He gave me a long
confused account of him, from which it appeared
that Mr. Dubellay was not an exact scholar.
Some of his derivations of place-names were
absurd—like St. Sant from Sancta Sanctorum—
and in quoting a line of Ausonius he made two
false quantities. He seemed to hope that I could
tell him something more about Vaunus, but I
said that my subject was Greek, and that I was
deeply ignorant about Roman Britain. I men-

tioned several books, and found that he had never heard of Haverfield.

One word he used, "hypocaust," which suddenly gave me a clue. He must have heated the temple, as he heated his house, by some very efficient system of hot air. I know little about science, but I imagined that the artificial heat of the portico, as contrasted with the cold outside, might create an air current. At any rate that explanation satisfied me, and my afternoon's adventure lost its uncanniness. The reaction made me feel friendly towards him, and I listened to his talk with sympathy, but I decided not to mention that I had visited his temple.

He told me about it himself in the most open way. "I couldn't leave the altar on the hillside," he said. "I had to make a place for it, so I turned the old front of the house into a sort of temple. I got the best advice, but architects are ignorant people, and I often wished I had been a better scholar. Still, the place satisfies me."

"I hope it satisfies Vaunus," I said jocularly.

"I think so," he replied quite seriously, and then his thoughts seemed to go wandering, and for a minute or so he looked through me with a queer abstraction in his eyes.

"What do you do with it now you've got it ? " I asked.

He didn't reply, but smiled to himself.

"I don't know if you remember a passage in Sidonius Apollinaris," I said, " a formula for consecrating pagan altars to Christian uses. You begin by sacrificing a white cock or something suitable, and tell Apollo with all friendliness that the old dedication is off for the present. Then you have a Christian invocation——"

He nearly jumped out of his chair.

"That wouldn't do—wouldn't do at all! . . . Oh Lord, no! . . . Couldn't think of it for one moment!"

It was as if I had offended his ears by some horrid blasphemy, and the odd thing was that he never recovered his composure. He tried, for he had good manners, but his ease and friendliness had gone. We talked stiffly for another half-hour about trifles, and then he rose to leave. I returned him his manuscript neatly parcelled up, and expanded in thanks, but he scarcely seemed to heed me. He stuck the thing in his pocket, and departed with the same air of shocked absorption.

After he had gone I sat before the fire and reviewed the situation. I was satisfied with my hypocaust theory, and had no more perturbation in my memory about my afternoon's adventure. Yet a slight flavour of unpleasantness hung about it, and I felt that I did not quite like Dubellay. I set him down as a crank who had tangled himself up with a half-witted hobby, like an old maid with her cats, and I was not sorry to be leaving the place.

My third and last visit to St. Sant was in the following June—the midsummer of 1914. I had

all but finished my Theocritus, but I needed
another day or two with the Vauncastle manuscript,
and, as I wanted to clear the whole thing off before
I went to Italy in July, I wrote to Dubellay and
asked if I might have another sight of it. The
thing was a bore, but it had to be faced, and I
fancied that the valley would be a pleasant place
in that hot summer.

I got a reply at once, inviting, almost begging
me to come, and insisting that I should stay at
the Hall. I couldn't very well refuse, though I
would have preferred the inn. He wired about my
train, and wired again saying he would meet me.
This time I seemed to be a particularly welcome
guest.

I reached Faxeter in the evening, and was met
by a car from a Faxeter garage. The driver was a
talkative young man, and, as the car was a closed
one, I sat beside him for the sake of fresh air.
The term had tired me, and I was glad to get out
of stuffy Cambridge, but I cannot say that I
found it much cooler as we ascended the Vaun
valley. The woods were in their summer magnificence, but a little dulled and tarnished by the heat,
the river was shrunk to a trickle, and the curious
hilltops were so scorched by the sun that they
seemed almost yellow above the green of the trees.
Once again I had the feeling of a landscape fan-
tastically un-English.

"Squire Dubellay's been in a great way about
your coming, sir," the driver informed me. "Sent
down three times to the boss to make sure it was

all right. He's got a car of his own, too, a nice little Daimler, but he don't seem to use it much. Haven't seen him about in it for a month of Sundays."

As we turned in at the Hall gates he looked curiously about him. "Never been here before, though I've been in most gentlemen's parks for fifty miles round. Rum old-fashioned spot, isn't it, sir?"

If it had seemed a shuttered sanctuary in midwinter, in that June twilight it was more than ever a place enclosed and guarded. There was almost an autumn smell of decay, a dry decay like touchwood. We seemed to be descending through layers of ever-thickening woods. When at last we turned through the iron gate I saw that the lawns had reached a further stage of neglect, for they were as shaggy as a hayfield.

The white-faced butler let me in, and there, waiting at his back, was Dubellay. But he was not the man whom I had seen in December. He was dressed in an old baggy suit of flannels, and his unwholesome red face was painfully drawn and sunken. There were dark pouches under his eyes, and these eyes were no longer excited, but dull and pained. Yes, and there was more than pain in them—there was fear. I wondered if his hobby were becoming too much for him.

He greeted me like a long-lost brother. Considering that I scarcely knew him, I was a little embarrassed by his warmth. "Bless you for coming, my dear fellow," he cried. "You want a wash

and then we'll have dinner. Don't bother to
change, unless you want to. I never do." He
led me to my bedroom, which was clean enough
but small and shabby like a servant's room. I
guessed that he had gutted the house to build his
absurd temple.

We dined in a fair-sized room which was a kind
of library. It was lined with old books, but they
did not look as if they had been there long ; rather
it seemed like a lumber room in which a fine collection had been stored. Once no doubt they had
lived in a dignified Georgian chamber. There was
nothing else, none of the antiques which I had
expected.

"You have come just in time," he told me.
"I fairly jumped when I got your letter, for I had
been thinking of running up to Cambridge to
insist on your coming down here. I hope you're
in no hurry to leave."

"As it happens," I said, "I *am* rather pressed
for time, for I hope to go abroad next week. I ought
to finish my work here in a couple of days. I
can't tell you how much I'm in your debt for your
kindness."

"Two days," he said. "That will get us over
midsummer. That should be enough." I hadn't
a notion what he meant.

I told him that I was looking forward to examining his collection. He opened his eyes.
"Your discoveries, I mean," I said, "the altar
of Vaunus . . ."

As I spoke the words his face suddenly con-

torted in a spasm of what looked like terror. He
choked and then recovered himself. "Yes, yes,"
he said rapidly. "You shall see it—you shall see
everything—but not now—not to-night. To-
morrow—in broad daylight—that's the time."

After that the evening became a bad dream.
Small talk deserted him, and he could only reply
with an effort to my commonplaces. I caught
him often looking at me furtively, as if he were
sizing me up and wondering how far he could go
with me. The thing fairly got on my nerves, and,
to crown all, it was abominably stuffy. The
windows of the room gave on a little paved court
with a background of laurels, and I might have
been in Seven Dials for all the air there was.

When coffee was served I could stand it no longer.
"What about smoking in the temple?" I said.
"It should be cool there with the air from the
lake."

I might have been proposing the assassination
of his mother. He simply gibbered at me. "No,
no," he stammered. "My God, no!" It was
half an hour before he could properly collect himself. A servant lit two oil-lamps, and we sat on in
the frowsty room.

"You said something when we met before," he
ventured at last, after many a sidelong glance at
me. "Something about a ritual for re-dedicating
an altar."

I remembered my remark about Sidonius
Apollinaris.

"Could you show me the passage? There is a

good classical library here, collected by my great-grandfather. Unfortunately my scholarship is not equal to using it properly."

I got up and hunted along the shelves, and presently found a copy of Sidonius, the Plantin edition of 1609. I turned up the passage, and roughly translated it for him. He listened hungrily, and made me repeat it twice.

" He says a cock," he hesitated. " Is that essential ? "

" I don't think so. I fancy any of the recognized ritual stuff would do."

" I am glad," he said simply. " I am afraid of blood."

" Good God, man," I cried out, " are you taking my nonsense seriously ? I was only chaffing. Let old Vaunus stick to his altar ! "

He looked at me like a puzzled and rather offended dog.

" Sidonius was in earnest . . ."

" Well, I'm not," I said rudely " We're in the twentieth century and not in the third. Isn't it about time we went to bed ? "

He made no objection, and found me a candle in the hall. As I undressed I wondered into what kind of lunatic asylum I had strayed. I felt the strongest distaste for the place, and longed to go straight off to the inn ; only I couldn't make use of a man's manuscripts and insult his hospitality. It was fairly clear to me that Dubellay was mad. He had ridden his hobby to the death of his wits and was now in its bondage. Good Lord ! he had talked of his precious Vaunus as a votary talks of a god. I believed he had come to worship some figment of his half-educated fancy.

I think I must have slept for a couple of hours. Then I woke dripping with perspiration, for the place was simply an oven. My window was as wide open as it would go, and, though it was a warm night, when I stuck my head out the air was fresh. The heat came from indoors. The room was on the first floor near the entrance and I was looking on to the overgrown lawns. The night was very dark and utterly still, but I could have sworn that I heard wind. The trees were as motionless as marble, but somewhere close at hand I heard a strong gust blowing. Also, though there was no moon, there was somewhere near me a steady glow of light ; I could see the reflection of it round the end of the house. That meant that it came from the temple. What kind of saturnalia was Dubellay conducting at such an hour ?

When I drew in my head I felt that if I was to get any sleep something must be done. There could be no question about it ; some fool had turned on the steam heat, for the room was a furnace. My temper was rising. There was no bell to be found, so I lit my candle and set out to find a servant.

I tried a cast downstairs and discovered the room where we had dined. Then I explored a passage at right angles, which brought me up against a great oak door. The light showed me that it was a new door, and that there was no apparent way of opening it. I guessed that it led into the temple, and, though it fitted close and there seemed to be no keyhole, I could hear through it a sound like a rushing wind. . . . Next I opened a door on my right and found myself in a big store cupboard. It had a funny, exotic, spicy smell, and, arranged very neatly on the floor and shelves, was a number of small sacks and coffers. Each bore a label, a square of stout paper with very black lettering. I read "*Pro servitio Vauni.*"

I had seen them before, for my memory betrayed me if they were not the very labels that Dubellay's servants had been attaching to the packages from the carrier's cart that evening in the past autumn. The discovery made my suspicions an unpleasant certainty. Dubellay evidently meant the labels to read " For the service of Vaunus." He was no scholar, for it was an impossible use of the word "*servitium,*" but he was very patently a madman.

However, it was my immediate business to find some way to sleep, so I continued my quest for a servant. I followed another corridor, and discovered a second staircase. At the top of it I saw an open door and looked in. It must have been Dubellay's, for his flannels were tumbled untidily on a chair ; but Dubellay himself was not there and the bed had not been slept in.

I suppose my irritation was greater than my alarm—though I must say I was getting a little scared—for I still pursued the evasive servant. There was another stair which apparently led to attics, and in going up it I slipped and made a great clatter. When I looked up the butler in his nightgown was staring down at me, and if ever a mortal face held fear it was his. When he saw who it was he seemed to recover a little.

"Look here," I said, "for God's sake turn off that infernal hot air. I can't get a wink of sleep. What idiot set it going?"

He looked at me owlishly, but he managed to find his tongue.

"I beg your pardon, sir," he said, "but there is no heating apparatus in this house."

There was nothing more to be said. I returned to my bedroom, and it seemed to me that it had grown cooler. As I leaned out of the window, too, the mysterious wind seemed to have died away, and the glow no longer showed from behind the corner of the house. I got into bed and slept heavily till I was roused by the appearance of my shaving water about half-past nine. There was no bathroom, so I bathed in a tin pannikin.

It was a hazy morning which promised a day of blistering heat. When I went down to breakfast I found Dubellay in the dining-room. In the daylight he looked a very sick man, but he seemed to have taken a pull on himself, for his manner was considerably less nervy than the night before. Indeed, he appeared almost normal, and I might have reconsidered my view but for the look in his eyes.

I told him that I proposed to sit tight all day over the manuscript, and get the thing finished.

He nodded. "That's all right. I've a lot to do myself, and I won't disturb you."

"But first," I said, "you promised to show me your discoveries."

He looked at the window where the sun was shining on the laurels and on a segment of the paved court.

"The light is good," he said—an odd remark. "Let us go there now. There are times and seasons for the temple."

He led me down the passage I had explored the previous night. The door opened, not by a key but by some lever in the wall. I found myself looking suddenly at a bath of sunshine with the lake below as blue as a turquoise.

It is not easy to describe my impressions of that place. It was unbelievably light and airy, as brilliant as an Italian colonnade in midsummer. The proportions must have been good, for the columns soared and swam, and the roof (which looked like cedar) floated as delicately as a flower on its stalk. The stone was some local limestone, which on the floor took a polish like marble. All around was a vista of sparkling water and summer woods and far blue mountains. It should have been as wholesome as the top of a hill.

And yet I had scarcely entered before I knew that it was a prison. I am not an imaginative man, and I believe my nerves are fairly good, but I could scarcely put one foot before the other, so strong was my distaste. I felt shut off from the world, as if I were in a dungeon or on an ice-floe.

And I felt, too, that though far enough from humanity, we were not alone.

On the inner wall there were three carvings. Two were imperfect friezes sculptured in low-relief, dealing apparently with the same subject. It was a ritual procession, priests bearing branches, the ordinary *dendrophori* business. The faces were only half-human, and that was from no lack of skill, for the artist had been a master. The striking thing was that the branches and the hair of the hierophants were being tossed by a violent wind, and the expression of each was of a being in the last stage of endurance, shaken to the core by terror and pain.

Between the friezes was a great roundel of a Gorgon's head. It was not a female head, such as you commonly find, but a male head, with the viperous hair sprouting from chin and lip. It had once been coloured, and fragments of a green pigment remained in the locks. It was an awful thing, the ultimate horror of fear, the last dementia of cruelty made manifest in stone. I hurriedly averted my eyes and looked at the altar.

That stood at the west end on a pediment with three steps. It was a beautiful piece of work, scarcely harmed by the centuries, with two words inscribed on its face—APOLL. VAUN. It was made of some foreign marble, and the hollow top was dark with ancient sacrifices. Not so ancient either, for I could have sworn that I saw there the mark of recent flame.

I do not suppose I was more than five minutes

in the place. I wanted to get out, and Dubellay wanted to get me out. We did not speak a word till we were back in the library.

"For God's sake give it up!" I said. "You're playing with fire, Mr. Dubellay. You're driving yourself into Bedlam. Send those damned things to a museum and leave this place. Now, now, I tell you. You have no time to lose. Come down with me to the inn straight off and shut up this house."

He looked at me with his lip quivering like a child about to cry.

"I will. I promise you I will. . . . But not yet. . . . After to-night. . . . To-morrow I'll do whatever you tell me. . . . You won't leave me?"

"I won't leave you, but what earthly good am I to you if you won't take my advice?"

"Sidonius . . ." he began.

"Oh, damn Sidonius! I wish I had never mentioned him. The whole thing is arrant nonsense, but it's killing you. You've got it on the brain. Don't you know you're a sick man?"

"I'm not feeling very grand. It's so warm to-day. I think I'll lie down."

It was no good arguing with him, for he had the appalling obstinacy of very weak things. I went off to my work in a shocking bad temper.

The day was what it had promised to be, blisteringly hot. Before midday the sun was hidden by a coppery haze, and there was not the faintest stirring of wind. Dubellay did not appear at luncheon—it was not a meal he ever ate, the butler told me. I slogged away all the afternoon, and had pretty well finished my job by six o'clock. That would enable me to leave next morning, and I hoped to be able to persuade my host to come with me.

The conclusion of my task put me into a better humour, and I went for a walk before dinner. It was a very close evening, for the heat haze had not lifted ; the woods were as silent as a grave, not a bird spoke, and when I came out of the cover to the burnt pastures the sheep seemed too languid to graze. During my walk I prospected the environs of the house, and saw that it would be very hard to get access to the temple except by a long circuit. On one side was a mass of outbuildings, and then a high wall, and on the other the very closest and highest quickset hedge I have ever seen, which ended in a wood with savage spikes on its containing wall. I returned to my room, had a cold bath in the exiguous tub, and changed.

Dubellay was not at dinner. The butler said that his master was feeling unwell and had gone to bed. The news pleased me, for bed was the best place for him. After that I settled myself down to a lonely evening in the library. I browsed among the shelves and found a number of rare editions which served to pass the time. I noticed that the copy of Sidonius was absent from its place.

I think it was about ten o'clock when I went to bed, for I was unaccountably tired. I remember wondering whether I oughtn't to go and visit

Dubellay, but decided that it was better to leave him alone. I still reproach myself for that decision. I know now I ought to have taken him by force and haled him to the inn.

Suddenly I came out of heavy sleep with a start. A human cry seemed to be ringing in the corridors of my brain. I held my breath and listened. It came again, a horrid scream of panic and torture.

I was out of bed in a second, and only stopped to get my feet into slippers. The cry must have come from the temple. I tore downstairs expecting to hear the noise of an alarmed household. But there was no sound, and the awful cry was not repeated.

The door in the corridor was shut, as I expected. Behind it pandemonium seemed to be loose, for there was a howling like a tempest—and something more, a crackling like fire. I made for the front door, slipped off the chain, and found myself in the still, moonless night. Still, except for the rending gale that seemed to be raging in the house I had left.

From what I had seen on my evening's walk I knew that my one chance to get to the temple was by way of the quickset hedge. I thought I might manage to force a way between the end of it and the wall. I did it, at the cost of much of my raiment and my skin. Beyond was another rough lawn set with tangled shrubberies, and then a precipitous slope to the level of the lake. I scrambled along the sedgy margin, not daring to lift my eyes till I was on the temple steps.

The place was brighter than day with a roaring blast of fire. The very air seemed to be incandescent and to have become a flaming ether. And yet there were no flames—only a burning brightness. I could not enter, for the waft from it struck my face like a scorching hand and I felt my hair singe. . . .

I am short-sighted, as you know, and I may have been mistaken, but this is what I think I saw. From the altar a great tongue of flame seemed to shoot upwards and lick the roof, and from its pediment ran flaming streams. In front of it lay a body—Dubellay's—a naked body, already charred and black. There was nothing else, except that the Gorgon's head in the wall seemed to glow like a sun in hell.

I suppose I must have tried to enter. All I know is that I found myself staggering back, rather badly burned. I covered my eyes, and as I looked through my fingers I seemed to see the flames flowing under the wall, where there may have been lockers, or possibly another entrance. Then the great oak door suddenly shrivelled like gauze, and with a roar the fiery river poured into the house.

I ducked myself in the lake to ease the pain, and then ran back as hard as I could by the way I had come. Dubellay, poor devil, was beyond my aid. After that I am not very clear what happened. I know that the house burned like a haystack. I found one of the men-servants on the lawn, and I think I helped to get the other down from his room by one of the rain-pipes. By the time the neigh-

bours arrived the house was ashes, and I was pretty
well mother-naked. They took me to the inn and
put me to bed, and I remained there till after the
inquest. The coroner's jury were puzzled, but
they found it simply death by misadventure;
a lot of country houses were burned that summer.
There was nothing found of Dubellay; nothing
remained of the house except a few blackened
pillars; the altar and the sculptures were so cracked
and scarred that no museum wanted them. The
place has not been rebuilt, and for all I know they
are there to-day. I am not going back to look for
them.

Nightingale finished his story and looked round
his audience.

"Don't ask me for an explanation," he said,
"for I haven't any. You may believe if you like
that the god Vaunus inhabited the temple which
Dubellay built for him, and, when his votary grew
scared and tried Sidonius's receipt for shifting the
dedication, became angry and slew him with his
flaming wind. That wind seems to have been a
perquisite of Vaunus. We know more about him
now, for last year they dug up a temple of his in
Wales."

"Lightning," some one suggested.

"It was a quiet night, with no thunderstorm,"
said Nightingale.

"Isn't the countryside volcanic?" Peckwether
asked. "What about pockets of natural gas or
something of the kind?"

"Possibly. You may please yourself in your explanation. I'm afraid I can't help you. All I know is, that I don't propose to visit that valley again ! "

"What became of your Theocritus ? "

"Burned, like everything else. However, that didn't worry me much. Six weeks later came the War, and I had other things to think about."

"Really, you now please speak in your explanation, and admit I don't help you. All I know is the I don't propose to risk the valley again."

With luncheon Mary Tr..... on.

"I mean, this every time clear. However, that didn't worry me much. But when the last came the War, and I had other things to think about."

V. "DIVUS" JOHNSTON

LORD LAMANCHA'S STORY

In deorum numerum relatus est non ore modo decernentium sed et persuasione vulgi.

SUETONIUS.

V. "DIVUS" JOHNSTON

W E were discussing the vagaries of ambition, and decided that most of the old prizes that humanity contended for had had their gilt rubbed off. Kingdoms, for example, which younger sons used to set out to conquer. It was agreed that nowadays there was a great deal of drudgery and very little fun in being a king.

"Besides, it can't be done," Leithen put in. "The Sarawak case. Sovereignty over territory can only be acquired by a British subject on behalf of His Majesty."

There was far more real power, some one argued, in the profession of prophet. Mass-persuasion was never such a force as to-day. Sandy Arbuthnot, who had known Gandhi and admired him, gave us a picture of that strange popular leader—ascetic, genius, dreamer, child. "For a little," he said, "Gandhi had more absolute sway over a bigger lump of humanity than anybody except Lenin."

"I once knew Lenin," said Fulleylove, the traveller, and we all turned to him.

"It must have been more than twenty years ago," he explained. "I was working at the British Museum and lived in lodgings in Bloomsbury, and he had a room at the top of the house. Ilyitch was the name we knew him by. He was a little, beetle-browed chap, with a pale face and the most amazing sleepy black eyes, which would suddenly twinkle and blaze as some thought passed through his mind. He was very pleasant and good-humoured, and would spend hours playing with the landlady's children. I remember I once took him down with me for a day into the country, and he was the merriest little grig. . . . Did I realize how big he was? No, I cannot say I did. He was the ordinary Marxist, and he wanted to resurrect Russia by hydraulics and electrification. He seemed to be a funny compound of visionary and *terre-à-terre* scientist. But I realized that he could lay a spell on his countrymen. I have been to Russian meetings with him—I talk Russian, you know—and it was astounding the way he could make his audience look at him like hungry sheep. He gave me the impression of utter courage and candour, and a kind of demoniac simplicity. . . . No, I never met him again, but oddly enough I was in Moscow during his funeral. Russian geographers were interesting themselves in the line of the old silk-route to Cathay, and I was there by request to advise them. I had not a very comfortable time, but everybody was very civil to me. So I saw Lenin's funeral, and unless you saw that you can have no notion of his power. A great black bier like an altar, and hundreds and thousands of people weeping and worshipping—yes, worshipping."

" The successful prophet becomes a kind of god,"

said Lamancha. "Have you ever known a god, Sandy ? . . . No more have I. But there is one living to-day somewhere in Scotland. Johnston is his name. I once met a very particular friend of his. I will tell you the story, and you can believe it or not as you like."

I had this narrative—he said—from my friend Mr. Peter Thomson of "Jessieville," Maxwell Avenue, Strathbungo, whom I believe to be a man incapable of mendacity, or, indeed, of imagination. He is a prosperous and retired ship's captain, dwelling in the suburbs of Glasgow, who plays two rounds of golf every day of the week, and goes twice every Sunday to a pink, new church. You may often see his ample figure, splendidly habited in broadcloth and finished off with one of those square felt hats which are the Scottish emblem of respectability, moving sedately by Mrs. Thomson's side down the avenue of "Balmorals" and "Belle-vues" where dwell the aristocracy of Strathbungo. It was not there that I met him, however, but in a Clyde steamboat going round the Mull, where I spent a comfortless night on my way to a Highland fishing. It was blowing what he called "a wee bit o' wind," and I could not face the odorous bunks which opened on the dining-room. Seated abaft the funnel, in an atmosphere of ham-and-eggs, bilge, and fresh western breezes, he revealed his heart to me, and this I found in it.

"About the age of forty " —said Mr. Thomson—

" I was captain of the steamer *Archibald McKelvie*, 1,700 tons burthen, belonging to Brock, Rattray, and Linklater, of Greenock. We were principally engaged in the China trade, but made odd trips into the Malay Archipelago and once or twice to Australia. She was a handy bit boat, and I'll not deny that I had many mercies vouchsafed to me when I was her skipper. I raked in a bit of salvage now and then, and my trading commission, paid regularly into the British Linen Bank at Maryhill, was mounting up to a fairish sum. I had no objection to Eastern parts, for I had a good constitution and had outgrown the daftnesses of youth. The berth suited me well, I had a decent lot for ship's company, and I would gladly have looked forward to spending the rest of my days by the *Archibald McKelvie*.

" Providence, however, thought otherwise, for He was preparing a judgment against that ship like the kind you read about in books. We were five days out from Singapore, shaping our course for the Philippines, where the Americans were then fighting, when we ran into a queer lown sea. Not a breath of air came out of the sky ; if you kindled a match the flame wouldna leap, but smouldered like touchwood ; and every man's body ran with sweat like a mill-lade. I kenned fine we were in for the terrors of hell, but I hadna any kind of notion how terrible hell could be. First came a wind that whipped away my funnel like a potato-peeling. We ran before it, and it was like the swee-gee we used to play at when we were laddies. One moment the muckle sea would get up on its hinder end and look at you, and the next you were looking at it as if you were on the top of Ben Lomond looking down on Luss. Presently I saw land in a gap of the waters, a land with great blood-red mountains, and, thinks I to myself, if we keep up the pace this boat of mine will not be hindered from ending two or three miles inland in some-body's kail-yard. I was just wondering how we would get the *Archibald McKelvie* back to her native element when she saved me the trouble ; for she ran dunt on some kind of a rock, and went straight to the bottom.

" I was the only man saved alive, and if you ask me how it happened I don't know. I felt myself choking in a whirlpool ; then I was flung through the air and brought down with a smack into deep waters ; then I was in the air again, and this time I landed amongst sand and tree-trunks and got a bash on the head which dozened my senses.

" When I came to it was morning, and the storm had abated. I was lying about half-way up a beach of fine white sand, for the wave that had carried me landwards in its flow had brought me some of the road back in its ebb. All round me was a sort of free-coup—trees knocked to match-wood, dead fish, and birds and beasts, and some boards which I jaloused came from the *Archibald McKelvie*. I had a big bump on my head, but otherwise I was well and clear in my wits, though empty in the stomach and very dowie in the heart. For I knew something about the islands of which I supposed this to be one. They were either barren wastes, with neither food nor water, or else they were inhabited by the bloodiest cannibals of the archipelago. It looked as if my choice lay between having nothing to eat and being eaten myself.

" I got up, and, after returning thanks to my Maker, went for a walk in the woods. They were full of queer painted birds, and it was an awful job climbing in and out of the fallen trees. By-and-by I came into an open bit with a burn where I slockened my thirst. It cheered me up, and I was just beginning to think that this was not such a bad island, and looking to see if I could find anything in the nature of coco-nuts, when I heard a whistle like a steam-siren. It was some sort of signal, for the next I knew I was in the grip of a dozen savages, my arms and feet were lashed together, and I was being carried swiftly through the forest.

" It was a rough journey, and the discomfort of that heathen handling kept me from reflecting upon my desperate position. After nearly three hours we stopped, and I saw that we had come to a city. The streets were not much to look at, and the houses were mud and thatch, but on a hillock in the middle stood a muckle temple not unlike a Chinese pagoda. There was a man blowing a horn, and a lot of folk shouting, but I paid no attention, for I was sore troubled with the cramp in my left leg. They took me into one of the huts, and made signs that I was to have it for my lodging. They brought me water to wash, and a very respectable dinner, which included a hen and a vegetable not unlike greens. Then they left me to myself, and I lay down and slept for a round of the clock.

" I was three days in that hut. I had plenty to eat and the folk were very civil, but they wouldna let me outbye and there was no window to look out of. I couldna make up my mind what they wanted with me. I was a prisoner, but they did not behave as if they bore any malice, and I might have thought I was an honoured guest, but for the guards at the door. Time hung heavy on my hands, for I had nothing to read and no light to read by. I said over all the chapters of the Bible and all the Scots songs I could remember, and I tried to make a poem about my adventures, but I stuck at the fifth line, for I couldna find a rhyme to McKelvie.

" On the fourth morning I was awakened by the most deafening din. I saw through the door that the streets were full of folk in holiday clothes, most of them with flowers in their hair and carrying palm branches in their hands. It was like something out of a Bible picture-book. After I had my breakfast four lads in long white gowns arrived, and in spite of all my protests they made a bonny spectacle of me. They took off my clothes, me blushing with shame, and rubbed me with a kind of oil that smelt of cinnamon. Then they shaved my chin, and painted on my forehead a mark like a freemason's. Then they put on me a kind of white nightgown with a red sash round the middle, and they wouldna be hindered from clapping on my head a great wreath of hothouse flowers, as if I was a funeral.

" And then like a thunder-clap I realized my horrible position. *I was a funeral.* I was to be offered up as a sacrifice to some heathen god—an awful fate for a Free Kirk elder in the prime of life.

" I was so paralytic with terror that I never tried to resist. Indeed, it would have done me little good, for outside there were, maybe, two hundred savages, armed and drilled like soldiers. I was put into a sort of palanquin, and my bearers started at a trot with me up the hill to the temple, the whole population of the city running alongside, and singing songs about their god. I was sick with fear, and I durstna look up, for I did not know what awesome sight awaited me.

" At last I got my courage back. ' Peter,' I says to myself, ' be a man. Remember your sainted Covenanting forefathers. You have been chosen to testify for your religion, though it's no likely that yon savages will understand what you say.' So I shut my jaw and resolved before I died to make a declaration of my religious principles, and to loosen some of the heathens' teeth with my fists.

" We stopped at the temple door and I was led through a court and into a muckle great place like a barn, with bats flying about the ceiling. Here there were nearly three thousand heathens sitting on their hunkers. They sang a hymn when they saw me, and I was just getting ready for action when my bearers carried me into another place, which I took to be the Holy of Holies. It was about half the size of the first, and at the end of it was a great curtain of leopards' skins hanging from roof to floor. My bearers set me in the middle of the room, and then rolled about on their stomachs in adoration before the curtain. After a bit they finished their prayers and crawled out backwards, and I was left alone in that fearsome place.

" It was the worst experience of my life. I believed that behind the skins there was a horrible idol, and that at any moment a priest with a knife would slip in to cut my throat. You may crack about courage, but I tell you that a man who can wait without a quiver on his murderers in the middle of a gloomy kirk is more than human. I am not ashamed to confess that the sweat ran over my brow, and my teeth were knocking in my head.

" But nothing happened. Nothing, except that as I sat there I began to notice a most remarkable smell. At first I thought the place was on fire. Then I thought it was the kind of stink called incense that they make in Popish kirks, for I once wandered into a cathedral in Santiago. But neither guess was right, and then I put my thumb on the proper description. It was nothing but the smell of the third-class carriages on the Coatbridge train on a Saturday night after a football match— the smell of plug tobacco smoked in clay pipes that were no just very clean. My eyes were getting accustomed to the light, and I found the place no that dark ; and as I looked round to see what caused the smell, I spied something like smoke coming from beyond the top of the curtain.

" I noticed another thing. There was a hole in the curtain, about six feet from the floor, and at that hole as I watched I saw an eye. My heart stood still, for, thinks I, that'll be the priest of Baal who presently will stick a knife into me. It was long ere I could screw up courage to look again, but I did it. And then I saw that the eye was not that of a savage, which would be black and blood-shot. It was a blue eye, and, as I looked, it winked at me.

" And then a voice spoke out from behind the curtain, and this was what it said. It said, ' God-sake, Peter, is that you ? And how did ye leave them a' at Maryhill ? '

" And from behind the curtain walked a muckle man, dressed in a pink blanket, a great red-headed man, with a clay pipe in his mouth. It was the god of the savages, and who do ye think it was ? A man Johnston, who used to bide in the same close as me in Glasgow. . . ."

Mr. Thomson's emotion overcame him, and he accepted a stiff drink from my flask. Wiping away a tear, which may have been of sentiment or of mirth, he continued :

" You may imagine that I was joyful and sur-prised to see him, and he, so to speak, fell on my neck like the father of the Prodigal Son. He hadna seen a Scotch face for four years. He raked up one or two high priests and gave instructions, and soon I was comfortably lodged in a part of the temple

close to his own rooms. Eh, man, it was a noble
sight to see Johnston and the priests. He was a
big, red-haired fellow, six foot four, and as strong
as a stot, with a voice like a north-easter, and yon
natives fair crawled like caterpillars in his presence.
I never saw a man with such a natural talent for
being a god. You would have thought he had been
bred to the job all his days, and yet I minded him
keeping a grocer's shop in the Dalmarnock Road.

"That night he told me his story. It seemed
that he had got a post at Shanghai in a trading
house, and was coming out to it in one of those God-
forgotten German tramps that defile the China
seas. Like me, he fell in with a hurricane, and,
like me, his ship was doomed. He was a powerful
swimmer, and managed to keep afloat until he
found some drifting wreckage, and after the wind
had gone down he paddled ashore. There he was
captured by the savages, and taken, like me, to
their city. They were going to sacrifice him, but
one chief, wiser than the rest, called attention to
his size and strength, and pointed out that they
were at war with their neighbours, and that a big
man would be of more use in the fighting line than
on an altar in the temple.

"So off went Johnston to the wars. He was
a bonny fighter, and very soon they made him
captain of the royal bodyguard, and a fortnight
later the general commanding-in-chief over the
whole army. He said he had never enjoyed himself
so much in his life, and when he got back from his
battles the population of the city used to meet

him with songs and flowers. Then an old priest
found an ancient prophecy about a Red God who
would come out of the sea and lead the people to
victory. Very soon there was a strong party for
making Johnston a god, and when, with the help
of a few sticks of trade dynamite, he had blown up
the capital of the other side and brought back his
army in triumph with a prisoner apiece, popular
feeling could not be restrained. Johnston was
hailed as divine. He hadna much grip of the
language, and couldna explain the situation, so he
thought it best to submit.

"'Mind you,' he said to me, 'I've been a good
god to these poor blind ignorant folk.' He had
stopped the worst of their habits and put down
human sacrifices, and got a sort of town council
appointed to keep the city clean, and he had made
the army the most efficient thing ever heard of in
the islands. And now he was preparing to leave.
This was what they expected, for the prophecy
had said that the Red God, after being the saviour
of his people, would depart as he had come across
the sea. So, under his directions, they had built
him a kind of boat with which he hoped to reach
Singapore. He had got together a considerable
fortune, too, chiefly in rubies, for as a god he had
plenty of opportunities of acquiring wealth honestly.
He said there was a sort of green-grocer's and
butcher's shop before his altar every morning, and
he got one of the priests, who had some business
notions, to sell off the goods for him.

"There was just one thing that bothered Mr.

Johnston. He was a good Christian man and had been an elder in a kirk in the Cowcaddens, and he was much in doubt whether he had not committed a mortal sin in accepting the worship of these heathen islanders. Often I argued it out with him, but I did not seem able to comfort him rightly. ' Ye see,' he used to say to me, ' if I have broken anything, it's the spirit and no the letter of the commandment. I havena set up a graven image, for ye canna call me a graven image.'

" I mind that I quoted to him the conduct of Naaman, who was allowed to bow in the house of Rimmon, but he would not have it. ' No, no,' he cried, ' that has nothing to do with the point. It's no a question of my bowing in the house of Rimmon. I'm auld Rimmon himself.' "

" That's a strange story, Mr. Thomson," I said. " Is it true ? "

" True as death. But you havena heard the end of it. We got away, and by-and-by we reached Singapore, and in course of time our native land. Johnston, he was a very rich man now, and I didna go without my portion ; so the loss of the *Archibald McKelvie* turned out the best piece of luck in my life. I bought a share in Brock's Line, but nothing would content Johnston but that he must be a gentleman. He got a big estate in Annandale, where all the Johnstons came from long ago, and one way and another he has spent an awful siller on it. Land will swallow up money quicker than the sea."

" And what about his conscience ? " I asked.

" It's keeping quieter," said Mr. Thomson. " He takes a great interest in Foreign Missions, to which he subscribes largely, and they tell me that he has given the funds to build several new kirks. Oh yes, and he's just been adopted as a prospective Liberal candidate. I had a letter from him no further back than yesterday. It's about his political career, as he calls it. He told me, what didna need telling, that I must never mention a word about his past. ' If discretion was necessary before,' he says, ' it's far more necessary now; for how could the Party of Progress have any confidence in a man if they heard he had once been a god ? ' "

VI. THE LOATHLY OPPOSITE

OLIVER PUGH'S STORY

How loathly opposite I stood
To his unnatural purpose.

King Lear.

VI. THE LOATHLY OPPOSITE

BURMINSTER had been to a Guildhall dinner the night before, which had been attended by many—to him—unfamiliar celebrities. He had seen for the first time in the flesh people whom he had long known by reputation, and he declared that in every case the picture he had formed of them had been cruelly shattered. An eminent poet, he said, had looked like a starting-price bookmaker, and a financier of world-wide fame had been exactly like the music-master at his preparatory school. Wherefore Burminster made the profound deduction that things were never what they seemed.

"That's only because you have a feeble imagination," said Sandy Arbuthnot. "If you had really understood Timson's poetry you would have realized that it went with close-cropped red hair and a fat body, and you should have known that Macintyre (this was the financier) had the music-and-metaphysics type of mind. That's why he puzzles the City so. If you understand a man's work well enough you can guess pretty accurately what he'll look like. I don't mean the colour of his eyes and his hair, but the general atmosphere of him."

It was Sandy's agreeable habit to fling an occasional paradox at the table with the view of starting an argument. This time he stirred up Pugh, who had come to the War Office from the Indian Staff Corps. Pugh had been a great figure in Secret Service work in the East, but he did not look the part, for he had the air of a polo-playing cavalry subaltern. The skin was stretched as tight over his cheek bones as over the knuckles of a clenched fist, and was so dark that it had the appearance of beaten bronze. He had black hair, rather beady black eyes, and the hooky nose which in the Celt often goes with that colouring. He was himself a very good refutation of Sandy's theory.

" I don't agree," Pugh said. " At least not as a general principle. One piece of humanity whose work I studied with the microscope for two aching years upset all my notions when I came to meet it."

Then he told us this story.

" When I was brought to England in November '17 and given a ' hush ' department on three floors of an eighteenth-century house in a back street, I had a good deal to learn about my business. That I learned it in reasonable time was due to the extraordinarily fine staff that I found provided for me. Not one of them was a regular soldier. They were all educated men—they had to be in that job —but they came out of every sort of environment. One of the best was a Shetland laird, another was an Admiralty Court K.C., and I had, besides, a metallurgical chemist, a golf champion, a leader-

writer, a popular dramatist, several actuaries, and
an East End curate. None of them thought of
anything but his job, and at the end of the War,
when some ass proposed to make them O.B.E.'s,
there was a very fair imitation of a riot. A more
loyal crowd never existed, and they accepted me
as their chief as unquestioningly as if I had been
with them since 1914.

"To the War in the ordinary sense they scarcely
gave a thought. You found the same thing in a
lot of other behind-the-lines departments, and I
daresay it was a good thing—it kept their nerves
quiet and their minds concentrated. After all, our
business was only to decode and decipher German
messages ; we had nothing to do with the use
which was made of them. It was a curious little
nest, and when the Armistice came my people were
flabbergasted—they hadn't realized that their job
was bound up with the War.

"The one who most interested me was my second-
in-command, Philip Channell. He was a man of
forty-three, about five foot four in height, weigh-
ing, I fancy, under nine stone, and almost as blind
as an owl. He was good enough at papers with his
double glasses, but he could hardly recognize you
three yards off. He had been a professor at some
Midland college—mathematics or physics, I think
—and as soon as the War began he had tried to
enlist. Of course they wouldn't have him—he was
about E5 in any physical classification, besides
being well over age—but he would take no refusal,
and presently he worried his way into the Govern-

ment service. Fortunately he found a job which he could do superlatively well, for I do not believe there was a man alive with more natural genius for cryptography.

" I don't know if any of you have ever given your mind to that heart-breaking subject. Anyhow, you know that secret writing falls under two heads —codes and ciphers, and that codes are combinations of words and ciphers of numerals. I remember how one used to be told that no code or cipher which was practically useful was really undiscoverable, and in a sense that is true, especially of codes. A system of communication which is in constant use must obviously not be too intricate, and a working code, if you get long enough for the job, can generally be read. That is why a code is periodically changed by the users. There are rules in worrying out the permutations and combinations of letters in most codes, for human ingenuity seems to run in certain channels, and a man who has been a long time at the business gets surprisingly clever at it. You begin by finding out a little bit, and then empirically building up the rules of decoding, till in a week or two you get the whole thing. Then, when you are happily engaged in reading enemy messages, the code is changed suddenly, and you have to start again from the beginning. . . . You can make a code, of course, that it is simply impossible to read except by accident—the key to which is a page of some book, for example—but fortunately that kind is not of much general use.

" Well, we got on pretty well with the codes, and read the intercepted enemy messages, cables and wireless, with considerable ease and precision. It was mostly diplomatic stuff, and not very important. The more valuable stuff was in cipher, and that was another pair of shoes. With a code you can build up the interpretation by degrees, but with a cipher you either know it or you don't—there are no half-way houses. A cipher, since it deals with numbers, is a horrible field for mathematical ingenuity. Once you have written out the letters of a message in numerals there are many means by which you can lock it and double-lock it. The two main devices, as you know, are transposition and substitution, and there is no limit to the ways one or other or both can be used. There is nothing to prevent a cipher having a double meaning, produced by two different methods, and, as a practical question, you have to decide which meaning is intended. By way of an extra complication, too, the message, when deciphered, may turn out to be itself in a difficult code. I can tell you our job wasn't exactly a rest cure."

Burminster, looking puzzled, inquired as to the locking of ciphers.

" It would take too long to explain. Roughly, you write out a message horizontally in numerals ; then you pour it into vertical columns, the number and order of which are determined by a key-word ; then you write out the contents of the columns horizontally, following the lines across. To unlock it you have to have the key-word, so as to put it back into the vertical columns, and then into the original horizontal form."

Burminster cried out like one in pain. "It can't be done. Don't tell me that any human brain could solve such an acrostic."

"It was frequently done," said Pugh.

"By you?"

"Lord bless you, not by me. I can't do a simple cross-word puzzle. By my people."

"Give me the trenches," said Burminster in a hollow voice. "Give me the trenches any day. Do you seriously mean to tell me that you could sit down before a muddle of numbers and travel back the way they had been muddled to an original that made sense?"

"I couldn't, but Channell could—in most cases. You see, we didn't begin entirely in the dark. We already knew the kind of intricacies that the enemy favoured, and the way we worked was by trying a variety of clues till we lit on the right one."

"Well, I'm blessed! Go on about your man Channell."

"This isn't Channell's story," said Pugh. "He only comes into it accidentally. . . . There was one cipher which always defeated us, a cipher used between the German General Staff and their forces in the East. It was a locked cipher, and Channell had given more time to it than to any dozen of the others, for it put him on his mettle. But he confessed himself absolutely beaten. He wouldn't admit that it was insoluble, but he declared that he would need a bit of real luck to solve it. I asked him what kind of luck, and he said a mistake and a repetition. That, he said, might give him a chance of establishing equations.

"We called this particular cipher 'P.Y.,' and we hated it poisonously. We felt like pygmies battering at the base of a high stone tower. Dislike of the thing soon became dislike of the man who had conceived it. Channell and I used to—I won't say amuse, for it was too dashed serious—but torment ourselves by trying to picture the fellow who owned the brain that was responsible for P.Y. We had a pretty complete *dossier* of the German Intelligence Staff, but of course we couldn't know who was responsible for this particular cipher. We knew no more than his code name, Reinmar, with which he signed the simpler messages to the East, and Channell, who was a romantic little chap for all his science, had got it into his head that it was a woman. He used to describe her to me as if he had seen her—a she-devil, young, beautiful, with a much-painted white face, and eyes like a cobra's. I fancy he read a rather low class of novel in his off-time.

"My picture was different. At first I thought of the histrionic type of scientist, the 'ruthless brain' type, with a high forehead and a jaw puckered like a chimpanzee's. But that didn't seem to work, and I settled on a picture of a first-class *Generalstabsoffizier*, as handsome as Falkenhayn, trained to the last decimal, absolutely passionless, with a mind that worked with the relentless precision of a fine machine. We all of us

at the time suffered from the bogy of this kind of
German, and, when things were going badly, as in
March '18, I couldn't sleep for hating him. The
infernal fellow was so water-tight and armour-
plated, a Goliath who scorned the pebbles from our
feeble slings.

"Well, to make a long story short, there came a
moment in September '18 when P.Y. was about the
most important thing in the world. It mattered
enormously what Germany was doing in Syria, and
we knew that it was all in P.Y. Every morning a
pile of the intercepted German wireless messages
lay on Channell's table, which were as meaningless
to him as a child's scrawl. I was prodded by my
chiefs and in turn I prodded Channell. We had a
week to find the key to the cipher, after which
things must go on without us, and if we had failed
to make anything of it in eighteen months of quiet
work, it didn't seem likely that we would succeed
in seven feverish days. Channell nearly went off
his head with overwork and anxiety. I used to
visit his dingy little room and find him fairly
grizzled and shrunken with fatigue.

"This isn't a story about him, though there is a
good story which I may tell you another time.
As a matter of fact, we won on the post. P.Y.
made a mistake. One morning we got a long message dated *en clair*, then a very short message,
and then a third message almost the same as the
first. The second must mean 'Your message of
to-day's date unintelligible, please repeat.' the
regular formula. This gave us a translation of a

bit of the cipher. Even that would not have brought it out, and for twelve hours Channell was on the verge of lunacy, till it occurred to him that Reinmar might have signed the long message with his name, as we used to do sometimes in cases of extreme urgency. He was right, and, within three hours of the last moment Operations could give us, we had the whole thing pat. As I have said, that is a story worth telling, but it is not this one.

" We both finished the War too tired to think of much except that the darned thing was over. But Reinmar had been so long our unseen but constantly pictured opponent that we kept up a certain interest in him. We would like to have seen how he took the licking, for he must have known that we had licked him. Mostly when you lick a man at a game you rather like him, but I didn't like Reinmar. In fact, I made him a sort of compost of everything I had ever disliked in a German. Channell stuck to his she-devil theory, but I was pretty certain that he was a youngish man with an intellectual arrogance which his country's *débâcle* would in no way lessen. He would never acknowledge defeat. It was highly improbable that I should ever find out who he was, but I felt that if I did, and met him face to face, my dislike would be abundantly justified.

" As you know, for a year or two after the Armistice I was a pretty sick man. Most of us were. We hadn't the fillip of getting back to civilized comforts, like the men in the trenches. We had always been comfortable enough in body, but our

minds were fagged out, and there is no easy cure
for that. My digestion went nobly to pieces, and
I endured a miserable space of lying in bed and
living on milk and olive-oil. After that I went
back to work, but the darned thing always returned,
and every leech had a different régime to advise. I
tried them all—dry meals, a snack every two hours,
lemon juice, sour milk, starvation, knocking off
tobacco—but nothing got me more than half-way
out of the trough. I was a burden to myself and
a nuisance to others, dragging my wing through life,
with a constant pain in my tummy.

"More than one doctor advised an operation,
but I was chary about that, for I had seen several
of my friends operated on for the same mischief
and left as sick as before. Then a man told me
about a German fellow called Christoph, who was
said to be very good at handling my trouble. The
best hand at diagnosis in the world, my informant
said—no fads—treated every case on its merits—
a really original mind. Dr. Christoph had a modest
kurhaus at a place called Rosensee in the Sächischen
Sweitz. By this time I was getting pretty desperate, so I packed a bag and set off for Rosensee.

"It was a quiet little town at the mouth of a
narrow valley, tucked in under wooded hills, a clean
fresh place with open channels of running water in
the streets. There was a big church with an onion
spire, a Catholic seminary, and a small tanning
industry. The kurhaus was half-way up a hill, and
I felt better as soon as I saw my bedroom, with its
bare scrubbed floors and its wide veranda looking

into a forest glade. I felt still better when I saw
Dr. Christoph. He was a small man with a grizzled
beard, a high forehead, and a limp, rather like what
I imagine the Apostle Paul must have been. He
looked wise, as wise as an old owl. His English
was atrocious, but even when he found that I
talked German fairly well he didn't expand in
speech. He would deliver no opinion of any kind
until he had had me at least a week under observation ; but somehow I felt comforted, for I concluded
that a first-class mind had got to work on me.

"The other patients were mostly Germans, with
a sprinkling of Spaniards, but to my delight I
found Channell. He also had been having a thin
time since we parted. Nerves were his trouble—
general nervous debility and perpetual insomnia,
and his college had given him six months' leave of
absence to try to get well. The poor chap was as
lean as a sparrow, and he had the large dull eyes
and the dry lips of the sleepless. He had arrived
a week before me, and like me was under observation. But his vetting was different from mine, for
he was a mental case, and Dr. Christoph used to
devote hours to trying to unriddle his nervous
tangles. 'He is a good man for a German,' said
Channell, 'but he is on the wrong tack. There's
nothing wrong with my mind. I wish he'd stick
to violet rays and massage, instead of asking me
silly questions about my great-grandmother.'

"Channell and I used to go for invalidish walks
in the woods, and we naturally talked about the
years we had worked together. He was living

mainly in the past, for the War had been the great
thing in his life, and his professorial duties seemed
trivial by comparison.   As we tramped among the
withered bracken and heather, his mind was always
harking back to the dingy little room where he had
smoked cheap cigarettes and worked fourteen hours
out of the twenty-four.   In particular, he was as
eagerly curious about our old antagonist, Reinmar,
as he had been in 1918.   He was more positive than
ever that she was a woman, and I believe that one
of the reasons that had induced him to try a cure
in Germany was a vague hope that he might get
on her track.   I had almost forgotten about the
thing, and I was amused by Channell in the part of
the untiring sleuth-hound.

"'You won't find her in the kurhaus,' I said.
'Perhaps she is in some old schloss in the neigh-
bourhood, waiting for you like the Sleeping
Beauty.'

"'I'm serious,' he said plaintively.   'It is purely
a matter of intellectual curiosity, but I confess I
would give a great deal to see her face to face.
After I leave here, I thought of going to Berlin to
make some inquiries.   But I'm handicapped, for
I know nobody and I have no credentials.   Why
don't you, who have a large acquaintance and far
more authority, take the thing up?'

"I told him that my interest in the matter had
flagged and that I wasn't keen on digging into the
past, but I promised to give him a line to our
Military Attaché if he thought of going to Berlin.
I rather discouraged him from letting his mind

dwell too much on events in the War. I said that he ought to try to bolt the door on all that had contributed to his present breakdown.

" ' That is not Dr. Christoph's opinion,' he said emphatically. ' He encourages me to talk about it. You see, with me it is a purely intellectual interest. I have no emotion in the matter. I feel quite friendly towards Reinmar, whoever she may be. It is, if you like, a piece of romance. I haven't had so many romantic events in my life that I want to forget this.'

" ' Have you told Dr. Christoph about Reinmar ? ' I asked.

" ' Yes,' he said, ' and he was mildly interested. You know the way he looks at you with his solemn grey eyes. I doubt if he quite understood what I meant; for a little provincial doctor, even though he is a genius in his own line, is not likely to know much about the ways of the Great General Staff. . . . I had to tell him, for I have to tell him all my dreams, and lately I have taken to dreaming about Reinmar.'

" ' What's she like ? ' I asked.

" ' Oh, a most remarkable figure. Very beautiful, but uncanny. She has long fair hair down to her knees.'

" Of course I laughed. ' You're mixing her up with the Valkyries,' I said. ' Lord, it would be an awkward business if you met that she-dragon in the flesh.'

" But he was quite solemn about it, and declared that his waking picture of her was not in the least

like his dreams. He rather agreed with my nonsense about the old schloss. He thought that she
was probably some penniless grandee, living solitary
in a moated grange, with nothing now to exercise
her marvellous brain on, and eating her heart out
with regret and shame. He drew so attractive a
character of her that I began to think that Channell
was in love with a being of his own creation, till
he ended with, ' But all the same she's utterly
damnable. She must be, you know.'

"After a fortnight I began to feel a different
man. Dr. Christoph thought that he had got on the
track of the mischief, and certainly, with his deep
massage and a few simple drugs, I had more internal
comfort than I had known for three years. He
was so pleased with my progress that he refused to
treat me as an invalid. He encouraged me to take
long walks into the hills, and presently he arranged
for me to go out roebuck-shooting with some of the
local junkers.

"I used to start before daybreak on the chilly
November mornings and drive to the top of one
of the ridges, where I would meet a collection of
sportsmen and beaters, shepherded by a fellow in
a green uniform. We lined out along the ridge, and
the beaters, assisted by a marvellous collection of
dogs, including the sporting dachshund, drove the
roe towards us. It wasn't very cleverly managed,
for the deer generally broke back, and it was chilly
waiting in the first hours with a powdering of snow
on the ground and the fir boughs heavy with frost
crystals. But later, when the sun grew stronger,

it was a very pleasant mode of spending a day.
There was not much of a bag, but whenever a roe
or a capercailzie fell, all the guns would assemble
and drink little glasses of *kirschwasser*. I had been
lent a rifle, one of those appalling contraptions
which are double-barrelled shot-guns and rifles in
one, and to transpose from one form to the other
requires a mathematical calculation. The rifle had
a hair-trigger too, and when I first used it I was
nearly the death of a respectable Saxon peasant.

" We all ate our midday meal together, and in
the evening, before going home, we had coffee and
cakes in one or other of the farms. The party
was an odd mixture, big farmers and small squires,
an hotel-keeper or two, a local doctor, and a couple
of lawyers from the town. At first they were a
little shy of me, but presently they thawed, and
after the first day we were good friends. They
spoke quite frankly about the War, in which every
one of them had had a share, and with a great deal
of dignity and good sense.

" I learned to walk in Sikkim, and the little
Saxon hills seemed to me inconsiderable. But they
were too much for most of the guns, and instead
of going straight up or down a slope they always
chose a circuit, which gave them an easy gradient.
One evening, when we were separating as usual,
the beaters taking a short cut and the guns a circuit,
I felt that I wanted exercise, so I raced the beaters
downhill, beat them soundly, and had the better
part of an hour to wait for my companions, before
we adjourned to the farm for refreshment. The

beaters must have talked about my pace, for as we walked away one of the guns, a lawyer called Meissen, asked me why I was visiting Rosensee at a time of year when few foreigners came. I said I was staying with Dr. Christoph.

" ' Is he then a private friend of yours ? ' he asked.

" I told him No, that I had come to his kurhaus for treatment, being sick. His eyes expressed polite scepticism. He was not prepared to regard as an invalid a man who went down a hill like an avalanche.

" But, as we walked in the frosty dusk, he was led to speak of Dr. Christoph, of whom he had no personal knowledge, and I learned how little honour a prophet may have in his own country. Rosensee scarcely knew him, except as a doctor who had an inexplicable attraction for foreign patients. Meissen was curious about his methods and the exact diseases in which he specialized. ' Perhaps he may yet save me a journey to Homburg ! ' he laughed. ' It is well to have a skilled physician at one's doorstep. The doctor is something of a hermit, and, except for his patients, does not appear to welcome his kind. Yet he is a good man, beyond doubt, and there are those who say that in the War he was a hero.'

" This surprised me, for I could not imagine Dr. Christoph in any fighting capacity, apart from the fact that he must have been too old. I thought that Meissen might refer to work in the base hospitals. But he was positive ; Dr. Christoph had been in the trenches ; the limping leg was a war wound.

" I had had very little talk with the doctor, owing to my case being free from nervous complications. He would say a word to me morning and evening about my diet, and pass the time of day when we met, but it was not till the very eve of my departure that we had anything like a real conversation. He sent a message that he wanted to see me for not less than one hour, and he arrived with a batch of notes from which he delivered a kind of lecture on my case. Then I realized what an immense amount of care and solid thought he had expended on me. He had decided that his diagnosis was right—my rapid improvement suggested that—but it was necessary for some time to observe a simple régime, and to keep an eye on certain symptoms. So he took a sheet of note-paper from the table, and in his small precise hand wrote down for me a few plain commandments.

" There was something about him, the honest eyes, the mouth which looked as if it had been often compressed in suffering, the air of grave goodwill, which I found curiously attractive. I wished that I had been a mental case like Channell, and had had more of his society. I detained him in talk, and he seemed not unwilling. By-and-by we drifted to the War, and it turned out that Meissen was right.

" Dr. Christoph had gone as medical officer in November '14 to the Ypres Salient with a Saxon regiment, and had spent the winter there. In '15 he had been in Champagne, and in the early months of '16 at Verdun, till he was invalided with rheumatic fever. That is to say, he had had about seventeen months of consecutive fighting in the worst areas with scarcely a holiday. A pretty good record for a frail little middle-aged man !

" His family was then at Stuttgart, his wife and one little boy. He took a long time to recover from the fever, and after that was put on home duty. ' Till the War was almost over,' he said, ' almost over, but not quite. There was just time for me to go back to the front and get my foolish leg hurt.' I must tell you that whenever he mentioned his war experience it was with a comical deprecating smile, as if he agreed with any one who might think that gravity like his should have remained in bed.

" I assumed that this home duty was medical, until he said something about getting rusty in his professional work. Then it appeared that it had been some job connected with Intelligence. ' I am reputed to have a little talent for mathematics,' he said. ' No. I am no mathematical scholar, but, if you understand me, I have a certain mathematical aptitude. My mind has always moved happily among numbers. Therefore I was set to construct and to interpret ciphers, a strange interlude in the noise of war. I sat in a little room and excluded the world, and for a little I was happy."

" He went on to speak of the *enclave* of peace in which he had found himself, and as I listened to his gentle monotonous voice, I had a sudden inspiration.

" I took a sheet of note-paper from the stand, scribbled the word *Reinmar* on it, and shoved it towards him. I had a notion, you see, that I might surprise him into helping Channell's researches.

"But it was I who got the big surprise. He stopped thunderstruck as soon as his eye caught the word, blushed scarlet over every inch of face and bald forehead, seemed to have difficulty in swallowing, and then gasped, 'How did you know?'

"I hadn't known, and now that I did, the knowledge left me speechless. This was the loathly opposite for which Channell and I had nursed our hatred. When I came out of my stupefaction I found that he had recovered his balance and was speaking slowly and distinctly, as if he were making a formal confession.

"'You were among my opponents . . . that interests me deeply. . . . I often wondered. . . . You beat me in the end. You are aware of that?'

"I nodded. 'Only because you made a slip,' I said.

"'Yes, I made a slip. I was to blame—very gravely to blame, for I let my private grief cloud my mind.'

"He seemed to hesitate, as if he were loath to stir something very tragic in his memory.

"'I think I will tell you,' he said at last. 'I have often wished—it is a childish wish—to justify my failure to those who profited by it. My chiefs understood, of course, but my opponents could not. In that month when I failed I was in deep sorrow. I had a little son—his name was Reinmar—you remember that I took that name for my code signature?'

" His eyes were looking beyond me into some vision of the past.

" ' He was, as you say, my mascot. He was all my family, and I adored him. But in those days food was not plentiful. We were no worse off than many million Germans, but the child was frail. In the last summer of the War he developed phthisis due to malnutrition, and in September he died. Then I failed my country, for with him some virtue seemed to depart from my mind. You see, my work was, so to speak, his also, as my name was his, and when he left me he took my power with him. . . . So I stumbled. The rest is known to you.'

" He sat staring beyond me, so small and lonely, that I could have howled. I put my hand on his shoulder and stammered some platitude about being sorry. We sat quite still for a minute or two, and then I remembered Channell. Channell must have poured his views of Reinmar into Dr. Christoph's ear. I asked him if Channell knew.

" A flicker of a smile crossed his face.

" ' Indeed no. And I will exact from you a promise never to breathe to him what I have told you. He is my patient, and I must first consider his case. At present he thinks that Reinmar is a wicked and beautiful lady whom he may some day meet. That is romance, and it is good for him to think so. . . . If he were told the truth, he would be pitiful, and in Herr Channell's condition it is important that he should not be vexed with such emotions as pity.' "

VII. SING A SONG OF SIXPENCE

SIR EDWARD LEITHEN'S STORY

The effect of night, of any flowing water, of lighted cities, of the peep of day, of ships, of the open ocean, calls up in the mind an army of anonymous desires and pleasures. Something, we feel, should happen; we know not what, yet we proceed in quest of it.

R. L. STEVENSON.

VII. SING A SONG OF SIXPENCE

LEITHEN'S face had that sharp chiselling of the jaw and that compression of the lips which seem to follow upon high legal success. Also an overdose of German gas in 1918 had given his skin a habitual pallor, so that he looked not unhealthy, but notably urban. As a matter of fact he was one of the hardest men I have ever known, but a chance observer might have guessed from his complexion that he rarely left the pavements.

Burminster, who had come back from a month in the grass countries with a face like a deep-sea mariner's, commented on this one evening.

"How do you manage always to look the complete Cit, Ned?" he asked. "You're as much a Londoner as a Parisian is a Parisian, if you know what I mean."

Leithen said that he was not ashamed of it, and he embarked on a eulogy of the metropolis. In London you met sooner or later everybody you had ever known; you could lay your hand on any knowledge you wanted; you could pull strings that controlled the innermost Sahara and the topmost Pamirs. Romance lay in wait for you at every street corner. It was the true City of the Caliphs.

"That is what they say," said Sandy Arbuthnot sadly, "but I never found it so. I yawn my head off in London. Nothing amusing ever finds me out—I have to go and search for it, and it usually costs the deuce of a lot."

"I once stumbled upon a pretty generous allowance of romance," said Leithen, "and it cost me precisely sixpence."

Then he told us this story.

It happened a good many years ago, just when I was beginning to get on at the Bar. I spent busy days in court and chambers, but I was young and had a young man's appetite for society, so I used to dine out most nights and go to more balls than were good for me. It was pleasant after a heavy day to dive into a different kind of life. My rooms at the time were in Down Street, the same house as my present one, only two floors higher up.

On a certain night in February I was dining in Bryanston Square with the Nantleys. Mollie Nantley was an old friend, and used to fit me as an unattached bachelor into her big dinners. She was a young hostess and full of ambition, and one met an odd assortment of people at her house. Mostly political, of course, but a sprinkling of art and letters, and any visiting lion that happened to be passing through. Mollie was a very innocent lion-hunter, but she had a partiality for the breed.

I don't remember much about the dinner, except that the principal guest had failed her. Mollie was loud in her lamentations. He was a South Ameri-

can President who had engineered a very pretty
coup d'état the year before, and was now in England
on some business concerning the finances of his
State. You may remember his name—Ramon
Pelem—he made rather a stir in the world for a
year or two. I had read about him in the papers,
and had looked forward to meeting him, for he had
won his way to power by extraordinary boldness
and courage, and he was quite young. There was
a story that he was partly English, and that his
grandfather's name had been Pelham. I don't
know what truth there was in that, but he knew
England well and Englishmen liked him.

Well, he had cried off on the telephone an hour
before, and Mollie was grievously disappointed.
Her other guests bore the loss with more fortitude,
for I expect they thought he was a brand of cigar.

In those days dinners began earlier and dances
later than they do to-day. I meant to leave soon,
go back to my rooms and read briefs, and then look
in at Lady Samplar's dance between eleven and
twelve. So at nine-thirty I took my leave.

Jervis, the old butler, who had been my ally from
boyhood, was standing on the threshold, and in the
square there was a considerable crowd now thinning
away. I asked what the trouble was.

"There's been an arrest, Mr. Edward," he said
in an awestruck voice. "It 'appened when I was
serving coffee in the dining-room, but our Albert
saw it all. Two foreigners, he said—proper rascals
by their look—were took away by the police just
outside this very door. The constables was very

nippy and collared them before they could use their pistols—but they 'ad pistols on them and no mistake. Albert says he saw the weapons."

" Did they propose to burgle you ? " I asked.

" I cannot say, Mr. Edward. But I shall give instructions for a very careful lock-up to-night."

There were no cabs about, so I decided to walk on and pick one up. When I got into Great Cumberland Place it began to rain sharply, and I was just about to call a prowling hansom, when I put my hand into my pocket. I found that I had no more than one solitary sixpence.

I could of course have paid when I got to my flat. But as the rain seemed to be slacking off, I preferred to walk. Mollie's dining-room had been stuffy, I had been in court all day, and I wanted some fresh air.

You know how in little things, when you have decided on a course, you are curiously reluctant to change it. Before I got to the Marble Arch it had begun to pour in downright earnest. But I still stumped on. Only I entered the Park, for even in February there is a certain amount of cover from the trees.

I passed one or two hurried pedestrians, but the place was almost empty. The occasional lamps made only spots of light in a dripping darkness, and it struck me that this was a curious patch of gloom and loneliness to be so near to crowded streets, for with the rain had come a fine mist. I pitied the poor devils to whom it was the only home. There was one of them on a seat which I passed. The collar of his thin shabby overcoat was turned up, and his shameful old felt hat was turned down, so that only a few square inches of pale face were visible. His toes stuck out of his boots, and he seemed sunk in a sodden misery.

I passed him and then turned back. Casual charity is an easy dope for the conscience, and I indulge in it too often. When I approached him he seemed to stiffen, and his hands moved in his pockets.

" A rotten night," I said. " Is sixpence any good to you ? " And I held out my solitary coin.

He lifted his face, and I started. For the eyes that looked at me were not those of a waster. They were bright, penetrating, authoritative—and they were young. I was conscious that they took in more of me than mine did of him.

" Thank you very much," he said, as he took the coin, and the voice was that of a cultivated man. " But I'm afraid I need rather more than sixpence."

" How much ? " I asked. This was clearly an original.

" To be accurate, five million pounds."

He was certainly mad, but I was fascinated by this wisp of humanity. I wished that he would show more of his face.

" Till your ship comes home," I said, " you want a bed, and you'd be the better of a change. Sixpence is all I have on me. But if you come to my rooms I'll give you the price of a night's lodging, and I think I might find you some old clothes."

" Where do you live ? " he asked.

" Close by—in Down Street." I gave the number.

He seemed to reflect, and then he shot a glance on either side into the gloom behind the road. It may have been fancy, but I thought that I saw something stir in the darkness.

" What are you ? " he asked.

I was getting abominably wet, and yet I submitted to be cross-examined by this waif.

" I am a lawyer," I said.

He looked at me again, very intently.

" Have you a telephone ? " he asked.

I nodded.

" Right," he said. " You seem a good fellow, and I'll take you at your word. I'll follow you. . . . Don't look back, please. It's important. . . . I'll be in Down Street as soon as you. . . . *Marchons*."

It sounds preposterous, but I did exactly as I was bid. I never looked back, but I kept my ears open for the sound of following footsteps. I thought I heard them, and then they seemed to die away. I turned out of the Park at Grosvenor Gate and went down Park Lane. When I reached the house which contained my flat, I looked up and down the street, but it was empty except for a waiting four-wheeler. But just as I turned in I caught a glimpse of some one running at the Hertford Street end. The runner came to a sudden halt and I saw that it was not the man I had left.

To my surprise I found the waif on the landing

outside my flat. I was about to tell him to stop outside, but as soon as I unlocked the door he rushed past me and entered. My man, who did not sleep on the premises, had left the light burning in the little hall.

"Lock the door," he said in a tone of authority. "Forgive me taking charge, but I assure you it is important."

Then to my amazement he peeled off the sopping overcoat, and kicked off his disreputable shoes. They were odd shoes, for what looked like his toes sticking out was really part of the make-up. He stood up before me in underclothes and socks, and I noticed that his underclothing seemed to be of the finest material.

"Now for your telephone," he said.

I was getting angry at these liberties.

"Who the devil are you?" I demanded.

"I am President Pelem," he said, with all the dignity in the world. "And you?"

"I?—oh, I am the German Emperor."

He laughed. "You know you invited me here," he said. "You've brought this on yourself." Then he stared at me. "Hullo, I've seen you before. You're Leithen. I saw you play at Lord's. I was twelfth man for Harrow that year. . . . Now for the telephone."

There was something about the fellow, something defiant and debonair and young, that stopped all further protest on my part. He might or might not be President Pelem, but he was certainly not a wastrel. Besides, he seemed curiously keyed up, as if the occasion were desperately important, and he infected me with the same feeling. I said no more, but led the way into my sitting-room. He flung himself on the telephone, gave a number, was instantly connected, and began a conversation in monosyllables.

It was a queer jumble that I overheard. Bryanston Square was mentioned, and the Park, and the number of my house was given—to somebody. There was a string of foreign names—Pedro and Alejandro and Manuel and Alcaza—and short breathless inquiries. Then I heard—" a good fellow—looks as if he might be useful in a row," and I wondered if he was referring to me. Some rapid Spanish followed, and then, " Come round at once—they will be here before you. Have policemen below, but don't let them come up. We should be able to manage alone. Oh, and tell Burton to ring up here as soon as he has news." And he gave my telephone number.

I put some coals on the fire, changed into a tweed jacket, and lit a pipe. I fetched a dressing-gown from my bedroom and flung it on the sofa. " You'd better put that on," I said when he had finished.

He shook his head.

" I would rather be unencumbered," he said. " But I should dearly love a cigarette . . . and a liqueur brandy, if you have such a thing. That Park of yours is infernally chilly."

I supplied his needs, and he stretched himself in an armchair, with his stockinged feet to the fire.

" You have been very good-humoured, Leithen,'

he said. " Valdez—that's my aide-de-camp—will
be here presently, and he will probably be preceded
by other guests. But I think I have time for the
short explanation which is your due. You believe
what I told you ? "

I nodded.

" Good. Well, I came to London three weeks
ago to raise a loan. That was a matter of life or
death for my big stupid country. I have succeeded.
This afternoon the agreement was signed. I think
I mentioned the amount to you—five million
sterling."

He smiled happily, and blew a smoke-ring into
the air.

" I must tell you that I have enemies. Among
my happy people there are many rascals, and I had
to deal harshly with them. ' So foul a sky clears
not without a storm '—that's Shakespeare, isn't it ?
I learned it at school. You see, I had Holy Church
behind me, and therefore I had against me all the
gentry who call themselves liberators. Red Masons,
anarchists, communists, that sort of crew. A good
many are now reposing beneath the sod, but some
of the worst remain. In particular, six followed me
to England with instructions that I must not return.

" I don't mind telling you, Leithen, that I have
had a peculiarly rotten time the last three weeks.
It was most important that nothing should happen
to me till the loan was settled, so I had to lead the
sheltered life. It went against the grain, I assure
you, for I prefer the offensive to the defensive.
The English police were very amiable, and I never

stirred without a cordon, your people and my own. The Six wanted to kill me, and as it is pretty easy to kill anybody if you don't mind being killed your-self, we had to take rather elaborate precautions. As it was, I was twice nearly done in. Once my carriage broke down mysteriously, and a crowd collected, and if I hadn't had the luck to board a passing cab, I should have had a knife in my ribs. The second was at a public dinner—something not quite right about the cayenne pepper served with the oysters. One of my staff is still seriously ill."

He stretched his arms.

" Well, that first stage is over. They can't wreck the loan, whatever happens to me. Now I am free to adopt different tactics, and take the offensive. I have no fear of the Six in my own country. There I can take precautions, and they will find it difficult to cross the frontier or to live for six hours thereafter if they succeed. But here you are a free people, and protection is not so easy. I do not wish to leave England just yet—I have done my work and have earned a little play. I know your land and love it, and I look forward to seeing something of my friends. Also I want to attend the Grand National. Therefore, it is necessary that my enemies should be confined for a little, while I take my holiday. So for this evening I made a plan. I took the offensive. I deliberately put myself in their danger."

He turned his dancing eyes towards me, and I have rarely had such an impression of wild and mirthful audacity.

" We have an excellent intelligence system," he went on, " and the Six have been assiduously shadowed. But as I have told you, no precautions avail against the fanatic, and I do not wish to be killed on my little holiday. So I resolved to draw their fire—to expose myself as ground bait, so to speak, that I might have the chance of netting them. The Six usually hunt in couples, so it was necessary to have three separate acts in the play, if all were to be gathered in. The first——"

" Was in Bryanston Square," I put in, " outside Lady Nantley's house ? "

" True. How did you know ? "

" I have just been dining there, and heard that you were expected. I saw the crowd in the square as I came away."

" It seems to have gone off quite nicely. We took pains to let it be known where I was dining. The Six, who mistrust me, delegated only two of their number for the job. They never put all their eggs in one basket. The two gentlemen were induced to make a scene, and, since they proved to be heavily armed, were taken into custody and may get a six months' sentence. Very prettily managed, but unfortunately it was the two that matter least—the ones we call Little Pedro and Alejandro the Scholar. Impatient, blundering children, both of them. That leaves four."

The telephone bell rang, and he made a long arm for the receiver. The news he got seemed to be good, for he turned a smiling face to me.

" I should have said two. My little enterprise

in the Park has proved a brilliant success. . . . But I must explain. I was to be the bait for my enemies, so I showed myself to the remaining four. That was really rather a clever piece of business. They lost me at the Marble Arch, and they did not recognize me as the scarecrow sitting on the seat in the rain. But they knew I had gone to earth there, and they stuck to the scent like terriers. Presently they would have found me, and there would have been shooting. Some of my own people were in the shadow between the road and the railings."

" When I saw you, were your enemies near ? " I asked.

" Two were on the opposite side of the road. One was standing under the lamp-post at the gate. I don't know where the fourth was at that moment. But all had passed me more than once. . . . By the way, you very nearly got yourself shot, you know. When you asked me if sixpence was any good to me. . . . That happens to be their pass-word. I take great credit to myself for seeing instantly that you were harmless."

" Why did you leave the Park if you had your trap so well laid ? " I asked.

" Because it meant dealing with all four together at once, and I do them the honour of being rather nervous about them. They are very quick with their guns. I wanted a chance to break up the covey, and your arrival gave it me. When I went off two followed, as I thought they would. My car was in Park Lane, and gave me a lift ; and one of them saw me in it. I puzzled them a little, but by now they must be certain. You see, my car has been waiting for some minutes outside this house."

" What about the other two ? " I asked.

" Burton has just telephoned that they have been gathered in. Quite an exciting little scrap. To your police it must have seemed a bad case of high-way robbery—two ruffianly looking fellows hold up a peaceful elderly gentleman returning from dinner. The odds were not quite like that, but the men I had on the job are old soldiers of the Indian wars and can move softly. . . . I only wish I knew which two they have got. Burton was not sure. Alcaza is one, but I can't be certain about the other. I hope it is not the Irishman."

My bell rang very loud and steadily.

" In a few seconds I shall have solved that problem," he said gaily. " I am afraid I must trouble you to open the door, Leithen."

" Is it your aide-de-camp ? "

" No. I instructed Valdez to knock. It is the residuum of the Six. Now listen to me, my friend. These two, whoever they are, have come here to kill me, and I don't mean to be killed. . . . My first plan was to have Valdez here—and others—so that my two enemies should walk into a trap. But I changed my mind before I telephoned. They are very clever men, and by this time they will be very wary. So I have thought of something else."

The bell rang again, and a third time insistently.

" Take these," and he held out a pair of cruel little bluish revolvers. " When you open the door, you will say that the President is at home and, in token of his confidence, offers them these. ' *Une espèce d'Irlandais, Messieurs. Vous commencez trop tard, et vous finissez trop tôt.*' Then bring them here. Quick now. I hope Corbally is one of them."

I did exactly as I was told. I cannot say that I had any liking for the task, but I was a good deal under the spell of that calm young man, and I was resigned to my flat being made a rendezvous for desperadoes. I had locked and chained and bolted the door, so it took me a few moments to open it.

I found myself looking at emptiness.

" Who is it ? " I called. " Who rang ? "

I was answered from behind me. It was the quickest thing I have ever seen, for they must have slipped through in the moment when my eyes were dazzled by the change from the dim light of the hall to the glare of the landing. That gave me some notion of the men we had to deal with.

" Here," said the voice. I turned and saw two men in waterproofs and felt hats, who kept their hands in their pockets and had a fraction of an eye on the two pistols I swung by the muzzles.

" M. le Président will be glad to see you, gentlemen," I said. I held out the revolvers, which they seemed to grasp and flick into their pockets with a single movement. Then I repeated slowly the piece of rudeness in French.

One of the men laughed. " Ramon does not forget," he said. He was a young man with sandy hair and hot blue eyes and an odd break in his long drooping nose. The other was a wiry little

fellow, with a grizzled beard and what looked like
a stiff leg.

I had no guess at my friend's plan, and was concerned to do precisely as I was told. I opened the
door of my sitting-room, and noticed that the
President was stretched on my sofa facing the door.
He was smoking and was still in his underclothes.
When the two men behind me saw that he was
patently unarmed they slipped into the room with
a quick cat-like movement, and took their stand
with their backs against the door.

" Hullo, Corbally," said the President pleasantly.
" And you, Manuel. You're looking younger than
when I saw you last. Have a cigarette ? " and he
nodded towards my box on the table behind him.
Both shook their heads.

" I'm glad you have come. You have probably
seen the news of the loan in the evening papers.
That should give you a holiday, as it gives me one.
No further need for the hectic oversight of each
other, which is so wearing and takes up so much
time."

" No," said the man called Manuel, and there
was something very grim about his quiet tones.
" We shall take steps to prevent any need for that
in the future."

" Tut, tut—that is your old self, Manuel. You
are too fond of melodrama to be an artist. You
are a priest at heart."

The man snarled. " There will be no priest at
your deathbed." Then to his companion. " Let
us get this farce over."

The President paid not the slightest attention, but looked steadily at the Irishman. " You used to be a sportsman, Mike. Have you come to share Manuel's taste for potting the sitting rabbit ? "

" We are not sportsmen, we are executioners of justice," said Manuel.

The President laughed merrily. " Superb ! The best Roman manner." He still kept his eyes on Corbally.

" Damn you, what's your game, Ramon ? " the Irishman asked. His freckled face had become very red.

" Simply to propose a short armistice. I want a holiday. If you must know, I want to go to the National."

" So do I."

" Well, let's call a truce. Say for two months or till I leave England—whichever period shall be the shorter. After that you can get busy again."

The one he had named Manuel broke into a spluttering torrent of Spanish, and for a little they all talked that language. It sounded like a commination service on the President, to which he good-humouredly replied. I had never seen this class of ruffian before, to whom murder was as simple as shooting a partridge, and I noted curiously the lean hands, the restless wary eyes, and the ugly lips of the type. So far as I could make out, the President seemed to be getting on well with the Irishman but to be having trouble with Manuel.

" Have ye really and truly nothing on ye ? " Corbally asked.

The President stretched his arms and revealed his slim figure in its close-fitting pants and vest.

"Nor him there?" and he nodded towards me.

"He is a lawyer; he doesn't use guns."

"Then I'm damned if I touch ye. Two months it is. What's your fancy for Liverpool?"

This was too much for Manuel. I saw in what seemed to be one movement his hand slip from his pocket, Corbally's arm swing in a circle, and a plaster bust of Julius Cæsar tumble off the top of my bookcase. Then I heard the report.

"Ye nasty little man," said Corbally, as he pressed him to his bosom in a bear's hug.

"You are a traitor," Manuel shouted. "How will we face the others? What will Alejandro say and Alcaza——"

"I think I can explain," said the President pleasantly. "They won't know for quite a time, and then only if you tell them. You two gentlemen are all that remain for the moment of your patriotic company. The other four have been the victims of the English police—two in Bryanston Square, and two in the Park close to the Marble Arch."

"Ye don't say!" said Corbally with admiration in his voice. "Faith, that's smart work!"

"They too will have a little holiday. A few months to meditate on politics, while you and I go to the Grand National."

Suddenly there was a sharp rat-tat at my door. It was like the knocking in *Macbeth* for dramatic effect. Corbally had one pistol at my ear in an instant, while a second covered the President.

"It's all right," said the latter, never moving a muscle. "It's General Valdez, whom I think you know. That was another argument which I was coming to if I hadn't had the good fortune to appeal to Mr. Corbally's higher nature. I know you have sworn to kill me, but I take it that the killer wants to have a sporting chance of escape. Well, there wouldn't have been the faintest shadow of a chance here. Valdez is at the door, and the English police are below. You are brave men, I know, but even brave men dislike the cold gallows."

The knocker fell again. "Let him in, Leithen," I was told, "or he will be damaging your valuable door. He has not the northern phlegm of you and me and Mr. Corbally."

A tall man in an ulster, which looked as if it covered a uniform, stood on the threshold. Some one had obscured the lights on the landing so that the staircase was dark, but I could see in the gloom other figures. "President Pelem . . ." he began.

"The President is here," I said. "Quite well and in great form. He is entertaining two other guests."

The General marched to my sitting-room. I was behind him and did not see his face, but I can believe that it showed surprise when he recognized the guests. Manuel stood sulkily defiant, his hands in his waterproof pockets, but Corbally's light eyes were laughing.

"I think you know each other," said the President graciously.

"My God!" Valdez seemed to choke at the sight. "These swine! Excellency, I have . . ."

"You have nothing of the kind. These are friends of mine for the next two months, and Mr. Corbally and I are going to the Grand National together. Will you have the goodness to conduct them downstairs and explain to the inspector of police below that all has gone well and that I am perfectly satisfied, and that he will hear from me in the morning? . . . One moment. What about a stirrup-cup? Leithen, does your establishment run to a whisky and soda all round?"

It did. We all had a drink, and I believe I clinked glasses with Manuel.

.   .   .   .   .   .

I looked in at Lady Samplar's dance as I had meant to. Presently I saw a resplendent figure arrive—the President, with the ribbon of the Gold Star of Bolivar across his chest. He was no more the larky undergraduate, but the responsible statesman, the father of his country. There was a considerable crowd in his vicinity when I got near him, and he was making his apologies to Mollie Nantley. She saw me and insisted on introducing me. "I so much wanted you two to meet. I had hoped it would be at my dinner—but anyhow I have managed it." I think she was a little surprised when the President took my hand in both of his. "I saw Mr. Leithen play at Lord's in '97," he said. "I was twelfth man for Harrow that year. It is delightful to make his acquaintance; I shall never forget this meeting."

" How English he is ! " Mollie whispered to me as we made our way out of the crowd.

They got him next year. They were bound to, for in that kind of business you can have no real protection. But he managed to set his country on its feet before he went down. . . . No, it was neither Manuel nor Corbally. I think it was Alejandro the Scholar.

VIII. SHIP TO TARSHISH

RALPH COLLATT'S STORY

Now the word of the Lord came unto Jonah the son of Amittai, saying, Arise, go to Nineveh. . . . But Jonah . . . found a ship going to Tarshish : so he paid the fare thereof, and went down into it, to go with them unto Tarshish from the presence of the Lord.

Jonah i. 1–3.

VIII. SHIP TO TARSHISH

THE talk one evening turned on the meta-physics of courage. It is a subject which most men are a little shy of discussing. They will heartily applaud a friend's pluck, but it is curious how rarely they will label a man a coward. Perhaps the reason is that we are all odd mixtures of strength and weakness, brave in certain things, timid in others ; and since each is apt to remember his private funks more vividly than the things about which he is bold, we are chary about dogmatizing.

Lamancha propounded the thesis that every-body had a yellow streak in them. We all, he said, at times shirk unpleasant duties, and invent an honourable explanation, which we know to be a lie.

Sandy Arbuthnot observed that the most temer-arious deeds were often done by people who had begun by funking, and then, in the shame of the rebound, did a good deal more than those who had no qualms. " The man who says I go not, and afterwards repents and goes, generally travels the devil of a long way."

" Like Jonah," said Lamancha, " who didn't like the job allotted him, and took ship to Tarshish to get away from it, and then repented and went like a raging lion to Nineveh."

Collatt, who had been a sailor and one of the Q-boat heroes in the War, demurred. "I wonder if Nineveh was as unpleasant as the whale's belly," he said. Then he told us a story in illustration, not, as one would have expected, out of his wild sea memories, but from his experience in the City, where he was now a bill-broker.

I got to know Jim Hallward first when he had just come down from the University. He was a tall, slim, fair-haired lad, with a soft voice and the kind of manners which make the ordinary man feel a lout. Eton and Christ Church had polished him till he fairly glistened. His clothes were sober works of art, and he was the cleanest thing you ever saw—always seemed to have just shaved and bathed after a couple of hours' hard exercise. We all liked him, for he was a companionable soul and had no frills, but in the City he was about as useless as a lily in a quickset hedge. Somebody called him an "apolaustic epicene," which sounded accurate, though I don't know what the words mean. He used to come down to business about eleven o'clock and leave at four—earlier in summer, when he played polo at Hurlingham.

This lotus-eating existence lasted for two years. His father was the head of Hallwards, the merchant-bankers who had been in existence since before the Napoleonic wars. It was an old-fashioned private firm with a tremendous reputation, but for some years it had been dropping a little out of the front rank. It had very few of the big issues, and,

though reckoned as solid as the Bank of England,
it had hardly kept pace with new developments.
But just about the time Jim came down from
Oxford his father seemed to get a new lease of life.
Hallwards suddenly became ultra-progressive, took
in a new manager from one of the big joint-stock
banks, and launched out into business which before
it would not have touched with the end of a barge-
pole. I fancy the old man wanted to pull up the
firm before he died, so as to leave a good thing to
his only child.

In this new activity Jim can't have been of much
use. His other engagements did not leave him a
great deal of time to master the complicated affairs
of a house like Hallwards. He spoke of his City
connection with a certain distaste. The set he had
got into were mostly eldest sons with political
ambitions, and if Jim had any serious inclination
it was towards Parliament, which he proposed to
enter in a year or two. For the rest he played
polo, and hunted, and did a little steeple-chasing,
and danced assiduously. Dancing was about the
only thing he did really well, for he was only a
moderate horseman and his politics were not to be
taken seriously. So he was the complete *flâneur*,
agreeable, popular, beautifully mannered, highly
ornamental, and the most useless creature on earth.
You see, he had slacked at school, and had just
scraped through college, and had never done a real
piece of work in his life.

In the autumn of 192—, whispers began to circu-
late about Hallwards. It seemed that they were

doing a very risky class of business, and people shrugged their shoulders. But no one was prepared for the almighty crash which came at the beginning of the New Year. The firm had been trying to get control of a colonial railway, and for this purpose was quietly buying up the ordinary stock. But an American group, with unlimited capital, was out on the same tack, and the result was that the price was forced up, and Hallwards were foolish enough to go on buying. They borrowed up to the limit of their capacity, and called a halt too late. If the thing had been known in time the City might have made an effort to keep the famous old firm on its legs, but it all came like a thunderclap. Hallwards went down, the American group got their railway stock at a knock-out price, and old Mr. Hallward, who had been ailing for some months, had a stroke of paralysis and died.

I was desperately sorry for Jim. The foundations of his world were upset, and he hadn't a notion what to do about it. You see, he didn't know the rudiments of the business, and couldn't be made to understand it. He went about in a dream, with staring, unseeing eyes, like a puzzled child. At first he screwed himself up to a sort of effort. He had many friends who would help, he thought, and he made various suggestions, all of a bottomless futility. Very soon he found that his Mayfair popularity was no sort of asset to him. He must have realized that people were beginning to turn a colder eye on a pauper than on an eligible young man, and his overtures were probably met with curt refusals. Anyhow, in a week he had given up hope. He felt himself a criminal and behaved as such. He saw nobody but his solicitors, and when he met a friend in the street he turned and ran. A perfectly unreasonable sense of disgrace took possession of him, and there was a moment when I was afraid he might put an end to himself.

This went on for the better part of a month, while I and one or two others were trying to save something from the smash. We put up a fund and bought some of the wreckage, with the idea of getting together a little company to nurse it. It was important to do something, for though Jim was an only child and his mother was dead, there were various elderly female relatives who had their incomes from Hallwards. The firm had been much respected and old Hallward had been popular, and Jim had no enemies. There is a good deal of camaraderie in the City, and a lot of us were willing to combine and keep Jim going. We were all ready to help him, if he would only sit down and put his back into the job.

But that was just what Jim would not do. He had got a horror of the City, and felt a pariah whenever he met anybody who knew about the crash. He had eyes like a hunted hare's, and one couldn't get any sense out of him. I don't think he minded the change in his comforts—the end of polo and hunting and politics, and the prospect of cheap lodgings and long office hours. I believe he welcomed all that as a kind of atonement. It was the disgrace of the thing that came between him and his sleep. He knew only enough of the City to have picked up a wrong notion of its standards, and imagined that everybody was pointing a finger at him as a fool, and possibly a crook.

It was very little use reasoning with him. I pointed out that the right thing for him to do was to shoulder the burden and retrieve his father's credit. He laughed bitterly.

"Much good I'd be at that," he said. "You know I'm a baby in business, though you're too polite to tell me so."

"You can have a try," I said. "We'll all lend you a hand."

It was no use. References to his father and the firm's ancient prestige and his old great-aunts only made him shiver. You could see that his misery made him blind to argument. Then I began to lose my temper. I told him that it was his duty as a man to face the music. I asked him what else he proposed to do.

He said he meant to go to Canada and start life anew. He would probably change his name. I got out of patience with his silliness.

"You're offered a chance here to make good," I told him. "In Canada you'll have to find your chance, and how in God's name are you going to do it ? You haven't been bred the right way to succeed in the Dominions. You'll probably starve."

"Quite likely," was his dismal answer. "I'll make my book for that. I don't mind anything as long as I'm in a place where nobody knows me."

"Remember, you are running away," I said,

"running away from what I consider your plain duty. You can't expect to win out if you begin by funking."

"I know, I know," he wailed. "I am a coward."

I said no more, for when a man is willing to admit that he is a coward his nerves have got the better of his reason. Well, the upshot was that Jim sailed for Canada with a little short of two hundred pounds in his pocket—what was left of his last allowance. He could have had plenty of introductions, but he wouldn't take them. He seemed to be determined to bury himself, and I daresay, too, he got a morbid satisfaction out of his discomfort. He had still the absurd notion of disgrace, and felt that any handicap he laid on himself was a kind of atonement.

He reached Montreal in the filthy weeks when the spring thaw begins—the worst sample of weather to be found on the globe. Jim had not procured any special outfit, and he landed with a kit consisting of two smart tweed suits, a suit of flannels, riding breeches, and knickerbockers—the remnants of his London wardrobe. It wasn't quite the rig for a poor man to go looking for a job in. He had travelled steerage, and, as might have been expected from one in his condition, had not made friends; but he had struck up a tepid acquaintanceship with an Irishman who was employed in a lumber business. The fellow was friendly, and was struck by Jim's obvious air of education and good-breeding, so, when he heard that he wanted work, he suggested that a clerkship might be got in his firm.

Jim applied, and was taken on as the clerk in charge of timber-cutting rights in Eastern Quebec. The work was purely mechanical and simply meant keeping a record of numbered lots, checking them off on the map, and filling in the details in the register as they came to hand. But it required accuracy and strict attention, and Jim had little of either. Besides, he wrote the vile fist which is the special privilege of our public schools. He held down the job for a fortnight and then was fired.

He had found cheap lodgings in a boarding-house down east, and trudged the two miles in the slush to his office. His fellow-lodgers were willing enough to be friendly—clerks and shop-boys and typists and newspaper reporters most of them. Jim wasn't a snob, but he was rapidly becoming a hermit, for all his nerves were exposed and he shrank from his fellows. His shyness was considered English swank, and the others invented nicknames for him and sniggered when he appeared. Luckily he was too miserable to pay much attention. He had no interest in their games, their visits to the movies and to cheap dance-halls, and their precocious sweethearting. He could not get the hang of their knowing commercial jargon. They set him down as a snob, and he shrank from them as barbarians.

But there was one lodger, a sub-editor on a paper which I shall call the *Evening Hawk*, who saw a little farther than the rest. He realized that Jim was an educated man—a "scholar" he called it, and he managed to get part of his confidence.

So when Jim lost his lumber job he was offered a billet on the *Hawk*. There was no superfluity of men of his type in local journalism, and the editor thought it might give tone to his paper to have some one on the staff who could write decent English and keep them from making howlers about Europe. The *Hawk* was a lively, up-to-date production, very much Americanized in its traditions and its literary style, but it had just acquired some political influence and it hankered after more.

But Jim was no sort of success in journalism. He was tried out in a variety of jobs—as reporter, special correspondent, sub-editor—but he failed to give satisfaction in any. To begin with he had no news-sense. Not many things interested him in his present frame of mind, and he had no notion what would interest the *Hawk's* readers. He couldn't compose snappy headlines, and it made him sick to try. His writing was no doubt a great deal more correct than that of his colleagues, but it was dull as ditch-water. To add to everything else he was desperately casual. It was not that he meant to be slack, but that he had no stimulus to make him concentrate his attention, and he was about the worst sub-editor, I fancy, in the history of the press.

Summer came, and sleet and icy winds gave place to dust and heat. Jim tramped the grilling streets, one vast ache of home-sickness. He had to stick to his tweeds, for his flannel suit had got lost in his journeys between boarding-houses, and, as he mopped his brow in the airless newspaper rooms smelling of printers' ink and shaken by the great presses, he thought of green lawns at Hurlingham, and cool back-waters of the Isis, and clipped yew hedges in old gardens, and a pleasant club window overlooking St. James's Street. He hungered for fresh air, but when on a Sunday morning he went for a long walk, he found no pleasure in the adjacent countryside. It all seemed dusty and tousled and unhomely. He wasn't complaining, for it seemed to him part of a rightful expiation, but he was very lonely and miserable.

I have said that he had landed with a couple of hundred pounds, and this he had managed to keep pretty well intact. One day at a quick-luncheon counter he got into talk with a man called McNee, a Manitoban who had fought in the War, and knew something about horses. McNee, like Jim, did not take happily to town life, and was very sick of his job with an automobile company, and looking about for a better. There was not much in common between the two men, except a dislike of Montreal, for I picture McNee as a rough diamond, an active enterprising fellow meant by Providence for a backwoodsman. He had heard of a big dam somewhere down in the Gaspé district, which was being constructed in connection with a pulp scheme. He knew one of the foremen, and believed that money might be made by any one who could put up a little capital and run a store in the construction camp. He told Jim that it was a fine wild country with plenty of game in the woods, and that, besides making money easily, a storekeeper could have a white man's life. But every bit of a thousand dollars capital would be needed, and he could only lay his hands on a couple of hundred. To Jim in his stuffy lodging-house the scheme offered a blessed escape. He wanted to make money, he wanted fresh air, and trees and running water, for your Englishman, though town-bred, always hankers after the country. So he gave up his job on the *Hawk*, just when it was about to give him up, and started out with McNee.

The place was his first disappointment. It was an ugly clearing in an interminable forest of dull spruces, which ran without a break to New Brunswick. However far you walked there was nothing to see except the low muffled hills and the monotonous green of the firs. The partners were given a big shack for their store, and made their sleeping quarters in one end of it. For stock they had laid in a quantity of tinned goods, tobacco, shirts and socks and boots, and a variety of musical instruments. But they found that most of their stuff was unmarketable, since the men were well fed and clothed by the company, and after a week their store had become a rough kind of café, selling hot-dogs and ice-cream and soft drinks. McNee was immensely proud of it, and ornamented the walls with " ideal faces " from the American magazines. He was a born restaurant-keeper, if he had got his chance, but unfortunately there was not much profit in coco-cola and gingerade.

In about a fortnight the place became half eating-house, half club, where the workmen gathered of an evening to play cards. McNee was in his element, but Jim was no more use than a sick pup. He didn't understand the lingo, and his shyness and absorption made him as unpopular as in the Montreal boarding-houses. He saw his little capital slipping away, and there was no compensation in the way of a pleasant life. He tried to imitate McNee's air of hearty bonhomie, and miserably failed. His partner was a good fellow, and stood up for him when an irate navvy consigned him to perdition as a " God-darned London dude," and Jim's own good temper and sense of only getting what he deserved did something to protect him. But he soon realized that he was a ghastly failure, and this knowledge prevented him expostulating with the other for his obvious shortcomings. For McNee soon became too much of a social success. Gaspé was not " dry," and there was more than soft drinks consumed in the store, especially by the joint-proprietor and his friend the foreman. Also McNee was a bit of a gambler, and was perpetually borrowing small sums from capital to meet his losses.

Now and then Jim took a holiday, and tramped all of a long summer day. The country around being only partially surveyed, there was no map to be had, and he repeatedly lost himself. Once he struck a lumber camp, and was given pork and beans by cheerful French-Canadians whose *patois* he could not follow. Once he had almost a happy day, when he saw his first moose. But generally he came back from stifling encounters with cedar swamps and *bois brulé*, weary but unrefreshed. He was not in the frame of mind to get much comfort out of the Canadian wilds, for he was always sore with longing for a different kind of landscape.

The river on which the camp lay was the famous Maouchi, and twelve miles down on the St. Lawrence shore was a big fishing-lodge owned by a rich New Yorker. Jim used to see members of the party—young men in marvellous knickerbockers and young women in jumpers like Joseph's coat, and he hid himself at the sight of them. Occasionally a big roadster would pass the store, conveying fishermen to some of the upper lakes. Once, when he was feeling specially dispirited after a long hot day, a car stopped at the door, and two people descended. They came into the store, and the young man asked for lemonade, declaring that their tongues were hanging out of their mouths. Happily McNee was there to serve them, while Jim sheltered behind the curtain of the sleeping-room. He knew them both. One was a subaltern in the cavalry with whom he had played bridge in the club, the other was a girl whom he had danced with. Their workmanlike English clothes, their quiet clear English voices gave him a bad dose of home-sickness. They were returning, he reflected, to hot baths and cool clean clothes and delicate food and civilized talk. For a moment he sickened at the sour stale effluvia of the eating-house, and the rank smell of the pork which McNee had been frying. Then he cursed himself for a fool and a child.

In the fall the work on the dam was shut down,

and the store was closed. The partners couldn't
remove their unsaleable goods, so the whole stock
was sold at junk prices among the nearest villages.
Jim found himself with about three hundred dollars
in the world, and the long Canadian winter to get
through. The fall on the other side of the Atlantic
is the pick of the year, and the beauty of the
flaming hillsides did a little to revive his spirits.
McNee wanted to get back to Manitoba, where he
had heard of a job, and Jim decided that he would
try Toronto, which was supposed to be rather more
healthy for Englishmen than the other cities. So
the two travelled west together, and Jim insisted
on paying McNee's fare to Winnipeg, thereby
leaving himself a hundred and fifty dollars or so on
which to face the world.

Toronto is the friendliest place on earth for the
man who knows how to make himself at home there.
There were plenty to help him if he had looked for
them, for nowhere will you find more warm-hearted
people to the square mile. But Jim's shyness and
prickliness put him outside the pale. He made no
effort to advertise the few assets he had, he was
desperately uncommunicative, and his self-absorp-
tion was not unnaturally taken for " side." Also
he made the mistake of letting himself get a little too
far down in the social scale. His clothes had become very shabby, and his boots were bad; when
the first snows came in November he bought himself
a thick overcoat, and that left him no money to
supplement the rest of his wardrobe, so that by
Christmas he was a very good imitation of a tramp.

He tried journalism first, but as he gave no information about himself except that he had been for a few weeks on the Montreal *Hawk*, he had some difficulty in getting a job. At last he got work on a weekly rag simply because he had some notion of grammar. It lasted exactly a fortnight. Then he tried tutoring, and spent some of his last dollars on advertising ; he had several nibbles, but always fell down at the interviews. One kind of parent jibbed at his superior manners, another at his inferior clothes. After that he jolted from one temporary job to another—a book-canvasser, an extra hand in a dry-goods store in the Christmas week, where the counter hid the deficiencies of his raiment, a temporary clerk during a municipal election, a packer in a fancy-stationery business, and finally a porter in a third-class hotel. His employment was not continuous, and between jobs he must have nearly starved. He had begun in the ordinary cheap boarding-house, but, before he found quarters in the attic of the hotel he worked at, he had sunk to a pretty squalid kind of doss-house. The physical discomfort was bad enough. He tramped the streets ill-clad and half-fed, and saw prosperous people in furs, and cheerful young parties, and fire-lit, book-lined rooms. But the spiritual trouble was worse. Sometimes, when things were very bad, he was fortunate enough to have his thoughts narrowed down to the obtaining of food and warmth. But at other times he would be tormented by a feeling that his misfortunes were deserved, and that Fate with a heavy hand was

belabouring him because he was a coward. H
trouble was no longer the idiotic sense of gui
about his father's bankruptcy; it was a much mo
rational penitence, for he was beginning to realia
that I had been right, and that he had behave
badly in running away from a plain duty. At fir
he choked down the thought, but all that miserab.
winter it grew upon him. His disasters were
direct visitation of the Almighty on one who ha
shown the white feather. He came to have a
almost mystical feeling about it. He felt that h
was branded like Cain, so that everybody knew tha
he had funked, and yet he realized that a rotte
morbid pride ironly prevented him from retracin
his steps.

The second spring found him thin from ba
feeding and with a nasty cough. He had the sens
to see that a summer in that hotel would be th
end of him, so, although he was in the depths o
hopelessness, the instinct of self-preservation drov
him to make a move. He wanted to get into th
country, but it was impossible to get work on
farm from Toronto, and he had no money to pa
for railway fares. In the end he was taken on a
a navvy on a bit of railway construction work i
the wilds of northern Ontario. He was given th
price of his ticket and ten dollars advance on hi
wages to get an outfit, and one day late in April h
found himself dumped at a railhead on a blue lak
with firs, firs, as far as the eye could reach. But i
was spring-time, the mating wildfowl were calling
the land was greening, and Jim drew long breath

f sweet air and felt that he was not going to die
ust yet.

But the camp was a roughish place, and he had no
McNee to protect him.   There was every kind of
oughneck and deadbeat there, and Jim was a bad
nixer.   He was an obvious softy and new chum
nd a natural butt, and, since he was being tortured
ll the time by his conscience, his good nature and
numble-mindedness were not so proof as they had
neen in Gaspé.   His poor physical condition made
nim a bad workman, and he came in for a good deal
f abuse as a slacker from the huskies who wrought
neside him.   The section boss was an Irishman
alled Malone with a tongue like a whip-lash, and
ne found plenty of opportunities for practising
nis gift on Jim.   But he was a just man, and after
a bit of rough-tonguing he saw that Jim was very
white about the gills and told him to show his hands.
Not being accustomed to the pick, these were one
nass of sores.   Malone cross-examined him, found
hat he had been at college, and took him off construction and put him in charge of stores.

There he had an easier life, but he was more
han ever the butt of the mess shack and the sleep-
ng quarters.   His crime was not only speaking
with an English accent and looking like Little
Willie, but being supposed to be a favourite of the
noss.   By-and-by the ragging became unbearable,
nd after his mug of coffee had been three times
struck out of his hand at one meal, Jim lost his
nemper and hit out.   In the fight which followed he
was ridiculously outclassed.   He had been fairly

good at games, but he had never boxed since hi
private school, and it is well for Jim's kind of ma
to think twice before he takes on a fellow who ha
all his life earned his living by his muscles.   But h
stood up pluckily, and took a good deal of punish
ment before he was knocked out, and he showed n
ill-will afterwards.   The incident considerably im
proved his position.   Malone, who heard of it, aske
him where in God's name he had been brought u
that he couldn't use his hands better, but didn'
appear ill-pleased.   The fight had another conse
quence.   It gave him just a suspicion of self-con
fidence, and helped him on his way to the decisio
to which he was slowly being compelled.

A week later he was sent a hundred miles int
the forest to take supplies to an advance surve
party.   It was something of a compliment tha
Malone should have picked him for the job, bu
Jim did not realize that.   His brain was beating
like a pendulum on his private trouble—that h
had run away, that all his misfortunes were th
punishment for his cowardice, and that, though h
confessed his fault, he could not make his shrinking
flesh go back.   He saw England as an Eden indeed
but with angels and flaming swords at every gate
He pictured the lifted eyebrows and the shrugge
shoulders as he crept into a clerk's job, with no
only his father's shame on his head, but the adde
disgrace of his own flight.   It had seemed impossibl
a year ago to stay on in London, but now it was
thousandfold more impossible to go home.

Yet the thought gave him no peace by day o

night. He had six men in his outfit, two of them
half-breeds, and the journey was partly by canoe—
with heavy portages—and partly on foot with the
stores in pack loads. It rained in torrents, the
river was in flood, and the first day they made a
bare twenty miles. The half-breeds were tough
old customers, but the other four were not much to
bank on, and on the third day, when they had to
hump their packs and foot it on a bad trail through
swampy woods in a cloud of flies, they decided
that they had had enough. There was a new gold
area just opened not so far away, and they announced that they intended to help themselves to
what they wanted from the stores and then make
a bee-line for the mines. They were an ugly type
of tough, and had physically the upper hand of
Jim and his half-breeds.

It was a nasty situation, and it shook Jim out of
his private vexations. He spoke them fair, and
proposed to make camp and rest for a day to talk
it out. Privately he sent one of the half-breeds
ahead to the survey party for help, while he kept
his ruffians in play. Happily he had some whisky
with him, and he had them drinking and playing
cards, which took him well into the afternoon.
Then they discovered the half-breed's absence, and
wouldn't believe Jim's yarn that he had gone off to
find fresh meat. His only chance was to bluff high,
and, since he didn't much care what happened to
him, he succeeded. He went to bed that night with
a tough beside him who had announced his intention of putting a bullet through his head if there was

any dirty work. Sometime after midnight his messenger arrived with help, and fortunately his bedside-companion's bullet went wide. The stores, a bit depleted, were safely delivered, and when Jim got back to his base he received a solid cursing from his boss for his defective stewardship. But Malone concluded with one of his rare compliments. "You'll train on, sonny," he said. "There's guts in you for all your goo-goo face."

That episode put an end to Jim's indecision. His time in Canada had been one long chapter of black disasters, and he was confident that they were sent to him as a punishment. His last adventure had somehow screwed up his manhood. He hated Canada like poison, but the thought of going back to England made him green with apprehension. Yet he was clear that he must do it or never have a moment's peace. So he wrote to me and told me that for a year he had been considering things, and had come to the conclusion that he had behaved like a cad. He was coming back to get into any kind of harness I directed, and would I advance him thirty pounds for his journey ?

Now the little company we had put together to nurse the wreckage of Hallwards had been doing rather well. One or two things had unexpectedly turned up trumps. There was enough money to keep the maiden aunts going, and it looked as if there would be a good deal presently for Jim. He had gone off leaving no address, so I had had no means of communicating with him. I cabled him a hundred pounds, and told him to come along.

One afternoon near the end of June he turned up in my office. He had crossed the Atlantic steerage, and his clothes were those of a docker who has been months out of work. The first thing he did was to plank eighty pounds on my desk. "You sent me too much," he said. "I don't want to owe more than is necessary. You can stop the twenty quid out of my wages."

At first sight I thought him very little changed in face. He was incredibly lean and tanned and his hair wanted cutting, but he had the same shy, hunted eyes as the boy who had bolted a year before. He did not seem to have won any self-confidence, except that the set of his mouth was a little firmer.

"I want to start work at once," he said. "I've come home to make atonement."

It took me a long time to make him understand the position of affairs—that he could count even now on a respectable income, and that, if he put his back into it, Hallwards might once again become a power in the City. "I was only waiting for you to come back," I said, "to revive the old name. Hallwards has a better sound than the Anglo-Orient Company."

"But I can't touch a penny," he said. "What about the people who suffered through the bankruptcy?"

"There were very few," I told him. "None of the widow-and-orphan business. The banks were amply secured. The chief sufferers were your aunts and yourself, and that's going to be all right now."

He listened with wide eyes, and slowly bewilderment gave place to relief, and relief to rapture. "The first thing you've got to do," I said, "is to go to your tailor and get some clothes. You'd better put up at an hotel till you can find a flat. I'll see about your club membership. If you want to play polo I'll lend you a couple of ponies. Come and dine with me to-night and tell me your story."

"My God!" he murmured. "Do you realize that for a year I've been on my uppers? That's my story."

The rest of that summer Jim walked about in a happy mystification. Once he was decently dressed, I could see that Canada had improved him. He was better-looking, tougher, manlier; his shyness was now wariness, and he had got a new and sounder code of values. He worked like a beaver in the office, and, though he was curiously slow and obtuse about some things, I began to see that he had his father's brains, and something, too, that old Hallward had never had, a sensitive, subtle imagination. For the rest he enjoyed himself. He came in for the end of the polo season, and he was welcomed back to his old set as if nothing had happened.

Then I ceased to see much of him. I had been overworking badly and needed a long holiday, so I went off to a Scotch deer forest in the middle of August and did not return till the beginning of October. Jim stuck tight to the office; he said that he had had all the holidays he wanted for a year or two.

On the second day after my return he came into

my room and said that he wanted to speak to me privately. He wished, he said, that nothing should be done about the restoring the name of Hallwards. He would like the Anglo-Orient to go on just as it was before he returned, and he did not want the directorship which had been arranged.

" Why in the world ? " I asked in amazement.

" Because I am going away. And I may be away for quite a time."

When I found words, and that took some time, I asked if he had grown tired of England.

" Bless you, no ! I love it better than any place on earth. The autumn scents are beginning, and London is snugging down for its blessed cosy winter, and the hunting will soon be starting, and last Sunday I heard the old cock pheasants shout-ing——"

" Where are you going ? Canada ? "

He nodded.

" Have you fallen in love with it ? "

" I hate it worse than hell," he said solemnly, and proceeded to say things which in the interest of Imperial good feeling I refrain from repeating.

" Then you must be mad ! "

" No," he said, " I'm quite sane. It's very simple, and I've thought it all out. You know I ran away from my duty eighteen months ago. Well, I was punished for it. I was a howling failure in Canada. . . . I haven't told you half . . . I pretty well starved . . . I couldn't hold down any job . . . I was simply a waif and a laughing-stock. And I loathed it—my God, how I loathed it !

But I couldn't come back—the very thought of facing London gave me a sick pain. It took me a year to screw up my courage to do what I knew was my manifest duty. Well, I turned up, as you know."

"Then that's all right, isn't it?" I observed obtusely. "You find London better than you thought?"

"I find it Paradise," and he smiled sadly. "But it's a Paradise I haven't deserved. You see, I made a failure in Canada and I can't let it go at that. I hate the very name of the place and most of the people in it. . . . Oh, I daresay there is nothing wrong with it, but one always hates a place where one has been a fool. . . . I have got to go back and make good. I shall take two hundred pounds, just what I had when I first started out."

I only stared, and he went on :

"I funked once, and that may be forgiven. But a man who funks twice is a coward. I funk Canada like the devil, and that is why I am going back. There was a man there—only one man—who said I had guts. I'm going to prove to that whole damned Dominion that I have guts, but principally I've got to prove it to myself. . . . After that I'll come back to you, and we'll talk business."

I could say nothing : indeed I didn't want to say anything. Jim was showing a kind of courage several grades ahead of old Jonah's. He had returned to Nineveh and found that it had no terrors, and was now going back to Tarshish, whales and all.

IX. SKULE SKERRY

ANTHONY HURRELL'S STORY

Who's there, besides foul weather ?

King Lear.

IX. SKULE SKERRY

MR. ANTHONY HURRELL was a small man, thin to the point of emaciation, but erect as a ramrod and wiry as a cairn terrier. There was no grey in his hair, and his pale far-sighted eyes had the alertness of youth, but his lean face was so wrinkled by weather that in certain lights it looked almost venerable, and young men, who at first sight had imagined him their contemporary, presently dropped into the " sir " reserved for indisputable seniors. His actual age was, I believe, somewhere in the forties. He had inherited a small property in Northumberland, where he had accumulated a collection of the rarer wildfowl; but much of his life had been spent in places so remote that his friends could with difficulty find them on the map. He had written a dozen ornithological monographs, was joint editor of the chief modern treatise on British birds, and had been the first man to visit the *tundras* of the Yenisei. He spoke little and that with an agreeable hesitation, but his ready smile, his quick interest, and the impression he gave of having a fathomless knowledge of strange modes of life, made him a popular and intriguing figure among his friends. Of his doings in the War he told us nothing; what we knew of them—and they were sensational enough in all conscience—we learned elsewhere. It was Nightingale's story which drew him from his customary silence. At the dinner following that event he made certain comments on current explanations of the super-normal. "I remember once," he began, and before we knew he had surprised us by embarking on a tale.

He had scarcely begun before he stopped. "I'm boring you," he said deprecatingly. "There's nothing much in the story. . . . You see, it all happened, so to speak, inside my head. . . . I don't want to seem an egotist. . . ."

"Don't be an ass, Tony," said Lamancha. "Every adventure takes place chiefly inside the head of somebody. Go on. We're all attention."

"It happened a good many years ago," Hurrell continued, "when I was quite a young man. I wasn't the cold scientist then that I fancy I am to-day. I took up birds in the first instance chiefly because they fired what imagination I possess. They fascinated me, for they seemed of all created things the nearest to pure spirit—those little beings with a normal temperature of 125°. Think of it. The goldcrest, with a stomach no bigger than a bean, flies across the North Sea! The curlew sandpiper, which breeds so far north that only about three people have ever seen its nest, goes to Tasmania for its holidays! So I always went bird-hunting with a queer sense of expectation and a bit of a tremor, as if I were walking very near the boundaries of the things we are not allowed to know. I felt this especially in the migration season. The small atoms, coming God knows whence and going God knows whither, were sheer mystery—they belonged to a world built in different dimensions from ours. I don't know what I expected, but I was always waiting for something, as much in a flutter as a girl at her first ball. You must realize that mood of mine to understand what follows.

" One year I went to the Norland Islands for the spring migration. Plenty of people do the same, but I had the notion to do something a little different. I had a theory that migrants go north and south on a fairly narrow road. They have their corridors in the air as clearly defined as a highway, and keep an inherited memory of these corridors, like the stout conservatives they are. So I didn't go to the Blue Banks or to Noop or to Hermaness or any of the obvious places, where birds might be expected to make their first landfall.

" At that time I was pretty well read in the sagas, and had taught myself Icelandic for the purpose. Now it is written in the Saga of Earl Skuli, which is part of the Jarla Saga or Saga of the Earls, that Skuli, when he was carving out his earldom in the Scots islands, had much to do with a place called the Isle of the Birds. It is mentioned repeatedly, and the saga-man has a lot to say about the amazing multitude of birds there. It couldn't have been an ordinary gullery, for the Northmen saw too many of these to think them worth mentioning. I got it into my head that it must have been one of the alighting places of the migrants, and was probably as busy a spot to-day as in the eleventh century. The saga said it was near Halmarsness, and that is on the west side of the island of Una, so to Una I decided to go. I fairly got that Isle of Birds on the brain. From the map it might be any one of a dozen skerries under the shadow of Halmarsness.

"I remember that I spent a good many hours in the British Museum before I started, hunting up the scanty records of those parts. I found—I think it was in Adam of Bremen—that a succession of holy men had lived on the isle, and that a chapel had been built there and endowed by Earl Rognvald, which came to an end in the time of Malise of Strathearn. There was a bare mention of the place, but the chronicler had one curious note. '*Insula Avium*,' ran the text, '*quæ est ultima insula et proxima Abysso*.' I wondered what on earth he meant. The place was not ultimate in any geographical sense, neither the farthest north nor the farthest west of the Norlands. And what was the 'abyss'? In monkish Latin the word generally means Hell—Bunyan's Bottomless Pit—and sometimes the grave; but neither meaning seemed to have much to do with an ordinary sea skerry.

"I arrived at Una about eight o'clock in a May evening, having been put across from Voss in a flitboat. It was a quiet evening, the sky without clouds but so pale as to be almost grey, the sea grey also but with a certain iridescence in it, and the low lines of the land a combination of hard

greys and umbers, cut into by the harder white of
the lighthouse. I can never find words to describe
that curious quality of light that you get up in the
North. Sometimes it is like looking at the world
out of deep water—Farquharson used to call it
' milky,' and one saw what he meant. Generally
it is a sort of essence of light, cold and pure and
distilled, as if it were reflected from snow. There
is no colour in it, and it makes thin shadows. Some
people find it horribly depressing—Farquharson
said it reminded him of a churchyard in the early
morning where all his friends were buried—but
personally I found it tonic and comforting. But it
made me feel very near the edge of the world.

" There was no inn, so I put up at the post office,
which was on a causeway between a fresh-water
loch and a sea voe, so that from the doorstep you
could catch brown trout on one side and sea-trout
on the other. Next morning I set off for Halmarsness, which lay five miles to the west over a flat
moorland all puddled with tiny lochans. There
seemed to be nearly as much water as land. Presently I came to a bigger loch under the lift of
ground which was Halmarsness. There was a gap
in the ridge through which I looked straight out
to the Atlantic, and there, in the middle distance,
was what I knew instinctively to be my island.

" It was perhaps a quarter of a mile long, low for
the most part, but rising in the north to a grassy
knoll beyond the reach of any tides. In parts it
narrowed to a few yards width, and the lower levels
must often have been awash. But it was an island,

not a reef, and I thought I could make out the remains of the monkish cell. I climbed Halmarsness, and there, with nesting skuas swooping angrily about my head, I got a better view. It was certainly my island, for the rest of the archipelago were inconsiderable skerries, and I realized that it might well be a resting-place for migrants, for the mainland cliffs were too thronged with piratical skuas and other jealous fowl to be comfortable for weary travellers.

" I sat for a long time on the headland looking down from the three hundred feet of basalt to the island half a mile off—the last bit of solid earth between me and Greenland. The sea was calm for Norland waters, but there was a snowy edging of surf to the skerries which told of a tide rip. Two miles farther south I could see the entrance to the famous Roost of Una, where, when tide and wind collide, there is a wall like a house, so that a small steamer cannot pass it. The only sign of human habitation was a little grey farm in the lowlands toward the Roost; but the place was full of the evidence of man—a herd of Norland ponies, each tagged with its owner's name—grazing sheep of the piebald Norland breed—a broken barbed-wire fence that drooped over the edge of the cliff. I was only an hour's walk from a telegraph office, and a village which got its newspapers not more than three days late. It was a fine spring noon, and in the empty bright land there was scarcely a shadow. . . . All the same, as I looked down at the island I did not wonder that it had been selected for attention by the saga-man and had been reputed holy. For it had an air of concealing something, though it was as bare as a billiard-table. It was an intruder, an irrelevance in the picture, planted there by some celestial caprice. I decided forthwith to make my camp on it, and the decision, inconsequently enough, seemed to me to be something of a venture.

"That was the view taken by John Ronaldson, when I talked to him after dinner. John was the postmistress's son, more fisherman than crofter, like all Norlanders, a skilful sailor and an adept at the dipping lug, and noted for his knowledge of the western coast. He had difficulty in understanding my plan, and when he identified my island he protested.

" ' Not Skule Skerry ! ' he cried. ' What would take ye there, man ? Ye'll get a' the birds ye want on Halmarsness and a far better bield. Ye'll be blawn away on the skerry, if the wund rises.'

"I explained to him my reasons as well as I could, and I answered his fears about a gale by pointing out that the island was sheltered by the cliffs from the prevailing winds, and could be scourged only from the south, south-west, or west, quarters from which the wind rarely blew in May. ' It'll be cauld,' he said, ' and wat.' I pointed out that I had a tent and was accustomed to camping. ' Ye'll starve '—I expounded my proposed methods of commissariat. ' It'll be an ill job getting ye on and off '—but after cross-examination he admitted that ordinarily the tides were not difficult, and that

I could get a rowboat to a beach below the farm I had seen—its name was Sgurravoe. Yet when I had said all this he still raised objections, till I asked him flatly what was the matter with Skule Skerry.

" ' Naebody gangs there,' he said gruffly.

" ' Why should they ? ' I asked. ' I'm only going to watch the birds.'

" But the fact that it was never visited seemed to stick in his throat, and he grumbled out something that surprised me. ' It has an ill name,' he said. But when I pressed him he admitted that there was no record of shipwreck or disaster to account for the ill name. He repeated the words ' Skule Skerry ' as if they displeased him. ' Folk dinna gang near it. It has aye had an ill name. My grandfather used to say that the place wasna canny.'

" Now your Norlander has nothing of the Celt in him, and is as different from the Hebridean as a Northumbrian from a Cornishman. They are a fine, upstanding, hard-headed race, almost pure Scandinavian in blood, but they have as little poetry in them as a Manchester Radical. I should have put them down as utterly free from superstition, and, in all my many visits to the islands, I have never yet come across a folk-tale—hardly even a historical legend. Yet here was John Ronaldson, with his weather-beaten face and stiff chin and shrewd blue eyes, declaring that an innocent-looking island ' wasna canny,' and showing the most remarkable disinclination to go near it.

" Of course all this only made me keener. Besides, it was called Skule Skerry, and the name could only come from Earl Skuli ; so it was linked up authentically with the oddments of information I had collected in the British Museum—the Jarla Saga and Adam of Bremen and all the rest of it. John finally agreed to take me over next morning in his boat, and I spent the rest of the day in collecting my kit. I had a small tent, and a Wolseley valise and half a dozen rugs, and, since I had brought a big box of tinned stuffs from the Stores, all I needed was flour and meal and some simple groceries. I learned that there was a well on the island, and that I could count on sufficient driftwood for my fire, but to make certain I took a sack of coals and another of peats. So I set off next day in John's boat, ran with the wind through the Roost of Una when the tide was right, tacked up the coast, and came to the skerry early in the afternoon.

" You could see that John hated the place. We ran into a cove on the east side, and he splashed ashore as if he expected to have his landing opposed, looking all the time sharply about him. When he carried my stuff to a hollow under the knoll, which gave a certain amount of shelter, his head was always twisting round. To me the place seemed to be the last word in forgotten peace. The swell lipped gently on the reefs and the little pebbled beaches, and only the babble of gulls from Halmarsness broke the stillness.

" John was clearly anxious to get away, but he

did his duty by me. He helped me to get the tent up, found a convenient place for my boxes, pointed out the well and filled my water bucket, and made a zareba of stones to protect my camp on the Atlantic side. We had brought a small dinghy along with us, and this was to be left with me, so that when I wanted I could row across to the beach at Sgurravoe. As his last service he fixed an old pail between two boulders on the summit of the knoll, and filled it with oily waste, so that it could be turned into a beacon.

"'Ye'll maybe want to come off,' he said, 'and the boat will maybe no be there. Kindle your flare, and they'll see it at Sgurravoe and get the word to me, and I'll come for ye though the Muckle Black Silkie himsel' was hunkerin' on the skerry.'

"Then he looked up and sniffed the air. 'I dinna like the set of the sky,' he declared. 'It's a bad weather-head. There'll be mair wund than I like in the next four-and-twenty hours.'

"So saying, he hoisted his sail, and presently was a speck on the waters towards the Roost. There was no need for him to hurry, for the tide was now wrong, and before he could pass the Roost he would have three hours to wait on this side of the Mull. But the man, usually so deliberate and imperturbable, had been in a fever to be gone.

"His departure left me in a curious mood of happy loneliness and pleasurable expectation. I was left solitary with the seas and the birds. I laughed to think that I had found a streak of superstition in the granite John. He and his Muckle Black Silkie! I knew the old legend of the North which tells how the Finns, the ghouls that live in the deeps of the ocean, can on occasion don a seal's skin and come to land to play havoc with mortals. But *diablerie* and this isle of mine were worlds apart. I looked at it as the sun dropped, drowsing in the opal-coloured tides, under a sky in which pale clouds made streamers like a spectral *aurora borealis*, and I thought that I had stumbled upon one of those places where Nature seems to invite one to her secrets. As the light died the sky was flecked as with the roots and branches of some great nebular tree. That would be the ' weather-head ' of which John Ronaldson had spoken.

" I set my fire going, cooked my supper, and made everything snug for the night. I had been right in my guess about the migrants. It must have been about ten o'clock when they began to arrive—after my fire had died out and I was smoking my last pipe before getting into my sleeping-bag. A host of fieldfares settled gently on the south part of the skerry. A faint light lingered till after midnight, but it was not easy to distinguish the little creatures, for they were aware of my presence and did not alight within a dozen yards of me. But I made out bramblings and buntings and what I thought was the Greenland wheatear; also jack snipe and sanderling ; and I believed from their cries that the curlew sandpiper and the whimbrel were there. I went to sleep in a state of high excitement, prom- ising myself a fruitful time on the morrow.

" I slept badly, as one often does one's first night in the open. Several times I woke with a start, under the impression that I was in a boat rowing swiftly with the tide. And every time I woke I heard the flutter of myriad birds, as if a velvet curtain were being slowly switched along an oak floor. At last I fell into deeper sleep, and when I opened my eyes it was full day.

" The first thing that struck me was that it had got suddenly colder. The sky was stormily red in the east, and masses of woolly clouds were banking in the north. I lit my fire with numbed fingers and hastily made tea. I could see the nimbus of seafowl over Halmarsness, but there was only one bird left on my skerry. I was certain from its forked tail that it was a Sabine's gull, but before I got my glass out it was disappearing into the haze towards the north. The sight cheered and excited me, and I cooked my breakfast in pretty good spirits.

" That was literally the last bird that came near me, barring the ordinary shearwaters and gulls and cormorants that nested round about Halmarsness. (There was not one single nest of any sort on the island. I had heard of that happening before in places which were regular halting-grounds for migrants.) The travellers must have had an inkling of the coming weather and were waiting somewhere well to the south. For about nine o'clock it began to blow. Great God, how it blew ! You must go to the Norlands if you want to know what wind can be. It is like being on a mountain-top, for there is no high ground to act as a wind-break. There was no rain, but the surf broke in showers and every foot of the skerry was drenched with it. In a trice Halmarsness was hidden, and I seemed to be in the centre of a maelstrom, choked with scud and buffeted on every side by swirling waters.

" Down came my tent at once. I wrestled with the crazy canvas and got a black eye from the pole, but I managed to drag the ruins into the shelter of the zareba which John had built, and tumble some of the bigger boulders on it. There it lay, flapping like a sick albatross. The water got into my food boxes, and soaked my fuel, as well as every inch of my clothing. . . . I had looked forward to a peaceful day of watching and medi- tation, when I could write up my notes ; and instead I spent a morning like a Rugger scrum. I might have enjoyed it, if I hadn't been so wet and cold, and could have got a better lunch than some clammy mouthfuls out of a tin. One talks glibly about being ' blown off ' a place, generally an idle exaggeration—but that day I came very near the reality. There were times when I had to hang on for dear life to one of the bigger stones to avoid being trundled into the yeasty seas.

" About two o'clock the volume of the storm began to decline, and then for the first time I thought about the boat. With a horrid sinking of the heart I scrambled to the cove where we had beached it. It had been drawn up high and dry, and its painter secured to a substantial boulder. But now there was not a sign of it except a ragged rope-end round the stone. The tide had mounted to its level, and tide and wind had smashed the rotten painter. By this time what was left of it would be tossing in the Roost.

"This was a pretty state of affairs. John was due to visit me next day, but I had a cold twenty-four hours ahead of me. There was of course the flare he had left me, but I was not inclined to use this. It looked like throwing up the sponge and confessing that my expedition had been a farce. I felt miserable, but obstinate, and, since the weather was clearly mending, I determined to put the best face on the business, so I went back to the wreckage of my camp, and tried to tidy up. There was still far too much wind to do anything with the tent, but the worst of the spindrift had ceased, and I was able to put out my bedding and some of my provender to dry. I got a dry jersey out of my pack, and, as I was wearing fisherman's boots and oilskins, I managed to get some slight return of comfort. Also at last I succeeded in lighting a pipe. I found a corner under the knoll which gave me a modicum of shelter, and I settled myself to pass the time with tobacco and my own thoughts.

"About three o'clock the wind died away completely. That I did not like, for a dead lull in the Norlands is often the precursor of a new gale. Indeed, I never remembered a time when some wind did not blow, and I had heard that when such a thing happened people came out of their houses to ask what the matter was. But now we had the deadest sort of calm. The sea was still wild and broken, the tides raced by like a mill-stream, and a brume was gathering which shut out Halmarsness —shut out every prospect except a narrow circuit of grey water. The cessation of the racket of the gale made the place seem uncannily quiet. The present tumult of the sea, in comparison with the noise of the morning, seemed no more than a mutter and an echo.

" As I sat there I became conscious of an odd sensation. I seemed to be more alone, more cut off, not only from my fellows but from the habitable earth, than I had ever been before. It was like being in a small boat in mid-Atlantic—but worse, if you understand me, for that would have been loneliness in the midst of a waste which was nevertheless surrounded and traversed by the works of man, whereas now I felt that I was clean outside man's ken. I had come somehow to the edge of that world where life is, and was very close to the world which has only death in it.

" At first I do not think there was much fear in the sensation—chiefly strangeness, but the kind of strangeness which awes without exciting. I tried to shake off the mood, and got up to stretch myself. There was not much room for exercise, and as I moved with stiff legs along the reefs I slipped into the water, so that I got my arms wet. It was cold beyond belief—the very quintessence of deathly Arctic ice, so cold that it seemed to sear and bleach the skin.

" From that moment I date the most unpleasant experience of my life. I became suddenly the prey of a black depression, shot with the red lights of terror. But it was not a numb terror, for my brain was acutely alive. . . . I had the sense to try to make tea, but my fuel was still too damp, and the best I could do was to pour half the contents of my brandy flask into a cup and swallow the stuff. That did not properly warm my chilled body, but —since I am a very temperate man—it speeded up my thoughts instead of calming them. I felt myself on the brink of a childish panic.

" One thing I thought I saw clearly—the meaning of Skule Skerry. By some alchemy of nature, at which I could only guess, it was on the track by which the North exercised its spell, a cableway for the magnetism of that cruel frozen Uttermost, which man might penetrate but could never subdue or understand. Though the latitude was only 61°, there were folds and tucks in space, and this isle was the edge of the world. Birds knew it, and the old Northmen, who were primitive beings like the birds, knew it. That was why an inconsiderable skerry had been given the name of a conquering Jarl. The old Church knew it, and had planted a chapel to exorcise the demons of darkness. I wondered what sights the hermit, whose cell had been on the very spot where I was cowering, had seen in the winter dusks.

" It may have been partly the brandy acting on an empty stomach, and partly the extreme cold, but my brain, in spite of my efforts to think rationally, began to run like a dynamo. It is difficult to explain my mood, but I seemed to be

two persons—one a reasonable modern man trying
to keep sane and scornfully rejecting the fancies
which the other, a cast-back to something elemental,
was furiously spinning.   But it was the second that
had the upper hand. . . . I felt myself loosed from
my moorings, a mere waif on uncharted seas.   What
is the German phrase ?   *Urdummheit*—Primal
Idiocy ?   That was what was the matter with me.
I had fallen out of civilization into the Outlands
and was feeling their spell. . . . I could not think,
but I could remember, and what I had read of the
Norse voyagers came back to me with horrid persistence.   They had known the outland terrors—
the Sea Walls at the world's end, the Curdled
Ocean with its strange beasts.   Those men did not
sail north as we did, in steamers, with modern food
and modern instruments, huddled into crews and
expeditions.   They had gone out almost alone, in
brittle galleys, and they had known what we could
never know.

   " And then, I had a shattering revelation.   I had
been groping for a word and I suddenly got it.   It
was Adam of Bremen's ' *proxima Abysso*.'   This
island was next door to the Abyss, and the Abyss
was that blanched world of the North which was
the negation of life.

   " That unfortunate recollection was the last
straw.   I remember that I forced myself to get up
and try again to kindle a fire.   But the wood was
still too damp, and I realized with consternation
that I had very few matches left, several boxes
having been ruined that morning.   As I staggered

about I saw the flare which John had left for me, and had almost lit it. But some dregs of manhood prevented me—I could not own defeat in that baby-ish way—I must wait till John Ronaldson came for me next morning. Instead I had another mouthful of brandy, and tried to eat some of my sodden bis-cuits. But I could scarcely swallow; the infernal cold, instead of rousing hunger, had given me only a raging thirst.

"I forced myself to sit down again with my face to the land. You see, every moment I was be-coming more childish. I had the notion—I cannot call it a thought—that down the avenue from the North something terrible and strange might come. My nervous state must have been pretty bad, for though I was cold and empty and weary I was scarcely conscious of physical discomfort. My heart was fluttering like a scared boy's; and all the time the other part of me was standing aside and telling me not to be a damned fool. . . . I think that if I had heard the rustle of a flock of migrants I might have pulled myself together, but not a blessed bird had come near me all the day. I had fallen into a world that killed life, a sort of Valley of the Shadow of Death.

"The brume spoiled the long northern twilight, and presently it was almost dark. At first I thought that this was going to help me, and I got hold of several of my half-dry rugs, and made a sleeping-place. But I could not sleep, even if my teeth had stopped chattering, for a new and per-fectly idiotic idea possessed me. It came from a recollection of John Ronaldson's parting words. What had he said about the Black Silkie—the Finn who came out of the deep and hunkered on this skerry ? Raving mania ! But on this lost island in the darkening night, with icy tides lapping about me, was any horror beyond belief ?

" Still, the sheer idiocy of the idea compelled a reaction. I took hold of my wits with both hands and cursed myself for a fool. I could even reason about my folly. I knew what was wrong with me. I was suffering from *panic*—a physical affection produced by natural causes, explicable, though as yet not fully explained. Two friends of mine had once been afflicted with it : one in a lonely glen in the Jotunheim, so that he ran for ten miles over stony hills till he found a sæter and human companionship ; the other in a Bavarian forest, where both he and his guide tore for hours through the thicket till they dropped like logs beside a highroad. This reflection enabled me to take a pull on myself and to think a little ahead. If my troubles were physical then there would be no shame in looking for the speediest cure. Without further delay I must leave this God-forgotten place.

" The flare was all right, for it had been set on the highest point of the island, and John had covered it with a peat. With one of my few remaining matches I lit the oily waste, and a great smoky flame leapt to heaven.

" If the half-dark had been eerie, this sudden brightness was eerier. For a moment the glare gave me confidence, but as I looked at the circle of moving waters evilly lit up all my terrors returned. . . . How long would it take John to reach me ? They would see it at once at Sgurravoe —they would be on the look-out for it—John would not waste time, for he had tried to dissuade me from coming—an hour—two hours at the most. . . .

" I found I could not take my eyes from the waters. They seemed to flow from the north in a strong stream, black as the heart of the elder ice, irresistible as fate, cruel as hell. There seemed to be uncouth shapes swimming in them, which were more than the flickering shadows from the flare. . . . Something portentous might at any moment come down that river of death. . . . Someone. . . .

" And then my knees gave under me and my heart shrank like a pea, for I saw that the someone had come.

" He drew himself heavily out of the sea, wallowed for a second, and then raised his head and, from a distance of five yards, looked me blindly in the face. The flare was fast dying down, but even so at that short range it cast a strong light, and the eyes of the awful being seemed to be dazed by it. I saw a great dark head like a bull's—an old face wrinkled as if in pain—a gleam of enormous broken teeth—a dripping beard—all formed on other lines than God has made mortal creatures. And on the right of the throat was a huge scarlet gash. The thing seemed to be moaning, and then from it came a sound—whether of anguish or wrath I cannot tell—but it seemed to be the cry of a tortured fiend.

"That was enough for me. I pitched forward in a swoon, hitting my head on a stone, and in that condition three hours later John Ronaldson found me.

"They put me to bed at Sgurravoe with hot earthenware bottles, and the doctor from Voss next day patched up my head and gave me a sleeping draught. He declared that there was little the matter with me except shock from exposure, and promised to set me on my feet in a week.

"For three days I was as miserable as a man could be, and did my best to work myself into a fever. I had said not a word about my experience, and left my rescuers to believe that my only troubles were cold and hunger, and that I had lit the flare because I had lost the boat. But during these days I was in a critical state. I knew that there was nothing wrong with my body, but I was gravely concerned about my mind.

"For this was my difficulty. If that awful thing was a mere figment of my brain, then I had better be certified at once as a lunatic. No sane man could get into such a state as to see such portents with the certainty with which I had seen that creature come out of the night. If, on the other hand, the thing was a real presence, then I had looked on something outside natural law, and my intellectual world was broken in pieces. I was a scientist, and a scientist cannot admit the supernatural. If with my eyes I had beheld the monster in which Adam of Bremen believed, which holy men had exorcised, which even the shrewd Norlanders shuddered at as the Black Silkie, then I must burn my books and revise my creed. I might take to poetry or theosophy, but I would never be much good again at science.

" On the third afternoon I was trying to doze, and with shut eyes fighting off the pictures which tormented my brain. John Ronaldson and the farmer of Sgurravoe were talking at the kitchen door. The latter asked some question, and John replied :

" ' Aye, it was a wall-ross and nae mistake. It cam ashore at Gloop Ness and Sandy Fraser has gotten the skin of it. It was deid when he found it, but no long deid. The puir beast would drift south on some floe, and it was sair hurt, for Sandy said it had a hole in its throat ye could put your nieve in. There hasna been a wall-ross come to Una since my grandfather's day.'

" I turned my face to the wall and composed myself to sleep. For now I knew that I was sane, and need not forswear science."

X. "TENDEBANT MANUS"

SIR ARTHUR WARCLIFF'S STORY

Send not on your soul before
To dive from that beguiling shore,
And let not yet the swimmer leave
His clothes upon the sands of eve.

                          A. E. HOUSMAN.

X. "TENDEBANT MANUS"

ONE night we were discussing Souldern, who had died a week before and whose memorial service had been held that morning in St. Margaret's. He had come on amazingly in Parliament, one of those sudden rises which were common in the immediate post-war years, when the older reputations were being questioned and the younger men were too busy making a livelihood to have time for hobbies. His speeches, his membership of a commission where he had shown both originality and courage, and his reputed refusal, on very honourable grounds, of a place in the Cabinet, had given him in the popular mind a flavour of mystery and distinction. The papers had devoted a good deal of space to him, and there was a general feeling that his death—the result of a motor smash—was a bigger loss to the country than his actual achievement warranted.

"I never met him," Palliser-Yeates said. "But I was at school with his minor. You remember Reggie Souldern, Charles? An uncommon good fellow—makings of a fine soldier, too—disappeared with most of his battalion in March '18, and was never heard of again. Body committed to the

pleasant land of France but exact spot unknown—
rather like a burial at sea."

"I knew George Souldern well enough," said
Lamancha, whom he addressed. "I sat in the
House with him for two years before the War.
That is to say, I knew as much of him as anybody
did, but there was very little you could lay hold of.
He used to be a fussy, ineffective chap, very fertile
in ideas which he never thought out, and always
starting hares that he wouldn't hunt. But just
lately he seems to have had a call, and he looked as
if he might have a career. Rotten luck that a
sharp corner and a lout of a motor-cyclist should
have put an end to it."

He turned to his neighbour. "Wasn't he a relation of yours, Sir Arthur?"

The man addressed was the oldest member of
the Club and by far the most distinguished. Sir
Arthur Warcliff had been a figure of note when
most of us were in our cradles. He began life in
the Sappers, and before he was thirty had been in
command of a troublesome little Somaliland expedition; then he had governed a variety of places
with such success that he was seriously spoken of
for India. In the War he would have liked to
return to soldiering, but they used him as the
Cabinet handy-man, and he had all the worst
diplomatic and administrative jobs to tackle.
You see, he was a master of detail, and had to
translate the generalities of policy into action.
He had never, as the jargon goes, got his personality over the footlights, so he was only a name to

the public—but a tremendous name, of which every party spoke respectfully. He had retired now, and lived alone with his motherless boy. Usually, for all his sixty-five years, he seemed a contemporary, for he was curiously young at heart, but every now and then we looked at his wise, worn face, realized what he had been and was, and sat at his feet.

" Yes," he said in reply to Lamancha. " George Souldern was my wife's cousin, and I knew him well for the last twenty years. Since the War I knew him better, and in the past eighteen months I was, I think, his only intimate friend."

" Was he a really big man ? " Sandy Arbuthnot asked. " I don't take much stock in his profession —but I thought—just for a moment—in that Irish row—that I got a glimpse of something rather out of the ordinary."

" He had first-class brains."

Sandy laughed. " That doesn't get you very far," he said. The phrase " first-class brains " had acquired at the time a flavour of comedy.

" No, it doesn't. If you had asked me the question six years ago I should have said that George was a brilliant failure. Immensely clever in his way, really well educated—which very few of us are—laborious as a beaver, but futile. The hare that is always being passed by every kind of tortoise. He had everything in his favour, but nothing ever came out as he wanted it. I only knew him after he came down from Oxford, but I believe that at the University he was a nonpareil."

"I was up with him," said Peckwether, the historian. "Oh yes, he was a big enough figure there. He was head of Winchester, and senior scholar of Balliol, and took two Firsts and several University prizes in his stride. He must have sat up all night, for he never appeared to work—you see, it was his pose to do things easily—a variety of the Grand Manner. He was a most disquieting undergraduate. In his political speeches he had the air of having just left a Cabinet meeting."

"Was he popular ? " some one asked.

"Not a bit," said Peckwether. " And for all his successes we didn't believe in him. He was too worldly-wise—what we used to call ' banausic '—too bent on getting on. We felt that he had all his goods in the shop window, and that there was no margin to him."

Sir Arthur smiled. "A young man's contemporaries are pretty shrewd judges. When I met him first I felt the same thing. He wasn't a prig, and he had a sense of humour, and he had plenty of ordinary decent feeling. But he was the kind of man who could never forget himself and throw his cap over the moon. One couldn't warm to him. . . . But, unlike you, I thought he would succeed. The one thing lacking was money, and within two years he had remedied that. He married a rich wife ; the lady died, but the fortune remained. I believe it was an honest love match, and for a long time he was heart-broken, and when he recovered he buried himself in work. You would have said that something was bound to happen. Young,

rich, healthy, incredibly industrious, able, present-
able—you would have said that any constituency
would have welcomed him, that his party would
have jumped at him, that he would have been a
prodigious success.

" But he wasn't. He made a bad candidate, and
had to stand three times before he got into the
House. And there he made no kind of impression, though he spoke conscientiously and always
on matters he knew about. He wrote a book on
the meaning of colonial nationalism—fluent, well-
expressed, sensible, even in parts eloquent, but
somehow it wasn't read. He was always making
speeches at public dinners and at the annual
meetings of different kinds of associations, but it
didn't seem to signify what he said, and he was
scarcely reported. There was no conspiracy of
silence to keep him down. for people rather liked
him. He simply seemed to have no clear boundary
lines and to be imperfectly detached from the
surrounding atmosphere. I could never understand why."

" Lack of personality," said Lamancha. " I
remember feeling that."

" Yes, but what is personality ? He had the
things that make it—brains and purpose. One
liked him—was impressed by his attainments, but,
if you understand me, one wasn't impressed by the
man. . . . It wasn't ordinary lack of confidence,
for on occasion he could be aggressive. It was the
lack of a continuity of confidence—in himself and
in other things. He didn't *believe* enough. Tha͏t

was why, as you said, he was always starting hares that he wouldn't hunt. Some excellent and unanswerable reason would occur to him why he should slack off. He was what I believe you call a good party man and always voted orthodoxly, but, after four years in the House, instead of being a leader he was rapidly becoming a mere cog in the machine. He didn't seem to be able to make himself count.

" That was his position eight years ago, and it was not far from a tragedy. He was as able as any man in the Cabinet, but he lacked the dæmonic force which even stupid people sometimes possess. I can only describe him in paradoxes. He was at once conceited and shy, inordinately ambitious and miserably conscious that he never got the value of his abilities out of life. . . . Then came the War."

" He served, didn't he ? " Leithen asked. " I remember running across him at G.H.Q."

" You may call it serving, if you mean that he was never out of uniform for four years. But he didn't fight. I wanted him to. I thought a line battalion might make a man of him, but he shrank from the notion. It wasn't lack of courage—I satisfied myself of that. But he hadn't the nerve to sink himself into the ranks of ordinary men. You understand why ? It would have meant the realization of what was the inmost fear of his heart. He had to keep up the delusion that he was some sort of a swell—had to have authority to buttress his tottering vanity.

" So he had a selection of footling staff jobs—
liaison with this and that, deputy-assistant to Tom,
Dick, and Harry, quite futile, but able to command
special passes and staff cars. He ranked, I think,
as a full colonel, but an Army Service Corps private
was more useful than ten of him. And he was as
miserable as a man could be. He liked people to
think that his trouble was the strain of the War, but
the real strain was that there was no strain. He
knew that he simply didn't matter. At least he
was candid with himself, and he was sometimes
candid with me. He rather hoped, I think, that
I would inspan him into something worth doing,
but in common honesty I couldn't, for you see I
too had come to disbelieve in him utterly.

" Well, that went on till March 1918, when his
brother Reggie was killed in the German push.
Ninth Division, wasn't it ? "

Palliser-Yeates nodded. " Ninth. South African Brigade. He went down at Marrières Wood,
but he and his lot stuck up the enemy for the best
part of a Sunday, and, I solemnly believe, saved our
whole front. They were at the critical point, you
see, the junction of Gough and Byng. His body
was never found."

" I know," said Sir Arthur, " and that is just the
point of my story."

He stopped. " I suppose I'm right to tell you
this. He left instructions that if anything happened to him I was to have his diary. He can't
have meant me to keep it secret. . . . No, I think
he would have liked one or two people to know."

He looked towards Palliser-Yeates. "You knew Reggie Souldern? How would you describe him?"

"The very best stamp of British regimental officer," was the emphatic reply.

"Clever?"

"Not a bit. Only average brains, but every ounce of them useful. Always cheery and competent, and a born leader of men. He was due for a brigade when he fell, and if the War had lasted another couple of years he might have had a corps. I never met the other Souldern, but from what you say he must have been the plumb opposite of Reggie."

"Just so. George had a great opinion of his brother—in addition to the ordinary brotherly love, for there were only the two of them. I thought the news of his death would break him altogether. But it didn't. He took it with extraordinary calm, and presently it looked as if he were actually more cheerful. . . . You see, they never found the body. He never saw him lying dead, or even the grave where he was buried, and he never met anybody who had. Reggie had been translated mysteriously out of the world, but the melancholy indisputable signs of death were lacking."

"You mean he thought he was only missing and might turn up some day?"

"No. He *knew* he was dead—the proof was too strong, the presumption was too heavy. . . . But while there was enough to convince his reason, there was too little for his imagination—no white face and stiff body, no wooden cross in the ceme-

tery.   He could *picture* him as still alive, and George
had a queer sensitive imagination about which most
people knew nothing."

Sir Arthur looked round the table and saw that
we were puzzled.

" It is a little difficult to explain. . . . Do you
remember a story of the French at Verdun making
an attack over ground they had been fighting on for
months ?   They shouted ' En avant, les morts,' and
they believed that the spirits of the dead responded
and redressed the balance.   I think it was the last
action at Vaux. . . . I don't suppose the *poilu*
thought the dead came back to help him, but he
pretended they were still combatants, and got a
moral support from the fancy. . . . That was
something like George Souldern's case.   If you had
asked him, you would have found that he had
no doubt that what was left of Reggie was somewhere in the churned-up wilderness north of Pér-
onne.   And there was never any nonsense about
visitations or messages from the dead. . . . But
the lack of *visible* proofs enabled his imagination
to picture Reggie as still alive, and going from
strength to strength.   He nursed the fancy till it
became as real to him as anything in his ordinary
life. . . . Reggie was becoming a great man and
would soon be the most famous man in the world,
and something of Reggie went into him and he
shared in Reggie's glory.   In March '18 a part-
nership began for George Souldern with his dead
brother, and the dead, who in his imagination was
alive and triumphant, lifted him out of the sticky

furrow which he had been ploughing since he left Oxford."

We were all silent except Pugh, who said that he had come across the same thing in the East—some Rajput prince, I think.

"How did you know this?" Lamancha asked.

"From the diary. George set down very fully every stage of his new career. But I very nearly guessed the truth for myself. You see, knowing him as I did, I had to admit a sudden and staggering change."

"How soon?"

"The week after the news came. I had been in Paris, and on my return ran across George in the Travellers' and said the ordinary banal words of sympathy. He looked at me queerly as he thanked me, and if I had not known how deeply attached the brothers were, I would have said that he was exhilarated by his loss. It was almost as if he had been given a drug to strengthen his arteries. He seemed to me suddenly a more substantial fellow, calmer, more at peace with himself. He said an odd thing too. 'Old Reggie has got his chance,' he said; and then, as if pulling himself up, 'I mean, he had the chance he wanted.'

"In June it was clear that something had happened to George Souldern. Do you remember how about that time a wave of dejection passed over all the Allied countries? It was partly the mess in Russia, partly in this country a slight loss of confidence in the Government, which seemed to have got to loggerheads with the soldiers, but mainly the ' drag ' that comes in all wars. It was the same in the American Civil War before Gettysburg. Foch was marking time, but he was doing it by retreating pretty fast on the Aisne. Well, our people needed a little cheering up, and our politicians tried their hand at it. There was a debate in Parliament, and far the best speech was George's. The rest were mere platitude and rhetoric, but he came down to the point like a steam-hammer."

" I know," said Lamancha. " I read it in the *Times* in a field hospital in Palestine."

" In his old days nobody would have paid much attention. He would have been clever and epigrammatic—sound enough, but ' precious.' His speech would have read well, if it had been reported, but it wouldn't have mattered a penn'orth to anybody. . . . Instead he said just the wise, simple, stalwart thing that every honest man had at the back of his head, and he said it with an air which made everybody sit up. For the first time in his life he spoke as one having authority. The press reported him nearly verbatim, for the journalists in the Gallery have a very acute sense of popular values.

" The speech put George, as the phrase goes, on the political map. The Prime Minister spoke to me about him, and there was some talk of employing him on a mission which never materialized. I met him one day in the street and congratulated him, and I remember that I was struck by the new vigour in his personality. He made me come home with him to tea, and to talk to him was like breathing ozone. He asked me one or two questions about numbers, and then he gave me his views on the War. At the time it was fashionable to think that no decision could be reached till the next summer, but George maintained that, if we played our cards right, victory was a mathematical certainty before Christmas. He showed a knowledge of the military situation which would have done credit to any soldier, and he could express himself, which few soldiers can do. His arguments stuck in my head, and I believe I used them in the War Cabinet. I left with a very real respect for one whom I had written off as a failure.

" Well, then came the last battle of the Marne, and Haig's great advance, and all the drama and confusion of the autumn months. I lost sight of George, for I was busy with the peace overtures, and I don't think I even heard of him again till the new year. . . . But the diary tells all about those months. I am giving you the bones of the story, but I am going to burn the diary, for it is too intimate for other eyes. . . . According to it Reggie finished the War as a blazing hero. It was all worked out in detail with maps and diagrams. He had become a corps commander by August, and in October he was the chief fighting figure on the British front, the conduit pipe of Foch's ideas, for he could work out in practice what the great man saw as a vision. It sounds crazy, but it was so convincingly done that I had to rub my eyes and make myself remember that Reggie was lying in a nameless grave on the Somme and not a household word in two hemispheres. . . . George, too, shared in his glory, but just how was not very clear. Anyway, the brothers were in the front of the stage, Reggie the bigger man, and George his civilian adviser and opposite number. I can see now how he got his confidence. He was no longer a struggler, but a made man ; he had arrived, he was proved, the world required him. Whatever he said or did must be attended to, and, because he believed this, it was."

Lamancha whistled long and low. " But how could his mind work, if he lived among fairy tales ? " he asked.

" He didn't," said Sir Arthur. " He lived very much in the real world. But he had all the time his private imaginative preserve, into which his normal mind did not penetrate. He drew his confidence from this preserve, and, having once got it, could carry it also into the real world."

" Wasn't he intolerably conceited ? " some one asked.

" No, for the great man was Reggie, and he was only a satellite. He was Reggie's prophet, and assured enough on that side, but there was no personal arrogance. His dead brother had become so to speak, his familiar spirit, his *dæmon*. ^de fact is that George was less of an egotist than ^had ever been before. His vanity was burne^p in a passion of service.

" I saw him frequently during the ^st half of '19, and had many talks with hi^rity, but he had been returned to Parliament by a b^didn't like the wasn't much in the public ey^

way things were going, but at the same time as a good citizen he declined to make things more difficult for the Government. The diary gives his thoughts at that time. He considered that the soldiers should have had the chief share in the settlement of the world—Foch and Haig and Hindenburg—and Reggie. He held that they would have made a cleaner and fairer job of it than the kind of circus that appeared at Versailles. Perhaps he was right—I can't be dogmatic, for I was a performer in the circus.

" That, of course, I didn't know till the other day. But the change in George Souldern was soon manifest to the whole world. There was the Irish business, when he went down to the worst parts of the South and West, and seemed to be simply asking for a bullet in his head. He was half Irish, you know. He wrote and said quite frankly that he didn't care a straw whether Ireland was inside or outside the British Empire, that the only thing which mattered was that she should find a soul, and that she had a long road to travel before she got one. He told her that at present she was one vast perambulating humbug, and that till she got a little discipline and sense of realities she would remain on the level of Hayti. Why some gunman didn't have a shot at him I can't imagine, except that such naked candour and courage was a new thing and had to be respected. . . . Then there was the Unemployment Commission. You remember the majority report—pious generalities and futile compromises. . . . 's dissenting report made him

for a month the best-abused man in Britain, for
he was impartially contemptuous of all sides.
To-day—well, I fancy most of us would agree with
George, and I observe that he is frequently quoted
by the Labour people.

" What struck me about his line of country was
that it was like that of a good soldier's. He had
the same power of seeing simple facts and of making
simple syllogisms, which the clever intellectual—
such as George used to be—invariably misses. And
there was the soldier's fidelity and sense of service.
George plainly had no axe to grind. He had intellectual courage and would back his views as a
general backs his strategy, but he kept always a
curious personal modesty. I tell you it seemed
nothing short of a miracle to one who had known
him in the old days.

" I accepted it as the act of God and didn't look
for any further explanation. I think that what
first set me questioning was his behaviour about
Reggie's memorial. The family wanted a stone put
up in the churchyard of the family place in Gloucestershire. George absolutely declined. He stuck
his toes into the ground and gave nothing but a flat
refusal. One might have thought that the brothers
had been estranged, but it was common knowledge
that they had been like twins and had written to
each other every day.

" Then there was the business about a memoir of
Reggie. The regiment wanted one, and his Staff
College contemporaries. Tollett—you remember
him, the man on the Third Army Staff—volun-

teered to write it, of course with George's assistance. George refused bluntly, and said that he felt the strongest distaste for the proposal. Tollett came to me about it, and I had George to luncheon and thrashed it out with him. I found his reasons very difficult to follow, for he objected even to a regimental history being compiled. He admitted that Tollett was as good a man as could be found for the job, but he said he hated the idea. Nobody understood Reggie but himself. Some day, he suggested, he might try to do justice to him in print—but not yet. I put forward all the arguments I could think of, but George was adamant.

" Walking home, I puzzled a good deal about the affair. It couldn't be merely the jealousy of a writer who wanted to reserve a good subject for himself—that wasn't George's character, and he had no literary vanity. Besides, that wouldn't explain his aversion to a prosaic regimental chronicle, and still less his objection to the cenotaph in the Gloucestershire churchyard. I wondered if there was not some quirk in George, some odd obsession about his brother. For a moment I thought that he might have been dabbling in spiritualism and have got some message from Reggie, till I remembered that I had heard him a week before declare his unbridled contempt for such mumbo-jumbo.

" I thought a good deal about it, and the guess I made was that George was living a double life— that in his subconsciousness Reggie was still alive for him. It was only a guess, but it was fairly near the truth, and last year I had it from his own lips.

"We were duck-shooting together on Crofts-moor, the big marsh near his home. That had been Reggie's pet game ; he used to be out at all hours in the winter dawns and dusks stalking wildfowl. George never cared for it, or indeed for any field sport. He would take his place at a covert shoot or a grouse drive and was useful enough with a gun, but he would have been the first to disclaim the title of sportsman. But now he was as keen and tireless as Reggie. He kept me out for eight hours in a filthy day of rain wading in trench boots in Gloucestershire mud.

"We did fairly well, and just before sunset the weather improved. The wind had gone into the north, and promised frost, and as we sat on an old broken-backed stone bridge over one of the dykes, waiting for the birds to be collected from the different stands, the western sky was one broad band of palest gold. We were both tired, and the sudden change from blustering rain to a cold still-ness, and from grey mist to colour and light, had a strange effect upon my spirits. I felt peaceful and solemnized. I lit a pipe, but let it go out, for my attention was held by the shoreless ocean in the west, against which the scarp of the Welsh hills showed in a dim silhouette. The sharp air, the wild marsh scents, the faint odour of tobacco awoke in me a thousand half-sad and half-sweet recollections.

"I couldn't help it. I said something about Reggie.

" George was sitting on the bridge with his eyes fixed on the sky. I thought he hadn't heard me, till suddenly he repeated ' Reggie. Yes, old Reggie.'

" ' This was what he loved,' I said.

" ' He still loves it,' was the answer, spoken very low. And then he repeated—to himself as it were :

" ' Fight on, fight on,' said Sir Andrew Barton.
   ' Though I be wounded I am not slain.
I'll lay me down and bleed awhile,
   And then I'll rise and fight again.' "

" He turned his fine-drawn face to me.

" ' You think Reggie is dead ? '

" I didn't know what to say. ' Yes,' I stammered, ' I suppose——'

" ' What do you mean by death ? ' His voice was almost shrill. ' We know nothing about it. What does it matter if the body is buried in a shell-hole——'

" He stopped suddenly, as a lamp goes out when you press the switch. I had the impression that those queer shrill words came not from George but from some other who had joined us.

" ' I believe that the spirit is immortal,' I began.

" ' The spirit——' again the shrill impersonal voice—' I tell you the whole man lives. . . . He is nearer to me than he ever was . . . we are never parted . . .'

" Again the light went out. He seemed to gulp, and when he spoke it was in his natural tones.

" ' I apologize,' he said. ' I must seem to you to be talking nonsense. . . . You don't understand. *You* would understand, if any one could, but I can't explain—yet—some day . . .'

" The head-keeper, the beaters, and the dogs came out of the reed beds, and at the same time the uncanny glow in the west was shrouded with the film of the coming night. It was almost dark when we turned to walk home, and I was glad of it, for neither of us wished to look at the other's face.

" I felt at once embarrassed and enlightened. I had been given a glimpse into the cloudy places of a man's soul, and had surprised his secret. My guess had been right. In George's subconscious mind Reggie was still alive—nay more, was progressing in achievement as if he had never disappeared in the March battle. It was no question of a disembodied spirit establishing communication with the living—that was a business I knew nothing about, nor George either. It was a question of life, complete life, in a peculiar world, companionship in some spiritual fourth dimension, and from that companionship he was drawing sustenance. He had learned Reggie's forthrightness and his happy simplicity. . . . I wondered and I trembled. There is a story of an early Victorian statesman who in his leisure moments played at being Emperor of Byzantium. The old Whig kept the two things strictly separate—he was a pious humanitarian in his English life, though he was a ruthless conqueror in the other. But in George's case the two were mingling. He was going about his daily duties with the power acquired from his secret world; that secret world, in which, with Reggie, he had become a master, was giving him a mastery over our common life. . . . I did not believe it would last. It was against nature that a man could continue to live as a parasite on the dead.

"I am almost at the end of my story. Two months later, George became a figure of national importance. It was he who chiefly broke up the Coalition at the Grafton House meeting, and thereby, I suppose, saved his party. His speech, you remember, clove through subtleties and irrelevances with the simple declaration that he could not work with what he could not trust, and, unless things changed, must go out of public life. That was Reggie's manner, you know—pure Reggie. Then came the General Election and the new Government, and George, very much to people's surprise, refused Cabinet office. The reason he gave was that on grounds of principle he had taken a chief part in wrecking the late Ministry, and he felt he could not allow himself to benefit personally by his action. We all thought him high-minded, if finical and quixotic, but the ordinary man liked it—it was a welcome change from the old gang of *arrivistes*. But it was not the real reason. I found that in the diary."

Sir Arthur stopped, and there was a silence while he seemed to be fumbling for words.

"Here we are walking on the edge of great mysteries," he continued. "The reason why he refused the Prime Minister's offer was Reggie. . . .

Somehow the vital force in that subconscious world
of his was ebbing. . . . I cannot explain how, but
Reggie was moving away from what we call realities
and was beckoning him to follow. . . . The Grafton House speech was George's last public utter-
ance. Few people saw him after that, for he rarely
attended the House. I saw him several times
in Gloucestershire. . . . Was he happy ? Yes, I
should say utterly happy, but too detached, too
peaceful, as if he had done with the cares of the
world. . . . I think I guessed what was happening,
when he told me that he had consented to the
cenotaph in the churchyard. He took a good deal
of pains about it, too, and choose an inscription,
which his maiden aunts thought irreligious. It was
Virgil's ' *Tendebant manus ripæ ulterioris amore.*'
. . . He withdrew his objection to the memoir too,
and Tollett got to work, but he gave him no help
—it was as if he had lost interest. . . . It is an odd
thing to say, but I have been waiting for the news
which was in last week's paper."

" You don't mean that he engineered the motor
smash ? " Lamancha asked.

" Oh no," said Sir Arthur gently. " As I said,
we are treading on the brink of great mysteries.
Say that it was predestined, fore-ordained, decreed
by the Master of Assembly. . . . I know that it had
to be. If you join hands with the dead they will
pull you over the stream."

XI. THE LAST CRUSADE

FRANCIS MARTENDALE'S STORY

It is often impossible, in these political inquiries, to find any proportion between the apparent force of any moral causes we may assign, and their known operation. We are therefore obliged to deliver up that operation to mere chance; or, more piously (perhaps more rationally), to the occasional interposition and the irresistible hand of the Great Disposer.

BURKE.

XI. THE LAST CRUSADE

ONE evening the talk at dinner turned on the Press. Lamancha was of opinion that the performances of certain popular newspapers in recent years had killed the old power of the anonymous printed word. "They bluffed too high," he said, "and they had their bluff called. All the Delphic oracle business has gone from them. You haven't to-day what you used to have—papers from which the ordinary man docilely imbibes all his views. There may be one or two still, but not more."

Sandy Arbuthnot, who disliked journalism as much as he liked journalists, agreed, but there was a good deal of difference of opinion among the others. Palliser-Yeates thought that the Press had more influence than ever, though it might not be much liked ; a man, he said, no longer felt the kind of loyalty towards his newspaper that he felt towards his club and his special brand of cigar, but he was mightily influenced by it all the same. He might read it only for its news, but in the selection of news a paper could wield an uncanny power.

Francis Martendale was the only journalist among us, and he listened with half-closed sleepy eyes. He had been a war correspondent as far back as the days of the South African War, and since then had seen every serious row on the face of the globe. In France he had risen to command a territorial battalion, and that seemed to have satisfied his military interest, for since 1919 he had turned his mind to business. He was part-owner of several provincial papers, and was connected in some way with the great Ladas news agency. He had several characters which he kept rigidly separate. One was a philosopher, for he had translated Henri Poincaré, and published an acute little study of Bergson; another was a yachtsman, and he used to race regularly in the twelve-metre class at Cowes. But these were his relaxations, and five days of the week he spent in an office in the Fleet Street neighbourhood. He was an enthusiast about his hobbies and a cynic about his profession, a not uncommon mixture; so we were surprised when he differed from Lamancha and Sandy and agreed with Palliser-Yeates.

"No doubt the power of the leader-writer has waned," he said. "A paper cannot set a Cabinet trembling because it doesn't like its policy. But it can colour the public mind most damnably by a steady drip of tendencious news."

"Lies?" Sandy asked.

"Not lies—truths judiciously selected—half-truths with no context. Facts—facts all the time. In these days the Press is obliged to stick to facts. But it can make facts into *news*, which is a very different class of goods. And it can interpret facts—don't forget that. It can report that Burminster fell asleep at a public dinner—which he did—in such a way as to make everybody think that he was drunk—which he wasn't."

" Rather a dirty game ? " some one put in.

"Sometimes—often perhaps. But now and then it works out on the side of the angels. Do any of you know Roper Willinck ? "

There was a general confession of ignorance.

" Pity. He would scarcely fit in here, but he is rather a great man and superbly good company. There was a little thing that Willinck once did— or rather helped to do, with about a million other people who hadn't a notion what was happening. That's the fun of journalism. You light a match and fling it away, and the fire goes smouldering round the globe, and ten thousand miles off burns down a city. I'll tell you about it if you like, for it rather proves my point."

It all began—said Martendale—with an old Wesleyan parson of the name of Tubb, who lived at a place called Rhenosterspruit on the east side of the Karroo. He had been a missionary, but the place had grown from a small native reserve to an ordinary up-country dorp ; the natives were all Christians now, and he had a congregation of store-keepers, and one or two English farmers, and the landlady of the hotel, and the workmen from an adjacent irrigation dam. Mr. Tubb was a man of over seventy, a devoted pastor with a gift of revivalist eloquence, but not generally considered very strong in the head. He was also a bachelor. He had caught a chill and had been a week in bed, but he rose on the Sunday morning to conduct service as usual.

Now about that time the Russian Government had been rather distinguishing themselves. They had had a great function at Easter, run by what they called the Living Church, which had taken the shape of a blasphemous parody of the Christian rites and a procession of howling dervishes who proclaimed that God was dead and Heaven and Hell wound up. Also they had got hold of a Patriarch, a most respected Patriarch, put him on trial for high treason, and condemned him to death. They had postponed the execution, partly by way of a refinement of cruelty, and partly, I suppose, to see just how the world would react; but there seemed not the slightest reason to doubt that they meant to have the old man's blood. There was a great outcry, and the Archbishop of Canterbury and the Pope had something to say, and various Governments made official representations, but the Bolshies didn't give a hoot. They felt that they needed to indulge in some little bit of extra blackguardism just to show what stout fellows they were.

Well, all this was in the cables from Riga and Warsaw and Helsingfors, and it got into the weekly edition of the *Cape Times*. There Mr. Tubb read it, as he lay sick in bed, and, having nothing else to worry about, it fretted him terribly. He could not bear to think of those obscene orgies in Moscow, and the story of the Patriarch made him frantic. This, it seemed to him, was a worse persecution than Nero's or Diocletian's, and the Patriarch was a nobler figure than any martyr of the Roman amphitheatre; and all the while the Christian peoples of the world were doing nothing. So Mr. Tubb got out of bed on that Sunday morning, and, having had no time to prepare a sermon, delivered his soul from the pulpit about the Bolshies and their doings. He said that what was needed was a new crusade, and he called on every Christian man and woman to devote their prayers, their money, and, if necessary, their blood to this supreme cause. Old as he was, he said, he would gladly set off for Moscow that instant and die beside the Patriarch, and count his life well lost in such a testimony of his faith.

I am sure that Mr. Tubb meant every word he said, but he had an unsympathetic audience, who were not interested in Patriarchs; and the hotel-lady slumbered, and the store-keepers fidgeted, and the girls giggled and whispered just as usual. There the matter would have dropped, had not a young journalist from Cape Town been spending his holidays at Rhenosterspruit and out of some caprice been present at the service. He was an ambitious lad, and next morning dispatched to his paper a brightly written account of Mr. Tubb's challenge. He wrote it with his tongue in his cheek, and headed it, "Peter the Hermit at Rhenosterspruit," with, as a sub-title, "The Last

Crusade." His editor cut it savagely, and left out all his satirical touches, so that it read rather bald and crude. Still, it got about a quarter of a column.

That week the Ladas representative at Cape Town was rather short of material, and just to fill up his budget of outgoing news put in a short message about Rhenosterspruit. It ran: "On Sunday Tubb Wesleyan minister Rhenosterspruit summoned congregation name Christianity release Patriarch announced intention personally lead crusade Moscow." That was the result of the cutting of the bright young correspondent's article. What he had meant as fantasy and farce was so summarized as to appear naked fact. Ladas in London were none too well pleased with the message. They did not issue it to the British Press, and they cabled to their Cape Town people that, while they welcomed "human interest" stories, they drew the line at that sort of thing. What could it matter to the world what a Wesleyan parson in the Karroo thought about Zinovieff? They wanted news, not nonsense.

Now behold the mysterious workings of the Comic Spirit. Ladas, besides their general service to the Canadian Press, made special services to several Canadian papers. One of these was called, shall we say, the *Toronto Watchman*. The member of the Ladas staff who had the compiling of the *Watchman* budget was often hard pressed, for he had to send news which was not included in the general service. That week he was peculiarly up against it, so he went through the files of the messages that had come in lately and had not already been transmitted to Canada, and in the Cape Town section he found the Rhenosterspruit yarn. He seized on it joyfully, for he did not know of the disfavour with which his chief had regarded it, and he dressed it up nicely for Toronto. The *Watchman*, he knew, was a family paper, with a strong religious connection, and this would be meat and drink to it. So he made the story still more matter-of-fact. Mr. Tubb had sounded a call to the Christian Church, and was himself on the eve of setting out against Trotsky like David against Goliath. He left the captions to the Toronto sub-editors, but of his own initiative he mentioned John Knox. That, he reflected comfortably, as he closed up and went off to play golf, would fetch the Presbyterian-minded *Watchman*.

It did. The editor of the *Watchman*, who was an elder of the Kirk and a Liberal Member of Parliament, had been getting very anxious about the ongoings in Russia. He was not very clear what a Patriarch was, but he remembered that various Anglican ecclesiastics had wanted to affiliate the English and Greek Churches, so he concluded that he was some kind of Protestant. He had, like most people, an intense dislike of Moscow and its ways, and he had been deeply shocked by the Easter sacrilege. So he went large on the Ladas message. It was displayed on his chief page, side by side with all the news he could collect about the Patriarch, and he had no less than two leaders on the subject.

The first, which he wrote himself, was headed "The Weak Things of the World and the Strong." He said that Mr. Tubb's clarion-call, "the voice of a simple man of God echoing from the lonely veld," might yet prove a turning-point in history, and he quoted Burke about a child and a girl at an inn changing the fate of nations. It might—it should —arouse the conscience of the Christian world, and inaugurate a new crusade, which would lift mankind out of the rut of materialism and open its eyes to the eternal verities. Christianity had been challenged by the miscreants in Russia, and the challenge must be met. I don't think he had any very clear idea what he meant, for he was strongly opposed to anything that suggested war, but it was a fine chance for "uplift" writing. The second leader was called "The Deeper Obligations of Empire," and, with a side glance at Mr. Tubb, declared that unless the British Empire was a spiritual and moral unity it was not worth talking about.

The rest of the Canadian Press did not touch the subject. They had not had the Rhenosterspruit message, and were not going to lift it. But the *Watchman* had a big circulation, and Mr. Tubb began to have a high, if strictly local, repute. Several prominent clergymen preached sermons on him, and a weekly paper printed a poem in which he was compared to St. Theresa and Joan of Arc.

The thing would have been forgotten in a fort-night, if McGurks had not chosen to take a hand. McGurks, as you probably know, is the biggest newspaper property in the world directed by a single hand. It owns outright well over a hundred papers, and has a controlling interest in perhaps a thousand. Its tone is strictly national, not to say chauvinistic ; its young men in Europe at that time were all hundred-per-cent. Americans, and returned to the States a hundred and twenty per cent., to allow for the difference in the exchange. McGurks does not love England, for it began with strong Irish connections, and it has done good work in pointing out to its immense public the predatory character of British Imperialism and the atrocities that fill the shining hours in India and Egypt. As a matter of fact, however, its politics are not very serious. What it likes is a story that can be told in thick black headlines, so that the stupidest of its free-born readers, glancing in his shirt-sleeves at the first page of his Sunday paper, can extract nourishment. Murders, rapes, fires, and drownings are its daily bread, and it fairly revels in details—measurements and plans, names and addresses of witnesses, and appalling half-tone blocks. Most unfairly it is called sensational, for the stuff is as dull as a directory.

With regard to Russia, McGurks had steered a wavy course. It had begun in 1917 by flaunting the banner of freedom, for it disliked all monarchies on principle. In 1919 it wanted America to recognize the Russian Government, and take hold of Russian trade. But a series of rebuffs to its special correspondents changed its view, and by 1922 it had made a speciality of Bolshevik horrors.

The year 1923 saw it again on the fence, from which in six months it had tumbled off in a state of anti-Bolshevik hysteria. It was out now to save God's country from foreign microbes, and it ran a good special line of experts who proved that what America needed was a *cordon sanitaire* to protect her purity from a diseased world. At the time of which I speak it had worked itself up into a fine religious enthusiasm. and had pretty well captured the " hick " public. McGurks was first and foremost a business proposition, and it had decided that crime and piety were the horses to back. I should add that, besides its papers, it ran a news agency, the P.U., which stood for Press Union, but which was commonly and affectionately known as Punk.

McGurks seized upon the story in the *Toronto Watchman* as a gift from the gods, and its headlines were a joy for ever. All over the States men read " Aged Saint Defies Demoniacs—Says That In God's Name He Will Move Mountains "—" Vengeance From The Veld "—" The First Trumpet Blast "—" Who Is On The Lord's Side—W H O ? " I daresay that in the East and beyond the Rockies people were only mildly interested, but in the Middle West and in the South the thing caught like measles. McGurks did not leave its stunts to perish of inanition. As soon as it saw that the public was intrigued it started out to organize that interest. It circularized every parson over big areas, it arranged meetings of protest and sympathy, it opened subscription lists, and, though it refrained from suggesting Government action, it made it clear that it wanted to create such a popular feeling that the Government would be bound to bestir itself. The home towns caught fire, the Bible Belt was moved to its foundations, every Methodist minister rallied to his co-religionist of Rhenosterspruit, the Sunday Schools uplifted their voice, and even the red-blooded he-men of the Rotary Clubs got going. The Holiness Tabernacle of Sarcophagus, Neb., produced twenty volunteers who were ready to join Mr. Tubb in Moscow, and the women started knitting socks for them, just as they did in the War. The First Consecration Church of Jumpersville, Tenn., followed suit, and McGurks made the most of the doings of every chapel in every one-horse township. Punk, too, was busy, and cabled wonderful stories of the new crusade up and down the earth. Old-established papers did not as a rule take the Punk service, so only a part of it was printed, but it all helped to create an atmosphere.

Presently Concord had to take notice. This, as you know, is the foremost American press agency—we call it the C.C.—and it had no more dealings with Punk than the Jews with the Samaritans. It was in close alliance with Ladas, so it cabled testily wanting to know why it had not received the Rhenosterspruit message. Ladas replied that they had considered the story too absurd to waste tolls on; but, since the C.C. was now carrying a lot of stuff about the new crusade, they felt obliged to cable to Cape Town to clear things up. Punk had

already got on to that job, and was asking its
correspondents for pictures of Rhenosterspruit,
interviews with the Reverend Tubb, details about
what he wore and ate and drank, news of his mother
and his childhood, and his premonitions of future
greatness.   Half a dozen anxious journalists con-
verged upon Rhenosterspruit.

But they were too late.   For Mr. Tubb was dead
—choked on a chicken-bone at his last Sunday
dinner. They were only in time to attend the
funeral in the little, dusty, sun-baked cemetery.
Very little was to be had from his congregation,
which, as I have said, had been mostly asleep
during the famous sermon ; but a store-keeper
remembered that the minister had not been quite
like himself on that occasion, and that he had
judged from his eyes that he had still a bad cold.
McGurks made a great fuss with this scrap of news.
The death of Mr. Tubb was featured like the demise
of a President or a film star, and there was a
moving picture of the old man, conscious that he
was near his end (the chicken-bone was never mentioned), summoning his failing strength to one
supreme appeal—" his eyes," said McGurks, " now
wet with tears for the world's sins, now shining
with the reflected radiance of the Better Country."

I fancy that the thing would have suddenly died
away, for there was a big prize-fight coming on, and
there seemed to be a risk of the acquittal of a nigger
who had knifed a bootlegger in Chicago, and an
Anti-Kink Queen was on the point of engaging
herself to a Dentifrice King, and similar stirring

public events were in the offing. But the death of
Mr. Tubb kept up the excitement, for it brought in
the big guns of the Fundamentalists. It seemed to
them that the old man had not died, but had been
miraculously translated, just like Elijah or William
Jennings Bryan after the Dayton trial. It was a
Sign, and they were bound to consider what it
signified.

This was much heavier metal than the faithful of
Sarcophagus and Jumpersville. The agitation was
now of national importance ; it had attained
" normalcy," as you might say, the " normalcy "
of the periodic American movement. Conventions
were summoned and addressed by divines whose
names were known even in New York. Senators
and congressmen took a hand, and J. Constantine
Buttrick, the silver trumpet of Wisconsin, gave
tongue, and was heard by several million wireless
outfits. Articles even appeared about it in the
intellectual weeklies. Congress wasn't in session,
which was fortunate, but Washington began to
be uneasy, for volunteers for the crusade were
enrolling fast. C.C. was compelled to carry long
dispatches, and Ladas had to issue them to the
English Press, which usually printed them in obscure corners with the names misspelt. England
is always apathetic about American news, and,
besides, she had a big strike on her hands at the
time. Those of us who get American press-
clippings realized that quite a drive was starting
to do something to make Moscow respectful to
religion, but we believed that it would be dropped

before any serious action could be taken. Meanwhile Zinovieff and Trotsky carried on as usual, and we expected any day to hear that the Patriarch had been shot and buried in the prison yard.

Suddenly Fate sent Roper Willinck mooning round to my office. I suppose Willinck is the least known of our great men, for you fellows have never even heard his name. But he *is* a great man in his queer way, and I believe his voice carries farther than any living journalist's, though most people do not know who is speaking. He doesn't write much in the Press here, only now and then a paper in the heavy monthlies; but he is the prince of special correspondents, and his " London Letters " in every known tongue are printed from Auckland to Seattle. He seems to have found the common denominator of style which is calculated to interest the whole human family. On the Continent he is the only English journalist whose name is known to the ordinary reader—rather like Maximilian Harden before the War. In America they reckon him a sort of Pope, and his stuff is syndicated in all the country papers. His enthusiasms make a funny hotch-potch—the League of Nations and the British Empire, racial purism and a sentimental socialism; but he is a devout Catholic, and Russia had become altogether too much for him. That was why I thought he would be interested in McGurks' stunt, of which he had scarcely heard; so he sat down in an armchair and, during the consumption of five caporal cigarettes, studied my clippings.

I have never seen a man so roused. "I see light," he cried, pushing his double glasses up on his forehead. "Martendale, this is a revelation. Out of the mouths of babes and sucklings. . . . Master Ridley, Master Ridley, we shall this day kindle a fire which will never be extinguished. . . ."

"Nonsense," I said. "The thing will fizzle out in a solemn protest from Washington to Moscow, with which old Trotsky will light his pipe. It has got into the hands of the highbrows, and in a week will be clothed in the jargon of the State Department, and the home towns will wonder what has been biting them."

"We must retrieve it," he said softly. "Get it back to the village green and the prayer-meeting. It was the prayer-meeting, remember, which brought America into the War."

"But how ? McGurks has worked that beat to death."

"McGurks ! " he cried contemptuously. "The time is past for slobber, my son. What they want is the prophetic, the apocalyptic, and by the bones of Habakkuk they shall have it. I am going to solemnize the remotest parts of the great Republic, and then," he smiled serenely, "I shall interpret that solemnity to the world. First the fact and then the moral—that's the lay-out."

He stuffed my clippings into his pocket and took himself off, and there was that in his eye which foreboded trouble. Some one was going to have to sit up when Willinck looked like that. My hope was that it would be Moscow, but the time was

getting terribly short. Any day might bring the
news that the Patriarch had gone to his reward.

I heard nothing for several weeks, and then Punk
suddenly became active, and carried some extraordinary stuff. It was mostly extracts from
respectable papers in the Middle West and the
South, reports of meetings which seemed to have
worked themselves into hysteria, and rumours of
secret gatherings of young men which suggested
the Ku-Klux-Klan. Moscow had a Press agency
of its own in London, and it began to worry Ladas
for more American news. Ladas in turn worried
C.C., but C.C. was reticent. There was a Movement, we were told, but the Government had it
well in hand, and we might disregard the scare
stuff Punk was sending ; everything that was important and reliable would be in its own service.
I thought I detected Willinck somewhere behind
the scenes, and tried to get hold of him, but learned
that he was out of town.

One afternoon, however, he dropped in, and I
noticed that his high-boned face was leaner than
ever, but that his cavernous eyes were happy.
" ' The good work goes cannily on,' " he said—he
was always quoting—and he flung at me a bundle
of green clippings.

They were articles of his own in the American
Press, chiefly the Sunday editions, and I noticed
that he had selected the really influential country
papers—one in Tennessee, one in Kentucky, and
a batch from the Corn States.

I was staggered by the power of his stuff—Wil-

linck had never to my knowledge written like this
before. He didn't rave about Bolshevik crimes—
people were sick of that—and he didn't bang the
religious drum or thump the harmonium. McGurks
had already done that to satiety. He quickly took
it for granted that the crusade had begun, and that
plain men all over the earth, who weren't looking
for trouble, felt obliged to start out and abolish
an infamy or never sleep peacefully in their beds
again. He assumed that presently from all corners of the Christian world there would be an
invading army moving towards Moscow, a thing
that Governments could not check, a people's
rising as irresistible as the change of the seasons.
Assuming this, he told them just exactly what
they would see.

I can't do justice to Willinck by merely describ-
ing these articles ; I ought to have them here to
read to you. Noble English they were, and as
simple as the Psalms. . . . He pictured the constitution of the army, every kind of tongue and
dialect and class, with the same kind of discipline
as Cromwell's New Model—Ironsides every one
of them, rational, moderate-minded fanatics, the
most dangerous kind. It was like *Paradise Lost*
—Michael going out against Belial. . . . And then
the description of Russia—a wide grey world, all
pale colours and watery lights, broken villages,
tattered little towns ruled by a few miscreants with
rifles, railway tracks red with rust, ruinous great
palaces plastered over with obscene posters, starv-
ing hopeless people, children with old vicious faces.

. . . God knows where he got the stuff from—
mainly his *macabre* imagination, but I daresay
there was a lot of truth in the details, for he had
his own ways of acquiring knowledge.

But the end was the masterpiece. He said that
the true rulers were not those whose names appeared
in the papers, but one or two secret madmen who
sat behind the screen and spun their bloody webs.
He described the crusaders breaking through shell
after shell, like one of those Chinese boxes which
you open only to find another inside till you end
with a thing like a pea. There were layers of Jew
officials and Lett mercenaries and camouflaging
journalists, and always as you went deeper the
thing became more inhuman and the air more fetid.
At the end you had the demented Mongol—that was
a good touch for the Middle West—the incarnation
of the back-world of the Orient. Willinck only
hinted at this ultimate camarilla, but his hints were
gruesome. To one of them he gave the name of
Uriel—a kind of worm-eaten archangel of the Pit,
but the worst he called Glubet. He must have got
the word out of a passage in Catullus which is not
read in schools, and he made a shuddering thing of
it—the rancid toad-man, living among half-lights
and blood, adroit and sleepless as sin, but cracking
now and then into idiot laughter.

You may imagine how this took hold of the Bible
Belt. I never made out what exactly happened,
but I have no doubt that there were the rudiments
of one of those mass movements, before which
Governments and newspapers, combines and Press

agencies, Wall Street and Lombard Street, and
common prudence are helpless. You could see it
in the messages C.C. sent and its agitated service
cables to its people. The Moscow Agency sat on
our doorstep and bleated for more news, and all
the while Punk was ladling out fire-water to every
paper that would take it.

"So much for the facts," Willinck said calmly.
"Now I proceed to point the moral in the proper
quarters!"

If he was good at kindling a fire he was better at
explaining just how hot it was and how fast it
would spread. I have told you that he was about
the only English journalist with a Continental
reputation. Well, he proceeded to exploit that
reputation in selected papers which he knew would
cross the Russian frontier. He was busy in the
Finnish and Latvian and Lithuanian Press, he
appeared in the chief Polish daily, and in Germany
his stuff was printed in one big Berlin paper and
—curiously enough—in the whole financial chain.
Willinck knew just how and where to strike. The
line he took was very simple. He quietly explained
what was happening in America and the British
Dominions—that the outraged conscience of Chris-
tendom had awakened among simple folk, and that
nothing on earth could hold it. It was a Puritan
crusade, the most deadly kind. From every corner
of the globe believers were about to assemble,
ready to sacrifice themselves to root out an infamy.
This was none of your Denikins and Koltchaks and
Czarist émigré affairs; it was the world's Christian

democracy, and a business democracy. No flag-waving or shouting, just a cold steady determination to get the job done, with ample money and men and an utter carelessness of what they spent on both. Cautious Governments might try to obstruct, but the people would compel them to toe the line. It was a militant League of Nations, with the Bible in one hand and the latest brand of munition in the other.

We had a feverish time at Ladas in those days. The British Press was too much occupied with the strike to pay full attention, but the Press of every other country was on its hind legs. Presently things began to happen. The extracts from *Pravda* and *Izvestia*, which we got from Riga and Warsaw, became every day more like the howling of epileptic wolves. Then came the news that Moscow had ordered a very substantial addition to the Red Army. I telephoned this item to Willinck, and he came round to see me.

"The wind is rising," he said. "The fear of the Lord is descending on the tribes, and that we know is the beginning of wisdom."

I observed that Moscow had certainly got the wind up, but that I didn't see why. "You don't mean to say that you have got them to believe in your precious crusade?"

He nodded cheerfully. "Why not? My dear Martendale, you haven't studied the mentality of those gentry as I have. Do you realize that the favourite reading of the Russian peasant used to be Milton? Before the War you could buy a

translation of *Paradise Lost* at every book kiosk
in every country fair. Those rootless intellectuals
have cast off all they could, but at the back of their
heads the peasant superstition remains. They are
afraid in their bones of a spirit that they think is in
Puritanism. That's why this American business
worries them so. They think they are a match for
Rome, and they wouldn't have minded if the racket
had been started by the Knights of Columbus or
that kind of show. But they think it comes from
the meeting-house, and that scares them cold."

"Hang it all," I said, "they must know the soft
thing modern Puritanism is—all slushy hymns and
inspirational advertising."

"Happily they don't. And I'm not sure that
their ignorance is not wiser than your knowledge,
my emancipated friend. I'm inclined to think that
something may yet come out of the Bible Christian that will surprise the world. . . . But not this
time. I fancy the trick has been done. You
might let me know as soon as you hear anything."
And he moved off, whistling contentedly through
his teeth.

He was right. Three days later we got the news
from Warsaw, and the Moscow Agency confirmed
it. The Patriarch had been released and sent
across the frontier, and was now being coddled and
fêted in Poland. I rang up Willinck, and listened
to his modest *Nunc dimittis* over the telephone.

He said he was going to take a holiday and go
into the country to sleep. He pointed out for my

edification that the weak things of the world—
meaning himself—could still confound the strong,
and he advised me to reconsider the foundations of
my creed in the light of this surprising miracle.

Well, that is my story. We heard no more of
the crusade in America, except that the Fundamentalists seemed to have got a second wind
from it and started a large-scale heresy hunt.
Several English bishops said that the release of the
Patriarch was an answer to prayer ; our Press
pointed out how civilization, if it spoke with one
voice, would be listened to even in Russia ; and
Labour papers took occasion to enlarge on the
fundamental reasonableness and urbanity of the
Moscow Government.

Personally I think that Willinck drew the right
moral. But the main credit really belonged to
something a great deal weaker than he—the aged
Tubb, now sleeping under a painted cast-iron grave-
stone among the dust-devils and meerkats of
Rhenosterspruit.

XII. FULLCIRCLE

MARTIN PECKWETHER'S STORY

Between the Windrush and the Colne
I found a little house of stone—
A little wicked house of stone.

XII. FULLCIRCLE

PECKWETHER, the historian, whose turn for story-telling came at our last dinner before the summer interregnum, apologized for reading his narrative. He was not good, he said, at impromptu composition. He also congratulated himself on Leithen's absence. "He comes into the story, and I should feel rather embarrassed talking about him to his face. But he has read my manuscript and approved it, so you have two reliable witnesses to a queerish tale."

In his precise academic voice he read what follows.

The October day was brightening towards late afternoon when Leithen and I climbed the hill above the stream and came in sight of the house. All morning a haze with a sheen of pearl in it had lain on the folds of downland, and the vision of far horizons, which is the glory of Cotswold, had been veiled, so that every valley seemed a place enclosed and set apart. But now a glow had come into the air, and for a little the autumn lawns had the tints of summer. The gold of sunshine was warm on the grasses, and only the riot of colour in the berry-laden edges of the fields and the slender woodlands told of the failing year.

We were looking into a green cup of the hills, and it was all a garden. A little place, bounded by slopes that defined its graciousness with no hint of barrier, so that a dweller there, though his view was but half a mile on any side, would yet have the sense of dwelling on uplands and commanding the world. Round the top edge ran an old wall of stones, beyond which the October bracken flamed to the skyline. Inside were folds of ancient pasture with here and there a thorn-bush, falling to rose gardens, and, on one side, to the smooth sward of a terrace above a tiny lake. At the heart of it stood the house, like a jewel well set. It was a miniature, but by the hand of a master. The style was late seventeenth century, when an agreeable classic convention had opened up to sunlight and comfort the dark magnificence of the Tudor fashion. The place had the spacious air of a great mansion, and was finished in every detail with a fine scrupulousness. Only when the eye measured its proportions with the woods and the hillside did the mind perceive that it was a small dwelling. The stone of Cotswold takes curiously the colour of the weather. Under thunder-clouds it will be as dark as basalt ; on a grey day it is grey like lava ; but in sunshine it absorbs the sun. At the moment the little house was pale gold, like honey.

Leithen swung a long leg across the stile.

"Pretty good, isn't it ?" he said. "It's pure authentic Sir Christopher Wren. The name is worthy of it, too. It is called Fullcircle."

He told me its story. It had been built after the

Restoration by the Carteron family, whose wide domains ran into these hills. The Lord Carteron of the day was a friend of the Merry Monarch, but it was not as a sanctuary for orgies that he built the house. Perhaps he was tired of the gloomy splendour of Minster Carteron, and wanted a home of his own and not of his ancestors' choosing. He had an elegant taste in letters, as we can learn from his neat imitations of Martial, his pretty *Bucolics*, and the more than respectable Latin hexameters of his *Ars Vivendi*. Being a great nobleman, he had the best skill of the day to construct his hermitage, and here he would retire for months at a time with like-minded friends to a world of books and gardens. He seems to have had no ill-wishers; contemporary memoirs speak of him charitably, and Dryden spared him four lines of encomium. "A selfish old dog," Leithen called him. "He had the good sense to eschew politics and enjoy life. His soul is in that little house. He only did one rash thing in his career—he anticipated the King, his master, by some years in turning Papist."

I asked about its later history.

"After his death it passed to a younger branch of the Carterons. It left them in the eighteenth century, and the Applebys got it. They were a jovial lot of hunting squires, and let the library go to the dogs. Old Colonel Appleby was still alive when I came to Borrowby. Something went wrong in his inside when he was nearly seventy, and the doctors knocked him off liquor. Not that he drank too much, though he did himself well. That

finished the poor old boy. He told me that it revealed to him the amazing truth that during a long
and, as he hoped, publicly useful life he had never
been quite sober. He was a good fellow, and I
missed him when he died. . . . The place went to
a remote cousin called Giffen."

Leithen's eyes, as they scanned the prospect,
seemed amused.

"Julian and Ursula Giffen. . . . I daresay you
know the names. They always hunt in couples,
and write books about sociology and advanced
ethics and psychics—books called either ' The New
This or That ' or ' Towards Something or Other.'
You know the sort of thing. They're deep in all
the pseudo-sciences. . . . Decent souls, but you
can guess the type. I came across them in a case
I had at the Old Bailey—defending a ruffian who
was charged with murder. I hadn't a doubt he
deserved hanging on twenty counts, but there
wasn't enough evidence to convict him on this one.
Dodderidge was at his worst—it was just before
they induced him to retire—and his handling of
the jury was a masterpiece of misdirection. Of
course there was a shindy. The thing was a
scandal, and it stirred up all the humanitarians,
till the murderer was almost forgotten in the ini-
quities of old Dodderidge. You must remember
the case. It filled the papers for weeks. Well, it
was in that connection that I fell in with the
Giffens. I got rather to like them, and I've been
to see them at their house in Hampstead. Golly,
what a place ! Not a chair fit to sit down on, and

colours that made you want to weep. I never met
people with heads so full of feathers."

I said something about that being an odd *milieu*
for him.

" Oh, I like human beings—all kinds. It's my
profession to study them, for without that the
practice of the law would be a lean affair. There
are hordes of people like the Giffens—only not so
good, for they really have hearts of gold. They are
the rootless stuff in the world to-day—in revolt
against everything and everybody with any ancestry. A kind of innocent self-righteousness—
wanting to be the people with whom wisdom begins
and ends. Thy are mostly sensitive and tender-
hearted, but they wear themselves out in an eternal
dissidence. Can't build, you know, for they object
to all tools, but very ready to crab. They scorn
any form of Christianity, but they'll walk miles to
patronize some wretched sect that has the merit of
being brand-new. ' Pioneers ' they call themselves
—funny little unclad people adventuring into the
cold desert with no maps. Giffen once described
himself and his friends to me as 'forward-look-
ing,' but that, of course, is just what they are not.
To tackle the future you must have a firm grip
of the past, and for them the past is only a path-
ological curiosity. They're up to their necks in
the mud of the present. . . . But good, after a
fashion ; and innocent—sordidly innocent. Fate
was in an ironical mood when she saddled them with
that wicked little house."

" Wicked " did not seem to me to be a fair word.

It sat honey-coloured among its gardens with the meekness of a dove. The sound of a bicycle on the road behind made us turn round, and Leithen advanced to meet a dismounting rider.

He was a tallish fellow, some forty years old perhaps, with one of those fluffy blond beards that have never been shaved. Short-sighted, of course, and wore glasses. Biscuit-coloured knickerbockers and stockings clad his lean limbs.

Leithen introduced me. " We are walking to Borrowby, and stopped to admire your house. Could we have just a glimpse inside ? I want Peckwether to see the staircase."

Mr. Giffen was very willing. " I've been over to Clyston to send a telegram. We have some friends for the week-end who might interest you. Won't you stay to tea ? "

There was a gentle formal courtesy about him, and his voice had the facile intonations of one who loves to talk. He led us through a little gate, and along a shorn green walk among the bracken to a postern which gave entrance to the garden. Here, though it was October, there was still a bright show of roses, and the jet of water from the leaden Cupid dripped noiselessly among fallen petals. And then we stood before the doorway, above which the old Carteron had inscribed a line of Horace.

I have never seen anything quite like the little hall. There were two, indeed, separated by a staircase of a wood that looked like olive. Both were paved with black and white marble, and the inner was oval in shape, with a gallery supported on

slender walnut pillars. It was all in miniature, but
it had a spaciousness which no mere size could give.
Also it seemed to be permeated by the quintessence
of sunlight. Its air was of long-descended, confident, equable happiness.

There were voices on the terrace beyond the hall.
Giffen led us into a room on the left. "You remember the house in Colonel Appleby's time,
Leithen. This was the chapel. It had always
been the chapel. You see the change we have made.
. . . I beg your pardon, Mr. Peckwether. You're
not by any chance a Roman Catholic ? "

The room had a white panelling, and on two sides
deep windows. At one end was a fine Italian
shrine of marble, and the floor was mosaic, blue and
white, in a quaint Byzantine pattern. There was
the same air of sunny cheerfulness as in the rest of
the house. No mystery could find a lodgment here.
It might have been a chapel for three centuries,
but the place was pagan. The Giffens' changes
were no sort of desecration. A green-baize table
filled most of the floor, surrounded by chairs like
a committee room. On new raw-wood shelves
were files of papers and stacks of blue-books and
those desiccated works into which reformers of
society torture the English tongue. Two type-
writers stood on a side-table.

"It is our workroom," Giffen explained, "where
we hold our Sunday moots. Ursula thinks that
a week-end is wasted unless it produces some piece
of real work. Often a quite valuable committee
has its beginning here. We try to make our home

a refuge for busy workers, where they need not idle, but can work under happy conditions."

" ' A college situate in a clearer air,' " Leithen quoted. But Giffen did not respond except with a smile; he had probably never heard of Lord Falkland.

A woman entered the room, a woman who might have been pretty if she had taken a little pains. Her reddish hair was drawn tightly back and dressed in a hard knot, and her clothes were horribly incongruous in a remote manor-house. She had bright eager eyes, like a bird, and hands that fluttered nervously. She greeted Leithen with warmth.

"We have settled down marvellously," she told him. "Julian and I feel as if we had always lived here, and our life has arranged itself so perfectly. My Mothers' Cottages in the village will soon be ready, and the Club is to be opened next week. Julian and I will carry on the classes ourselves for the first winter. Next year we hope to have a really fine programme. . . . And then it is so pleasant to be able to entertain one's friends. . . . Won't you stay to tea ? Dr. Swope is here, and Mary Elliston, and Mr. Percy Blaker—you know, the Member of Parliament. Must you hurry off ? I'm so sorry. . . . What do you think of our workroom ? It was utterly terrible when we first came here—a sort of decayed chapel, like a withered tuberose. We have let the air of heaven into it."

I observed that I had never seen a house so full of space and light.

"Ah, you notice that ? It is a curiously happy

place to live in. Sometimes I'm almost afraid to
feel so light-hearted. But we look on ourselves as
only trustees. It is a trust we have to administer
for the common good. You know, it's a house on
which you can lay your own impress. I can imagine places which dominate the dwellers, but Fullcircle is plastic, and we can make it our own just
as much as if we had planned and built it. That's
our chief piece of good fortune."

We took our leave, for we had no desire for the
company of Dr. Swope and Mr. Percy Blaker.
When we reached the highway we halted and looked
back on the little jewel. Shafts of the westering
sun now caught the stone and turned the honey to
ripe gold. Thin spires of amethyst smoke rose into
the still air. I thought of the well-meaning restless
couple inside its walls, and somehow they seemed
out of the picture. They simply did not matter.
The house was the thing, for I had never met in
inanimate stone such an air of gentle masterfulness.
It had a personality of its own, clean-cut and secure,
like a high-born old dame among the females of
profiteers. And Mrs. Giffen claimed to have given
it her impress !

That night in the library at Borrowby, Leithen
discoursed of the Restoration. Borrowby, of which,
by the expenditure of much care and a good deal
of money, he has made a civilized dwelling, is a
Tudor manor of the Cotswold type, with high-
pitched narrow roofs and tall stone chimneys, rising
sheer from the meadows with something of the
massiveness of a Border keep. He nodded towards

the linen-fold panelling and the great carven chimney-piece.

" In this kind of house you have the mystery of the elder England. What was Raleigh's phrase ? ' High thoughts, and divine contemplations.' The people who built this sort of thing lived close to another world, and they thought bravely of death. It doesn't matter who they were—Crusaders or Elizabethans or Puritans—they had all poetry in them, and the heroic, and a great unworldliness. They had marvellous spirits, and plenty of joys and triumphs ; but they had also their hours of black gloom. Their lives were like our weather— storm and sun. One thing they never feared— death. He walked too near them all their days to be a bogy.

" But the Restoration was a sharp break. It brought paganism into England—paganism and the art of life. No people have ever known better the secret of a bland happiness. Look at Fullcircle. There are no dark corners there. The man that built it knew all there was to be known about how to live. . . . The trouble was that they did not know how to die. That was the one shadow on the glass. So they provided for it in the pagan way. They tried magic. They never became true Catholics—they were always pagan to the end, but they smuggled a priest into their lives. He was a kind of insurance premium against unwelcome mystery."

It was not till nearly two years later that I saw

the Giffens again. The May-fly season was near its close, and I had snatched a day on a certain limpid Cotswold river. There was another man on the same beat, fishing from the opposite bank, and I watched him with some anxiety, for a duffer would have spoilt my day. To my relief I recognized Giffen. With him it was easy to come to terms, and presently the water was parcelled out between us.

We forgathered for luncheon, and I stood watching while he neatly stalked, rose, and landed a trout. I confessed to some surprise—first, that Giffen should be a fisherman at all, for it was not in keeping with my old notion of him ; and second, that he should cast such a workmanlike line. As we lunched together, I observed several changes. He had shaved his fluffy beard, and his face was notably less lean, and had the clear even sunburn of the countryman. His clothes, too, were different. They also were workmanlike, and looked as if they belonged to him—no more the uneasy knicker-bockers of the Sunday golfer.

" I'm desperately keen," he told me. " You see it's only my second May-fly season, and last year I was no better than a beginner. I wish I had known long ago what good fun fishing was. Isn't this a blessed place ? " And he looked up through the canopy of flowering chestnuts to the June sky.

" I'm glad you've taken to sport," I said. " Even if you only come here for the week-ends, sport lets you into the secrets of the countryside."

" Oh, we don't go much to London now," was his answer. " We sold our Hampstead house a year ago. I can't think how I ever could stick that place. Ursula takes the same view. . . . I wouldn't leave Oxfordshire just now for a thousand pounds. Do you smell the hawthorn ? Last week this meadow was scented like Paradise. D'you know, Leithen's a queer fellow ? "

I asked why.

" He once told me that this countryside in June made him sad. He said it was too perfect a thing for fallen humanity. I call that morbid. Do you see any sense in it ? "

I knew what Leithen meant, but it would have taken too long to explain.

" I feel warm and good and happy here," he went on. " I used to talk about living close to Nature. Rot! I didn't know what Nature meant. Now——" He broke off. " By Jove, there's a kingfisher. That is only the second I've seen this year. They're getting uncommon with us."

" With us "—I liked the phrase. He was becoming a true countryman.

We had a good day—not extravagantly successful, but satisfactory, and he persuaded me to come home with him to Fullcircle for the night, explaining that I could catch an early train next morning at the junction. So we extricated a little two-seater from a thicket of lilacs, and he drove me through four miles of sweet-scented dusk, with nightingales shouting in every thicket. I changed into a suit of his flannels in a bedroom looking out on the little lake where trout were rising, and I remember that I whistled from pure lightheartedness. In that adorable house one seemed to be still breathing the air of the spring meadows.

Dinner was my first big surprise. It was admirable—plain but perfectly cooked, and with that excellence of basic material which is the glory of a well-appointed country house. There was wine too, which, I am certain, was a new thing. Giffen gave me a bottle of sound claret, and afterwards some more than decent port. My second surprise was my hostess. Her clothes, like her husband's, must have changed, for I did not notice what she was wearing, and I had noticed it only too clearly the last time we met. More remarkable still was the difference in her face. For the first time I realized that she was a pretty woman. The contours had softened and rounded, and there was a charming well-being in her eyes, very different from the old restlessness. She looked content—infinitely content.

I asked about her Mothers' Cottages. She laughed cheerfully.

" I gave them up after the first year. They didn't mix well with the village people. I'm quite ready to admit my mistake, and it was the wrong kind of charity. The Londoners didn't like it—felt lonesome and sighed for the fried-fish shop ; and the village women were shy of them—afraid of infectious complaints, you know. Julian and I have decided that our business is to look after our own people."

It may have been malicious, but I said something about the wonderful scheme of village education.

" Another relic of Cockneyism," laughed the lady ; but Giffen looked a trifle shy.

" I gave it up because it didn't seem worth while. What is the use of spoiling a perfectly wholesome scheme of life by introducing unnecessary complications ? Medicine is no good unless a man is sick, and these people are not sick. Education is the only cure for certain diseases the modern world has engendered, but if you don't find the disease the remedy is superfluous. The fact is, I hadn't the face to go on with the thing. I wanted to be taught rather than to teach. There's a whole world round me of which I know very little, and my first business is to get to understand it. Any village poacher can teach me more of the things that matter than I have to tell him."

" Besides, we have so much to do," his wife added. " There's the house and the garden, and the home-farm and the property. It isn't large, but it takes a lot of looking after."

The dining-room was long and low-ceilinged, and had a white panelling in bold relief. Through the windows came odours of the garden and a faint tinkle of water. The dusk was deepening, and the engravings in their rosewood frames were dim, but sufficient light remained to reveal the picture above the fireplace. It showed a middle-aged man in the clothes of the later Carolines. The plump tapering fingers of one hand held a book, the other was hidden in the folds of a flowered waistcoat. The long, curled wig framed a delicate face, with something of the grace of youth left to it. There were quizzical lines about the mouth, and the eyes smiled pleasantly yet very wisely. It was the face of a man I should have liked to dine with. He must have been the best of company.

Giffen answered my question.

"That's the Lord Carteron who built the house. No. No relation. Our people were the Applebys, who came in 1753. We've both fallen so deep in love with Fullcircle that we wanted to see the man who conceived it. I had some trouble getting it. It came out of the Minster Carteron sale, and I had to give a Jew dealer twice what he paid for it. It's a jolly thing to live with."

It was indeed a curiously charming picture. I found my eyes straying to it till the dusk obscured the features. It was the face of one wholly at home in a suave world, learned in all the urbanities. A good friend, I thought, the old lord must have been, and a superlative companion. I could imagine neat Horatian tags coming ripely from his lips. Not a strong face, but somehow a dominating one. The portrait of the long-dead gentleman had still the atmosphere of life. Giffen raised his glass of port to him as we rose from the table, as if to salute a comrade.

We moved to the room across the hall, which had once been the Giffens' workroom, the cradle of earnest committees and weighty memoranda. This was my third surprise. Baize-covered table and raw-wood shelves had disappeared. The place was now half smoking-room, half library. On the walls hung a fine collection of coloured sporting prints, and below them were ranged low Hepplewhite book-cases. The lamplight glowed on the ivory walls, and the room, like everything else in the house, was radiant. Above the mantelpiece was a stag's head —a fair eleven-pointer.

Giffen nodded proudly towards it. "I got that last year at Machray. My first stag."

There was a little table with an array of magazines and weekly papers. Some amusement must have been visible in my face as I caught sight of various light-hearted sporting journals, for he laughed apologetically. "You mustn't think that Ursula and I take in that stuff for ourselves. It amuses our guests, you know."

I dared say it did, but I was convinced that the guests were no longer Dr. Swope and Mr. Percy Blaker.

One of my many failings is that I can never enter a room containing books without scanning the titles. Giffen's collection won my hearty approval. There were the very few novelists I can read myself —Miss Austen and Sir Walter and the admirable Marryat ; there was a shelf full of memoirs, and a good deal of seventeenth and eighteenth century poetry ; there was a set of the classics in fine editions, Bodonis and Baskervilles and suchlike ; there was much county history, and one or two valuable old herbals and itineraries. I was certain that two years before Giffen would have had no use for literature except some muddy Russian oddments, and I am positive that he would not have known the name of Surtees. Yet there stood the tall octavos recording the unedifying careers of Mr. Jorrocks, Mr. Facey Romford, and Mr. Soapy Sponge.

I was a little bewildered as I stretched my legs in a very deep armchair. Suddenly I had a strong impression of looking on at a play. My hosts seemed to be automata, moving docilely at the orders of a masterful stage-manager, and yet with no sense of bondage. And as I looked on they faded off the scene, and there was only one personality—that house so serene and secure, smiling at our modern antics, but weaving all the while an iron spell round its lovers. For a second I felt an oppression as of something to be resisted. But no. There was no oppression. The house was too well-bred and disdainful to seek to captivate. Only those who fell in love with it could know its mastery, for all love exacts a price. It was far more than a thing of stone and lime ; it was a creed, an art, a scheme of life—older than any Carteron, older than England. Somewhere far back in time—in Rome, in Attica, or in an Ægean island—there must have been such places ; but then they called them temples, and gods dwelt in them.

I was roused by Giffen's voice discoursing of his books. " I've been rubbing up my classics again," he was saying. " Queer thing, but ever since I left Cambridge I have been out of the mood for them. And I'm shockingly ill-read in English literature. I wish I had more time for reading, for it means a lot to me."

" There is such an embarrassment of riches here," said his wife. " The days are far too short for all there is to do. Even when there is nobody staying in the house I find every hour occupied. It's delicious to be busy over things one really cares for."

"All the same I wish I could do more reading," said Giffen. "I've never wanted to so much before."

"But you come in tired from shooting and sleep sound till dinner," said the lady, laying an affectionate hand on his shoulder.

They were happy people, and I like happiness. Self-absorbed perhaps, but I prefer selfishness in the ordinary way of things. We are most of us selfish dogs, and altruism makes us uncomfortable. But I had somewhere in my mind a shade of uneasiness, for I was the witness of a transformation too swift and violent to be wholly natural. Years, no doubt, turn our eyes inward and abate our heroics, but not a trifle of two or three. Some agency had been at work here, some agency other and more potent than the process of time. The thing fascinated and partly frightened me. For the Giffens—though I scarcely dared to admit it—had deteriorated. They were far pleasanter people. I liked them infinitely better. I hoped to see them often again. I detested the type they used to represent, and shunned it like the plague. They were wise now, and mellow, and most agreeable human beings. But some virtue had gone out of them. An uncomfortable virtue, no doubt, but a virtue, something generous and adventurous. Before, their faces had had a sort of wistful kindness. Now they had geniality—which is not the same thing.

What was the agency of this miracle ? It was all around me : the ivory panelling, the olive-wood staircase, the lovely pillared hall. I got up to go to bed with a kind of awe on me. As Mrs. Giffen lit my candle, she saw my eyes wandering among the gracious shadows.

" Isn't it wonderful," she said, " to have found a house which fits us like a glove ? No ! Closer. Fits us as a bearskin fits the bear. It has taken our impress like wax."

Somehow I didn't think that the impress had come from the Giffens' side.

A November afternoon found Leithen and myself jogging homewards from a run with the Heythrop. It had been a wretched day. Twice we had found and lost, and then a deluge had set in which scattered the field. I had taken a hearty toss into a swamp, and got as wet as a man may be, but the steady downpour soon reduced every one to a like condition. When we turned towards Borrowby the rain ceased, and an icy wind blew out of the east which partially dried our sopping clothes. All the grace had faded from the Cotswold valleys. The streams were brown torrents, the meadows lagoons, the ridges bleak and grey, and a sky of scurrying clouds cast leaden shadows. It was a matter of ten miles to Borrowby : we had long ago emptied our flasks, and I longed for something hot to take the chill out of my bones.

" Let's look in at Fullcircle," said Leithen, as we emerged on the highroad from a muddy lane.

" We'll make the Giffens give us tea. You'll find changes there." I asked what changes, but he only smiled and told me to wait and see.

My mind was busy with surmises as we rode up the avenue. I thought of drink or drugs, and promptly discarded the notion. Fullcircle was above all things decorous and wholesome. Leithen could not mean the change in the Giffens' ways which had so impressed me a year before, for he and I had long ago discussed that. I was still puzzling over his words when we found ourselves in the inner hall, with the Giffens making a hospitable fuss over us.

The place was more delectable than ever. Outside was a dark November day, yet the little house seemed to be transfused with sunshine. I do not know by what art the old builders had planned it, but the airy pilasters, the perfect lines of the ceiling, the soft colouring of the wood seemed to lay open the house to a clear sky. Logs burned brightly on the massive steel andirons, and the scent and the fine blue smoke of them strengthened the illusion of summer.

Mrs. Giffen would have had us change into dry things, but Leithen pleaded a waiting dinner at Borrowby. The two of us stood by the fireplace drinking tea, the warmth drawing out a cloud of vapour from our clothes to mingle with the wood-smoke. Giffen lounged in an armchair, and his wife sat by the tea-table. I was looking for the changes of which Leithen had spoken.

I did not find them in Giffen. He was much as

I remembered him on the June night when I had slept here, a trifle fuller in the face perhaps, a little more placid about the mouth and eyes. He looked a man completely content with life. His smile came readily and his easy laugh. Was it my fancy, or had he acquired a look of the picture in the dining-room? I nearly made an errand to go and see it. It seemed to me that his mouth had now something of the portrait's delicate complacence. Lely would have found him a fit subject, though he might have boggled at his lean hands.

But his wife! Ah, there the changes were unmistakable. She was comely now rather than pretty, and the contours of her face had grown heavier. The eagerness had gone from her eyes and left only comfort and good-humour. There was a suspicion, ever so slight, of rouge and powder. She had a string of good pearls—the first time I had seen her wear jewels. The hand that poured out the tea was plump, shapely, and well cared for. I was looking at a most satisfactory mistress of a country house, who would see that nothing was lacking to the part.

She talked more and laughed oftener. Her voice had an airy lightness which would have made the silliest prattle charming.

"We are going to fill the house with young people and give a ball at Christmas," she announced. "This hall is simply clamouring to be danced in. You must come both of you. Promise me. And, Mr. Leithen, it would be very kind if you brought a party from Borrowby. Young men, please. We are overstocked with girls in these parts. . . . We must do something to make the country cheerful in winter-time."

I observed that no season could make Fullcircle other than cheerful.

"How nice of you!" she cried. "To praise a house is to praise the householders, for a dwelling is just what its inmates make it. Borrowby is you, Mr. Leithen, and Fullcircle us."

"Shall we exchange?" Leithen asked.

She made a mouth. "Borrowby would crush me, but it suits a Gothic survival like you. Do you think you would be happy here?"

"Happy?" said Leithen thoughtfully. "Happy? Yes, undoubtedly. But it might be bad for my soul. . . . There's just time for a pipe, Giffen, and then we must be off."

I was filling my pipe as we crossed the outer hall, and was about to enter the smoking-room I so well remembered when Giffen laid a hand on my arm.

"We don't smoke there now," he said hastily.

He opened the door and I looked in. . . . The place had suffered its third metamorphosis. The marble shrine which I had noticed on my first visit had been brought back, and the blue mosaic pavement and the ivory walls were bare. At the eastern end stood a little altar, with above it a copy of a Correggio Madonna.

A faint smell of incense hung in the air and the fragrance of hothouse flowers. It was a chapel, but, I swear, a more pagan place than when it had been work-room or smoking-room.

Giffen gently shut the door. " Perhaps you didn't know, but some months ago my wife became a Catholic. It is a good thing for women, I think. It gives them a regular ritual for their lives. So we restored the chapel. It had always been there in the days of the Carterons and the Applebys."

" And you ? " I asked.

He shrugged his shoulders. " I don't bother much about these things. But I propose to follow suit. It will please Ursula and do no harm to anybody."

.   .   .   .   .   .

We halted on the brow of the hill and looked back on the garden valley. Leithen's laugh, as he gazed, had more awe than mirth in it.

" That little wicked house ! I'm going to hunt up every scrap I can find about old Tom Carteron. He must have been an uncommon clever fellow. He's still alive down there and making people do as he did. . . . In that kind of place you may expel the priest and sweep it and garnish it. But he always returns."

The wrack was lifting before the wind and a shaft of late watery sun fell on the grey walls. It seemed to me that the little house wore an air of gentle triumph.

THE END

Printed in Great Britain by
Thomas Nelson and Sons Ltd, Edinburgh